Scarecrow

A Chief Inspector Pointer Mystery

By A. E. Fielding

Originally published in 1937

Scarecrow

© 2014 Resurrected Press
www.ResurrectedPress.com

Published by Intrepid Ink, LLC

Intrepid Ink, LLC provides full publishing services to authors of fiction and non-fiction books, eBooks and websites. From editing to formatting, to publishing, to marketing, Intrepid Ink gets your creative works into the hands of the people who want to read them.
Find out more at www.IntrepidInk.com.

ISBN 13: 978-1-937022-78-5

Printed in the United States of America

Other Resurrected Press Books in *The Chief Inspector Pointer Mystery* Series

The Eames-Erskine Case
The Footsteps that Stopped
The Clifford Affair
The Cluny Problem
The Craig Poisoning Mystery
The Tall House Mystery
Tragedy at Beechcroft
The Case of the Two Pearl Necklaces
Mystery at the Rectory
Scarecrow

RESURRECTED PRESS CLASSIC MYSTERY CATALOGUE

Journeys into Mystery
Travel and Mystery in a More Elegant Time

The Edwardian Detectives
Literary Sleuths of the Edwardian Era

Gems of Mystery
Lost Jewels from a More Elegant Age

Anne Austin
One Drop of Blood
The Black Pigeon
Murder at Bridge

E. C. Bentley
Trent's Last Case: The Woman in Black

Ernest Bramah
Max Carrados Resurrected:
The Detective Stories of Max Carrados

Agatha Christie
The Secret Adversary
The Mysterious Affair at Styles

Octavus Roy Cohen
Midnight

Freeman Wills Croft
The Ponson Case
The Pit Prop Syndicate

The Uttermost Farthing: A Savant's Vendetta

Arthur Griffiths
The Passenger From Calais
The Rome Express

Fergus Hume
The Mystery of a Hansom Cab
The Green Mummy
The Silent House
The Secret Passage

Edgar Jepson
The Loudwater Mystery

A. E. W. Mason
At the Villa Rose

A. A. Milne
The Red House Mystery

Baroness Emma Orczy
The Old Man in the Corner

Edgar Allan Poe
The Detective Stories of Edgar Allan Poe

Arthur J. Rees
The Hampstead Mystery
The Shrieking Pit
The Hand In The Dark
The Moon Rock
The Mystery of the Downs

Mary Roberts Rinehart
Sight Unseen and The Confession

Dorothy L. Sayers

Whose Body?

Sir William Magnay
The Hunt Ball Mystery

Mabel and Paul Thorne
The Sheridan Road Mystery

Louis Tracy
The Strange Case of Mortimer Fenley
The Albert Gate Mystery
The Bartlett Mystery
The Postmaster's Daughter
The House of Peril
The Sandling Case: What Would You Have Done?

Charles Edmonds Walk
The Paternoster Ruby

John R. Watson
The Mystery of the Downs
The Hampstead Mystery

Edgar Wallace
The Daffodil Mystery
The Crimson Circle

Carolyn Wells
Vicky Van
The Man Who Fell Through the Earth
In the Onyx Lobby
Raspberry Jam
The Clue
The Room with the Tassels
The Vanishing of Betty Varian
The Mystery Girl
The White Alley
The Curved Blades

Anybody but Anne
The Bride of a Moment
Faulkner's Folly
The Diamond Pin
The Gold Bag
The Mystery of the Sycamore
The Come Back

Raoul Whitfield
Death in a Bowl

And much more!
Visit ResurrectedPress.com
for our complete catalogue

FOREWORD

The period between the First and Second World Wars has rightly been called the "Golden Age of British Mysteries." It was during this period that Agatha Christie, Dorothy L. Sayers, and Margery Allingham first turned their pens to crime. On the male side, the era saw such writers as Anthony Berkeley, John Dickson Carr, and Freeman Wills Crofts join the ranks of writers of detective fiction. The genre was immensely popular at the time on both sides of the Atlantic, and by the end of the 1930's one out of every four novels published in Britain was a mystery.

While Agatha Christie and a few of her peers have remained popular and in print to this day, the same cannot be said of all the authors of this period. With so many mysteries published in the period, it is inevitable that many of them would become obscure or worse, forgotten, often with no justification than changing public tastes. The case of Archibald Fielding is one such, an author, who though popular enough to have a career spanning two decades and more than two dozen mysteries has become such a cipher that his, or as seems more likely, her real identity has become as much a mystery as the books themselves.

While the identity of the author may forever remain an unsolved puzzle, there are some facts that may be inferred from the texts. It is likely that the author had an upbringing and education typical of the British upper middle class in the period before the Great War with all that implies; a familiarity with the classics, the arts, and music, a working knowledge of French, an appreciation of the finer things in life. The author has also traveled abroad, primarily in the south of France, but probably to Belgium, Spain, and Italy as well, as portions of several of the books are set in those locales.

The books attributed to Archibald Fielding, A. E. Fielding, or Archibald E. Fielding, are quintessential Golden Age British mysteries. They include all the attributes, the country houses, the tangled webs of relationships, the somewhat feckless cast of characters who seem to have nothing better to do with themselves than to murder or be murdered. Their focus is on a middle class and upper class struggling to find themselves in the new realities of the post war era while still trying to live the lifestyle of the Edwardian era. Things are never as they seem, red herrings are distributed liberally through the pages as are the clues that will ultimately lead to the solution of "the puzzle," for the British mysteries of this period are centered on the puzzle element which both the reader and the detective must solve before the last page.

A majority of the Fielding mysteries involve the character of Chief Inspector Pointer. Unlike the eccentric Belgian Hercule Poirot, the flamboyant Lord Peter Wimsey, or the somewhat mysterious Albert Campion, Pointer is merely a competent, sometimes clever, occasionally intuitive policeman. And unlike, as with Inspector French in the stories of Freeman Wills Croft, the emphasis is on the mystery itself, not the process of detection.

Pointer is nearly as much of a mystery as the author. Very little of his personal life is revealed in the books. He is described as being vaguely of Scottish ancestry. He is well read and educated, though his duties at Scotland Yard prevent him from enjoying those pursuits. His success as a detective depends on his willingness to "suspect everyone" and to not being tied to any one theory. He is fluent in French and familiar with that country. He is, at least in the first book, unmarried, sharing lodgings with a bookbinder named O'Connor, in much the manner of Holmes and Watson, though O'Connor disappears in the subsequent volumes.

While the early books fall plainly in the "humdrum" school with Pointer appearing almost immediately and much of story revolving on the business of tracking down various clues, the later novels are much more concerned with the lives of the characters surrounding the mystery. Pointer is much less center stage, often arriving instead at mid-book to clean up the pieces and insure that the guilty do not escape justice. It is, perhaps, this lack of focus on the detective, which has caused the works of Fielding to fade away while the likes of Poirot seem to attract the interest of each new generation.

One intriguing feature of the Pointer mysteries is that they all involve an unexpected twist at the end, wherein the mystery finally solved is not the mystery invoked at the beginning of the book. I leave it to the reader to judge whether Fielding is "playing by the rules" in this, but it does keep the books interesting up to the last chapter.

Scarecrow, published in 1937, was one of the last mysteries by Fielding. Only two more were published, and one of those, *Pointer to a Crime*, may have been published after the author's death. In a clue to Fielding's life, much of the mystery takes place in the Provence region in the south of France, and demonstrates a familiarity with both the language and customs of the area. It's quite clear from this and several other books that the author must have spent a considerable time in France before settling down in Kensington to garden and write mystery novels.

Scarecrow finds Chief Inspector Pointer at his deductive best as he must first establish the identity of a nameless body found on Dover beach, and then trace the victim's recent movements to discover how he came to have his head smashed in. Along the way, in typical Fielding fashion, he discovers ties to an older case of murder, one that had long been considered solved. For fans of the classic British "puzzle" mystery, *Scarecrow* will be one of Fielding's most satisfying.

Despite their obscurity, the mysteries of Archibald Fielding, whoever he or she might have been, are well written, well crafted examples of the form, worthy of the interest of the fans of the genre. It is with pleasure, then, that Resurrected Press presents this new edition of *Scarecrow* and others in the series to its readers.

About the Author

The identity of the author is as much a mystery as the plots of the novels. Two dozen novels were published from 1924 to 1944 as by Archibald Fielding, A. E. Fielding, or Archibald E. Fielding, yet the only clue as to the real author is a comment by the American publishers, H.C. Kinsey Co. that A. E. Fielding was in reality a "middle-aged English woman by the name of Dorothy Feilding whose peacetime address is Sheffield Terrace, Kensington, London, and who enjoys gardening." Research on the part of John Herrington has uncovered a person by that name living at 2 Sheffield Terrace from 1932-1936. She appears to have moved to Islington in 1937 after which she disappears. To complicate things, some have attributed the authorship to Lady Dorothy Mary Evelyn Moore nee Feilding (1889-1935), however, a grandson of Lady Dorothy denied any family knowledge of such authorship. The archivist at Collins, the British publisher, reports that any records of A. Fielding were presumably lost during WWII. Birthdates have been given variously as 1884, 1889, and 1900. Unless new information comes to light, it would appear that the real authorship must remain a mystery.

Greg Fowlkes
Editor-In-Chief
Resurrected Press
www.ResurrectedPress.com

CHAPTER 1: THE FARM OF THE GOLDEN GOAT

"Jack you're infernally lazy." Florence Rackstraw, hands on narrow hips, looked at Inskipp with an air of impatience. "Come along. The walk back will do you good."

It was now nearly five o'clock.

"I don't need to be done good to," murmured Inskipp, his felt hat tilted over his eyes. "I'm perfect."

"Same here," said Elsie Cameron drowsily. She was seated on the rocks beside him. "Don't let us keep you, Florence."

Florence shot Inskipp an angry look. He caught it and closed his eyes promptly. Her brother joined the little group of three on the Menton promenade.

"Well, haven't we dallied long enough in Babylon?" he asked, shifting a handful of stones to another pocket.

"In Bosio, you mean," chaffed Elsie. Honore Bosio keeps the best cake shop in Menton, and the Rackstraws loved a good feed.

"Shake a leg, Inskipp," adjured Rackstraw. "I want to discuss an episode in Haroun with you."

Inskipp yawned. The two were writing a scenario. They were to share the profits of the film between them, and each talked as though they had a gold mine under their hats.

"Haroun is tired," announced Inskipp firmly. "Very tired. He won't be at home to visitors until to-morrow. Besides, Elsie and I are going to drive up to the farm with Norbury."

"You are an idler," said Florence with a nip-in of her thin lips, as, with a wave of the hand that looked angry instead of friendly, she led the way at a good pace along the *Promenade du Midi* to where the road started that would bring them after a three hours' ramble to Norbury's farm, La Chevre d'Or, high up in the hills behind Menton. The four were his paying guests.

Elsie and Inskipp watched them disappear.

"There, but for the grace of God—" murmured Inskipp unctuously.

"I don't think any one should be as ugly as those two are," said Elsie. She spoke meditatively, objectively. She was an artist, and, incidentally, a very pretty girl.

And as though to give her another look at them, the brother and sister suddenly reappeared, walking briskly towards them. As usual, Florence Rackstraw was in the lead. She was very tall. Her head was too large for her bony body, and seemed to be all face, a face the colour of mottled mahogany. Her hair, straight as that of a mouse, was looped in two curtains over her ears and gathered into a tight little bun on her long, scraggy neck. Her eyes protruded. Her chin retreated. Her nose was hooked. Her mouth consisted of two thin, pale lines that slanted up to one side.

Her brother resembled her closely, with rougher features, and a still harsher voice. He, too, had her air of absolute self-satisfaction.

"As you're driving with Norbury, take these up for us, will you?" The coats were tossed at the two before they could reply. Then the Rackstraws wheeled and strode off once more.

"You're treading on dangerous ground when you talk of ugliness to me," said Inskipp meaningly. And he certainly could not be considered handsome.

"But you're honest," objected Elsie at once. "You're straight. You can't be ugly when you look that. That's what I'm trying to get at, I think, that it doesn't matter if you look ugly, as long as you don't look as though you really were ugly—you yourself—in yourself."

"That's a bit difficult to grasp," said Inskipp with a grin that showed his strong teeth. "That's too much in Laroche's line for me." Laroche was a Frenchman, a writer of psychological studies, who was also staying at the Golden Goat.

"What I mean is that I think only ugly thoughts can make faces so plain. The Rackstraws look mean and malicious—and I think they are both those things."

She spoke with her eyes on the incredible blue of the sea in front of her. Inskipp altered his position to face her more directly. He was a young man, and Florence Rackstraw had made a dead set at him when he had first come to the farm two months ago. He had drifted into a quasi intimacy with her before he saw his danger and struck out for safety.

"They're very intelligent," said Inskipp a trifle awkwardly. "Very clever."

"They are," agreed Elsie in a tone that said that that quality counted for little. "But they could be very dangerous, both of them."

"In what way?" he asked.

"I haven't the faintest idea," was the prompt reply. "I don't reason about people. I feel them."

"And never, never make a mistake," he finished with mock solemnity.

"Never when I dislike people. It sounds cynical, but it's true. It's only when I like people that I may be all wrong."

They were lounging on the *Promenade du Midi*, that broad walk that runs along the sea at Menton, sometimes with neither parapet nor railing to protect it from the water. A grand walk when the sea is rough, and the green waves come roaring in over the foundations of the wall. White wings were wheeling and circling over their heads. One gull, more adventurous than his mates, nipped the bread from Inskipp's fingers in his swift glide past, banked—a lovely flash of silver —and came back for

more. The hot sun flooded everything. The air was cool
and fresh. The sea ran in broad washes of deep blue and
bright green. The sky was the true sky of Menton, high,
and blue, and soft, and deep. The donkey and ponies, kept
at a corner of the casino for children to ride, stamped a
little. They were as bored as Inskipp felt. A few notes
from the orchestra playing outside the casino reached
them. It was all like a scene at a theatre, Inskipp
thought, something which he watched, but in which he
had no part. As for Elsie, she was at grips with a curious,
a quite contrary feeling to his. It was as though
something were trying to rouse her to a sense of the
moment's importance. She got up, ostensibly the better to
watch the gulls whirl overhead, in reality to give herself
room. What was this sudden impulse which was sweeping
through her as the gulls swept through the air around
her—an impulse to fight and win the man beside her, a
sudden awareness of powers within her which, if used—of
qualities which, if shown—would draw John Inskipp to
her side and keep him there. He was a lonely man. She
knew herself to be his complement. Should she make him
realise this? She could. She knew that she could. What
she did not know was that the fate of Inskipp depended
on that moment— that Atropos with her shears paused
for a second to wait for her. Had she obeyed her
innermost craving Inskipp would have been saved. But,
unfortunately, Elsie came of a race of women who were
won, not who did the winning. She told herself the truth,
that she cared for him much more than he did for her.
She flung off the odd feeling that the moment held some
opportunity which would never come again—and turned
to see a man hurrying towards them along the
promenade.

"Here's Du-Metri," she said in a welcoming voice.

"Two-Yards" was the nickname of the Norburys'
factotum. A tall wiry figure, he came swinging along the
Promenade from the nearby *Halles*. "Ohe!" he hailed, and
waved a long, lean arm. Elsie liked the man. Two-Yards

was a character. She sat smiling as he strode up and made a jerky little bow. "Il padrone sends this message," he said, drawing himself erect. "Not to wait for him here, as he must go to Gorbio. He will have to pick you up at the old Carnoles Olive Mill."

Two-Yards looked as though carved from pliable teak, his features were so salient, his colouring so uniform and dark a brown. His lean, clean-shaven face was good looking, with regular features, and dark eyes that were at once keen and veiled. He knew every star that hung in the Menton heavens, and he knew their courses, the hour of their rising and the time of their setting. He knew all the flowers of the fields, and the birds in the woods, as he knew his own herds. Born in the hills behind Hyeres, Two-Yards was steeped in Provencal legends and folk-lore. It was from him that Inskipp had first heard the legend of Haroun, the Moslem Corsair who had turned Christian for love of a captive maid.

"Are you coming up to the Mill, too?" Inskipp asked.

Two-Yards threw up his chin in sign of negation. He had still some purchases to make for the farm, and would follow later in the day in the farm cart. His eyes on the horizon, he stood a minute looking out to sea.

Leaning far out of a boat painted green and yellow, a fisherman was beating the waves with all his strength, and at the full stretch of his long arms.

"To drive the fish into the net," Two-Yards said in reply to Elsie's inquiring look.

"Is there anything you don't know, Du-Metri?" she asked him.

"Yes. I don't know who gives my Sabe her silk handkerchiefs," he said suddenly.

Sabe—short for Isabella—was his daughter. She was a flirt, and Du-Metri was a Spartan parent.

"Well, I must be off." And he took his cap off again, while Elsie laughed silently.

The two caught the next Gorbio bus and were whirled along to the old mill at its opening.

Green and cool and very lovely, the road wound past gardens where geraniums hung in thick mounds the size of cartwheels on the stone walls, or climbed half-way up the trunks of the palms, where roses and carnations filled the air with fragrance, where the bougainvillea covered walls and roofs with its magnificent purple. They got out at the Old Mill and sat down to wait for Norbury on the rocks which dot the entrance to the little hamlet. The ruined Maulessena Castle was to one side, the great new sanatorium was hidden by a group of olive trees fifty feet high. Where they were sitting, they had pines on one side and palms on the other. It was typical of this corner of the world. The rustle of the palm fronds sounded like heavy rain in the breeze. Below them lay Menton looking what architecturally, as well as historically, it was—pure Italian, as it curved around the Gulf of Peace, a horseshoe of emerald and cobalt. Eastward, two lines of lavender and violet mountains carried the eye to Bordighera, whose houses glittered like dice on the farthermost spur of land. Up here, one even caught a glimpse of the Gulf of Genoa on the other side of the first line of purple hills, like a stroke of sapphire. To the west, the green ridge of Cap Martin ran an arm into the sea with one white hotel catching the light.

Elsie drew a deep breath. Things must surely come right between her and Inskipp in such a world. And if that was not to be, then beauty such as this can fill the heart like love. The sunshine flooded all her being, luminous and strong and vital.

She crumbled some of the earth between her fingers. "It's wonderful soil. You've heard, of course, of the man who, by an oversight, left his umbrella sticking in the ground hereabouts. When he went to look for it a week later, he found it a small tree in full bloom."

Inskipp laughed outright.

"Did Two-Yards tell you that one?"

"No. Mr. Norbury." Getting to her feet, she looked about her, her felt hat in her hand.

"I don't think there's anything in the world more beautiful, in its own way, than is this region."

Her eyes were shining, her whole little face alight and glowing. It was a whimsical, irregular face under a mop of tawny hair that had streaks of red, like flames, in it.

"I suppose not." After a pause Inskipp added: "But it doesn't mean anything to me. Does it to you?"

"Mean?" She was puzzled, and her transparent, candid face showed it.

He made a vague gesture. "It's lovely—as a set scene at a theatre is lovely. But it's not real—to me. Palms—they can't take the place of beeches. I'd rather look at an oak than an olive, any day—-"

"And you'd rather watch rain than sunshine— is that it?" she laughed. "Nothing like patriotism!"

But he was not laughing.

Inskipp's sallow face was a melancholy one. Something about it suggested the seeker who had never yet even caught sight of anything worthy of his search, the visionary who had never yet had a vision. In age, he was under thirty.

His brow was narrow and low, not the brow of a clever, or even of a well-read, man. His dark, deep-set eyes were his best feature; they were unsatisfied looking, but well cut and well opened. His nose was thin, with generous nostrils, his mouth also suggested generosity as well as firmness, his chin was dogged and masterful. Elsie's quick eyes had put it down correctly as the face of a dreamer; but Inskipp did not look at all like a dreamer who could not be wakened. You might fool him without any great difficulty, possibly, but most assuredly you would have to pay for it afterwards if he learnt the truth. He was under medium height and slenderly built, with a narrow chest which was the reason for his being out of England. A bad attack of pneumonia had sent him to Menton, and a chance stroll up among the hills had suddenly brought him, some eight weeks ago, to a low Provencal farmhouse. Twin cedars stood at the gateway—

one standing for *Prosperity*, one for *Peace*. Its roof was of
the red, fluted Provencal tiles, its garden hedges were of
rosemary and juniper and lavender.

Inskipp had spelled out the farm's name on the gate,
and wondered at it: *La Domaine de la Chevre d'Or*. Two-
Yards had seen him, and promptly asked him to hold the
gate open for a pig which was intent on double-crossing
him. In the pig-hunt which followed, Inskipp, Two-Yards,
the pig, and a tall, rangy man of middle age who swore
heartily in English, all got thoroughly well mixed up.
When the pig was back where he belonged, instead of
where he wanted to be, the Englishman introduced
himself as the owner of the farm, and asked Inskipp in to
taste some of his new wine. Inskipp met the other guests
who were staying at the place, and had promptly
arranged with Two-Yards to fetch his things from below.
He had not regretted it. The farm was simple, but it was
cheap, and the scenery was magnificent.

Inskipp liked Mrs. Norbury, too. So did Elsie
Cameron, who had been at the farm since early spring.
She, also, had to spend the winter in warm and sheltered
nooks, and the farm was securely tucked away alike from
Bise or Mistral.

Norbury's yodel came ringing down the green valley
above them. Inskipp answered with one of Two-Yards'
strange shouts. Such a shout as the Provencal herdsmen
give at dawn and at nightfall. A shout which has come
down from the Phoenicians, said Laroche. It stirs the
hearer strangely. Some old tumult of the blood beyond
our present-day reason or understanding answers it.
Elsie never listened to it without a feeling that the enemy
tribes were at the stockade, that javelins were flying
around her.

Norbury drew up his Ford close to them.

He was a big, sunburnt man in the early forties, with
a pleasant enough but very non-committal face, out of
which would come at times a glance, chill and keen as a
north-easter.

They clambered in over bags of flour, sugar and salt. Then they were off.

"How's the marketing been?" asked Inskipp as they had to slow down for a herd of cows.

"So-so," was the reply. "They say the weather is going to break. Hope it won't, or it'll be a bad look-out for my oranges."

Norbury had not many oranges on his farm, but he overlooked no source of profit, and an orange-tree bears easily three thousand oranges in twelve months, and choice ones yield four times that.

It did not take long to reach his *Domaine*, or farm, and for a moment the three of them looked down at a sea of grey-green olives which hid the lemons and vines planted below them.

Norbury's chief source of income was from his lemon-trees. The Mentonais claim that Eve's last act when leaving Paradise was to pick a lemon to carry with her. She decided to give it to the most beautiful country which she and Adam should find on their wanderings. When she came to Menton, she flung it on a terrace, telling it to grow and multiply and turn the land into another Garden of Eden, which—according to the legend—it promptly proceeded to do.

Norbury called for a couple of the farm hands to help him unload the car, while Elsie and Inskipp walked round a corner to the house. As they did so, a good-looking young couple came sauntering up to the open door. The woman in front, with something very graceful, though weary, in her gait. Edna Blythe always walked like that, though she never seemed to go farther than the nearest sunny corner. She was a tall, slender woman, not pretty, exactly, but with something about her rather sad, very bored-looking face that suggested that she could be pretty if she chose. She was fair, with fine brown eyes, and a low forehead. Her features were well cut. A straight nose, a small, curiously tight mouth which yet looked as though when relaxed it could be very sweet, an obstinate little chin, and a firm jaw. Her hands were nervous and suggested illness.

Her brother, who followed her in, was tall and fair, too. Otherwise there was no resemblance between them.

Mrs. Norbury joined them with one of her ginger cakes which she wanted to put out of doors to dry off. She rated Norbury sharply for letting the car cut across the grass. Inskipp sometimes fancied that her big burly husband was a little afraid of his dot of a wife, and indeed Mrs. Norbury could be very forthright and unbending at times. There had been that affair of the Italian count and the lady he called his wife just after Inskipp's own arrival. Mrs. Norbury had learnt from the young man himself that he and his companion were not yet married, though they intended to have this done soon. The car took the two down to Menton the same day, Mrs. Norbury driving, and looking calm and unflustered, in spite of the fact that the count and future countess on the back seat seemed to have turned into two geysers.

"If you tolerate a thing, you aid it," was her only comment on the matter, in answer to a chaffing remark of Rackstraw's, who thought her attitude distinctly comic.

She asked Inskipp and Elsie about Menton as she carefully set the cake level.

"It was very close," said Inskipp, "and very enervating."

"As always—" threw in Elsie.

"And as always," he went on, "full of Voronoff's patients, or would-be patients."

"We women score when it comes to old age," said Mrs. Norbury meditatively. "We accept it more placidly."

"Not while there's a paint-pot to be had!" retorted Elsie, laughing.

"A woman has to accept so much," Mrs. Norbury maintained, "that old age seems a trifle." She spoke bitterly. Her voice was bitter, too. But, then, Mrs. Norbury did not have a pleasant voice at any time. Over the telephone, that tester of tone, it sounded very hard always, and could sound distinctly grating.

CHAPTER 2: INSKIPP HEARS OF MIREILLE, AND LEARNS WHAT THE GOLDEN GOAT STANDS FOR

For Inskipp, the next fortnight was one of outward peace and inward battle. He won. At the end of the time Florence Rackstraw treated him as a very unpleasant insect, and Inskipp was glad. He had found it harder than he thought to get out of the atmosphere of the suitor in which Florence had very subtly wrapped him and all his words. He had had to be really rude at the last to cut the cord which, she insisted, linked them. Elsie had watched his struggles with approval, but with no overt help. She told herself that, as he had got himself into the false position, he must get out of it by himself, too. But when he was out, he was no nearer to Elsie.

One night, when the other men were off helping to drive some young bulls to Castellar, whence they were going to be sent to Aries and Nimes for the bull fights, he and Mrs. Rackstraw had sat talking on the verandah. Oddly enough, Mrs. Rackstraw had been Inskipp's secret ally in the struggle with her daughter. Inskipp had thought more than once that she had no love for either of her children. Had he known the story of her life with their father, and how much these two resembled that unpleasant gentleman, now dead and buried, he would not have been astonished. As it was, after Inskipp, beguiled by the singing of the nightjar in a nearby tree, and by Mrs. Rackstraw's words on companionship had drifted into what was practically a description of his ideal woman, Mrs. Rackstraw had said significantly:

"I know a girl who fits that description of yours, Mr. Inskipp. All but the loveliness, which you think means a beautiful soul—and that's Elsie Cameron."

Florence Rackstraw, who had slipped unnoticed into a chair in the corner, sat very still.

Inskipp was amused. How little people understood, he thought. Here had he been indiscreet enough to give a glimpse of his heart's ideal, and what he showed had been identified with Elsie Cameron! Elsie was a nice girl, a very nice girl. He would be a lucky chap who would win her one day for his wife; but as to her resembling the dream creature he had described Inskipp gave a suppressed smile, then he made for his own room. He wanted to jot down his impressions of the herd of bulls this evening as they had gone roaring, stamping, snorting down the valley. Just such an incident could have happened at the castle of Anna's father—Anna was the Christian maid who had converted Haroun to Christianity, said the tale. Inskipp had never up till now written anything, but he was bored at the farm, and boredom is the best incentive to writing.

He had worked for about an hour, when a knock came at his door.

In answer to his curt "*Entrez,*" Florence Rackstraw came in.

"I've got something that would fit wonderfully into your film," said Florence. "It's in a book on Provence castles—an old French book that I picked up in Menton last time we were there. I've been reading it."

A week ago Inskipp would have made an excuse but she had altered—she had retired defeated, and he followed her without another thought to the large room which the Rackstraws used as a sitting-room.

"Light your pipe, and I'll get it," said Florence as she stepped on to her own bedroom. "Matches are on the mantel—"she called back. Her tone was friendly, though detached.

Inskipp strolled to the fireplace, where some logs of olive wood were still smouldering.

He suddenly picked up a photograph standing by the

clock. He had never seen it there before. He had never seen it anywhere before. This lovely oval. This beautiful small head set so proudly on its slender shoulders.

He still had it in his hand when Florence came back.

"Isn't she beautiful? She's my greatest pal! And she wants to go into a convent when she has secured her divorce!"

"It's the loveliest face I have ever seen," he said slowly.

"And as good as she is beautiful," Florence said warmly. "I want her to come here. It would do Mireille good to have to interest herself in the affairs of this life for a while. She is too unworldly."

"Mireille?" Inskipp repeated questioningly. What a charming name, he thought.

"Yes. Mireille de Pra is her name. Madame de Pra. She was married some three years ago, but she never lived with her husband. He had a fit as they were walking down the aisle after the wedding; he rolled right off the steps, they say—I wasn't there—and for a while they thought he was dead. But unfortunately he wasn't. For when he came round finally he was raving mad, and has remained mad ever since. Isn't it terrible!"

"It's a crime—marriage such as that!" Inskipp was fairly stuttering.

"I have another photograph of her. Would you like to see it?"

Florence felt in a drawer and handed him a portrait as lovely as the other, if not more so, for it showed a figure as beautiful as was the face. It showed the same girl—she looked barely nineteen —in what seemed to be a convent garden bending over a great spread of Madonna lilies. Inskipp's heart contracted, and expanded, and did all sorts of queer things inside him.

He said nothing, only looked at the two photographs.

She has to stay in the convent in Brittany for the present," Florence went on. "But, then, frankly I'm not keen on Harry meeting her. He isn't her sort at all, and it might spoil our friendship. I usually keep these photographs safely tucked away for that reason. He doesn't know about her, and—well, I don't see why he should. He may have left here before she comes."

She put the photographs carefully into a drawer. Then she showed him the book with the descriptions of the old castle that had interested her. Inskipp barely understood what she was saying, but he thanked her effusively, and, taking the book, went out of the room, his head in a whirl. He felt like a man who has most unexpectedly stumbled on a treasure. A sense of excitement filled him, an impatience for the weeks to pass till that wonderful creature should stand before him in the flesh as she stood in the photograph. He felt as though the world were a marvellous place, as though to each of us had been offered a ticket in a wonderful lottery. The feeling stayed with him next morning when he woke up. But as he dressed, and when he sat down to his writing, doubts began to rise. He told himself not to be a fool. Girls such as that one in the photographs would not give him a second glance. Or even one. He laughed aloud in scorn at his ugly, dull self.

"Glad you're in such a cheerful mood, Inskipp," said a voice behind him. "The fact is, I was wondering whether you would help me out again—just for the next few days. I don't like to keep the Norburys waiting."

Rackstraw had come in through a side door.

Inskipp took out his pocket-book. A bit over two hundred francs should settle Rackstraw's debt to the Norburys. Inskipp was anything but a wealthy man, but he had set aside a thousand pounds for odds and ends when he had invested the remainder of his money. So far, he had spent very little of it. Money could not buy happiness—could not prevent acute loneliness, for bought companionship is no companionship. Inskipp had tried that out thoroughly already.

"I'd ask the Norburys to let it run on for a bit," Rackstraw said, "but they're having a hard time to make ends meet, let alone lap."

Inskipp said that this was news to him. Rackstraw made a little face.

"It wouldn't be if you slept in my room. Mrs. Norbury wants the money back that she put into the farm, and Norbury can't run to it."

Inskipp handed over the notes now, but he had an uncomfortable feeling that Rackstraw was meditating a further request for a loan. Something biggish. He fancied that Rackstraw had been trying to get up his courage for it for some days.

He slipped away out of doors. The orange trees were too compact and tidy for his taste. Inskipp preferred lemon trees. By the back door was a charming specimen. A sudden desire to paint it came over him. He could sketch in an amateurish way in water-colours, and he went indoors now for his sketching-block, and box of colours. He chose his pencil carefully, and set to work.

Not for him was the one-line of the real artist, but by patient work he achieved a very accurate drawing of the little tree. Its beauty grew on him as he studied it. Its airy grace, the delicate spacing of its fine leaves which decorate but never hide branch or fruit. Its shape as it grows older is much like that of a pear tree, but the abundant, daffodil yellow fruit hangs so clear of branch or leaf, that it seems to be backed only by the bright blue of the sky, and against that sky the effect is enchanting.

Inskipp enjoyed the work. Unlike the writer, the artist, however poor, finds that if he is patient he enters into a life within life, a world within the world. Colours become more than something seen by the eye—they have a meaning—they have a magic—

Inskipp decided to put in the kitchen door, the maize field with its tassels and the scarecrow that stood in one corner, and a tiny lemon sapling which grew at the base of the second lemon tree, with its little fruit the size of an acorn, but perfect in colour and shape, dotted like fairy lamps all over the slender branches.

"*Tiens!* You sketch? Well, perhaps?" It was Monsieur Laroche, sipping a glass of Chateauneuf du Pape. As for the local stuff, Laroche maintained that it was not wine at all, but merely vinegar in the making.

Monsieur Laroche repeated his remark. His mother had been Irish, and he spoke English as though born in Dublin.

"Why should I not sketch?" Inskipp asked, putting his drawing away.

Laroche had a way of making him feel as though he were under a microscope, than which there is no sensation more distasteful to a Briton.

"I agree that it is in character." Ah, there he was again! Laroche could talk by the hour on what was in a man's character and what was not.

Miss Blythe came towards them.

"Has the noon-gun gone yet?" she asked. They all set their watches by the cannon fired from Menton fort.

Inskipp thought she had a pretty but rather vacant face. She was very dull to talk to, very heavy in conversation, and she had a habit, which embarrassed him, of listening with her eyes rivetted intently on the speaker, as though she would never see him again, and the memory of each feature and of each expression might make all the difference to her own future.

The gun boomed. Miss Blythe set her watch, and passed on.

"What's *her* character?" he asked Laroche under his breath as the Frenchman stared meditatively after her.

"Ah!" said Laroche between his teeth. "That is the thing she hides with all her skill. But I have my ideas!"

Inskipp was amused. Poor quiet, dull Miss Blythe!

"I can't think what you see of interest in her," he said truthfully.

"I see a most uncommon sight," said Laroche almost sadly. "I see a person afraid of themselves. Yes, just that. Not, as I thought, merely afraid to show herself to others, but afraid of some weakness—or some impulse—in herself. I suspect drink," he said finally.

"Mind you," said the writer apologetically, "that is only a guess. Chiefly because of the choice of this farm. No temptations here. Mr. Norbury keeps no cellar. His *eau de vie* is only useful as an embrocation." The farm had its own still, a perfectly respectable farmhouse appurtenance in France, where every windfall finds its way ultimately into it. "I wish I could clear her up," he added; "but it might take years."

"How about asking her brother?" suggested Inskipp.

The Frenchman considered a moment, then he shook his head. "I think not. He is born a bully under his varnish of the public school. And, by the way, how he avoids saying what school he was at."

A sound of voices made them look up. Rackstraw and Du-Metri were walking together towards them. Mrs. Norbury was behind them.

"Another painter! Here's Du-Metri with a pot." Laroche stepped aside to avoid its swing.

"For the Golden Goat," said Two-Yards, with a gleam of his strong teeth, making for the gate, where he began to repaint the name. As he did so, he started one of his songs of which the refrain was:

Apres aco, su anac. (After which I left.)

Laroche listened to it with delight. He wondered what Mrs. Norbury would say if she could understand the words of the Rabelaisian old ditty.

Mrs. Norbury, as it happened, was thinking of the painting that was being done, not of the song.

"I do so dislike the farm's name." She looked at the gate frowningly. "I wanted to change it to *Lou Lavandou*, or *Las Mimosas*. Provencal names, too, both of them, but you can't change things in Provence. Not even though the last owner was gored to death in a field over there by one of his bulls."

"But the name wouldn't alter the luck, surely." Inskipp's voice was amused.

"It's supposed to be unlucky," said Mrs. Norbury

shortly, turning back into the house; "but my husband doesn't believe in luck."

"I thought *La Chevre d'Or* is a beneficent creature who guards the hidden treasures left by the Saracens," said Elsie, who, together with Rackstraw, had come out after Mrs. Norbury.

"And I thought he was the defender of Provencal relics, butting away the archaeologist who got too close to anything interesting," said Rackstraw.

"One of its duties, certainly," allowed Laroche. "That Chevre d'Or is evidently in the pay of the Department of Public Works. But he has another side. A more mysterious side. He is also The Unattainable. The Impossible-to-realise. And to see *that* Chevre d'Or is to die shortly afterwards."

"They would get that side of him from the Greeks, who settled all this part of the coast and built their temples and theatres here," said Rackstraw, who was an archaeologist.

"Yes, in many places he is Pan. But he is other things, too. A blending of many old superstitions." Laroche made a gesture as the luncheon bell sounded. "Unless you are a Provencal—and even then—it is better to leave the mysterious creature alone."

CHAPTER 3: INSKIPP WRITES TO MIREILLE, AND AN ACCIDENT HAPPENS TO FLORENCE

By the end of the month Inskipp was corresponding with the beauty of the photograph. It came about through Florence having come down one morning with her hand and arm in a sling. A bad attack of neuritis, she called it. She sought him out later in his room, and explained that she was sending some flowers to her friend Mireille de Pra, and now could not write the letter for her birthday that should go with them. She did not care to ask her mother to do it for her, for, as Inskipp knew, she did not want Harry to get to know Mireille, and she could not ask her mother to keep the letter a secret.

"He would fall in love with her. She would loathe him. And our friendship would never be the same again," she said for the second time. "Would you write a letter to my dictation?" she asked, and Inskipp, trying not to flush with pleasure, said he would be happy to do so.

"It must go by the afternoon's post," she told him, and suggested three o'clock for the work, but at two she looked in to his room to say that she had a raging toothache, and was going to drive down to Menton to have the tooth out. Would he write instead, and explain that she—Florence— had a bad attack of neuritis? Mireille knew that she was subject to them.

Inskipp had spent a whole afternoon over the letter until it was a monument of the stilted and the stiff.

He received a charming reply, but all too short.

As a reply to this reply, Inskipp ventured to send a basket of mimosa, accompanied by a little very carefully written note entirely about Florence and the farm.

He received another charming letter, and a very

delightful correspondence started, though on Madame de Pra's part the letters were all too brief, and not very frequent. Yet, even so, they brought an unaccustomed look of happiness to Inskipp's face.

In the first ones, Madame de Pra had written as to an elderly man—an invalid—and Inskipp had hardly dared speak of his real age, but he had done so. The interval that followed this had been longer than the first one, and the next letter from Mrs. de Pra was very short and stiff, but that coolness was now wearing off, and when they met it would be without awkward explanations. As to when that meeting would be, Mireille said that when she had finally obtained her divorce she wanted a long change up on the hills that she knew so well. Florence had told Inskipp that Mireille was born in the Esterels, the daughter of a small proprietor named Briancard, a scholarly man, who had paid too much attention to his books and too little to his land. His wife, an Englishwoman, had died a year after the marriage of Mireille, their only child, and Madame de Pra was now an orphan.

Florence made no secret of her hope that Mireille could eventually come to the farm, and Inskipp made no secret of his sharing that hope. He wondered how he could ever have disliked Florence as he had just before his break with her. Evidently he had taken her far too seriously. Evidently it had just been a whim of hers— passing—quickly forgotten—to try to make a fool of him.

Even at the time of his break with her he had thought that it was love of domination rather than affection. He was sure of it now. Yet there was another side to Florence, and this morning it was very charmingly in evidence. She had used some phrase that had startled him, for it was word for word what Mireille had written him in his last letter. Seeing his start, Florence had at once explained that she had heard the sentence from Mireille herself apropos of the bond between a writer and his pen. And from that she had gone on to talk of Mireille in a way that enchanted him. He diffidently told her what her friend's letters meant to him, what character, what heart they revealed. Florence listened with a very soft look on her face—a look that touched him.

"I believe you would have fallen in love with her from her letters, even if you had never seen her picture," she said finally, turning away to choose her gloves.

"No," Inskipp said honestly, for the vision of that lovely face was ever with him. And on that he now ventured to ask her if he might have one of the photographs of Madame de Pra which she had. Florence refused absolutely and curtly. Inskipp told himself that he had roused her jealousy as a friend. But Florence explained that she would feel it to be treachery to Mireille to hand on her picture to any one else. "But if you ask her, she might send you one. Perhaps a later one still," Florence said, turning at the door. And Inskipp realised afresh how ugly she was.

He thought of what Elsie had said. Theoretically he, too, held that faces are records of thoughts and emotions, but poor Florence's face was surely just a freak of nature.

"Upon my word, Inskipp," said Laroche, as he and Rackstraw came on him a moment later. "I think you have had a glimpse of golden hoofs and horns, eh? You look as though you had. If so, beware!"

Inskipp flushed.

"I think he has seen *Mireille*," suggested Rackstraw with a grin. "I don't mean the film of that name; I meant the damsel herself."

"Then you *have* met her?" Inskipp said instantly.

The two men roared their amusement in great peals. As for Elsie, she had gone on into the house.

"*Touche!*" Laroche ejaculated, laughing afresh. "Ah, *Mireio*! If a lady is the reason, then indeed!" And he threw up his hands.

"What are you two talking about?" Inskipp was vexed. "You mention a lady's name whom I don't think you know?" He looked at Rackstraw questioningly. "And you and Laroche seem to think I've made a special-sized joke."

Rackstraw hastened to apologise. "Sorry, my dear chap, sorry! I don't know the lady. I merely mentioned the name of Mistral's famous heroine as a chance explanation for your look of general content these days. I've evidently hit some mark."

"Mistral? That's the damned wind that gives every one the pip, surely?"

"It's also the name of the great Provencal poet — Frederic Mistral. Or was," Laroche explained. "His *Mireio* is a Provencal epic. Though personally I prefer *Calandau*. But *Mireio* is Provencal for Mireille, the name of his heroine, a name used long before his day for any pretty girl."

"I only meant that you must have met some village charmer—no offence, Inskipp." Rackshaw was feeling very amiable this morning.

Inskipp was already appeased. He Was glad to be assured that Harry Rackstraw had never met his sister's lovely friend, and he hummed to himself as he too went indoors.

These were the days of the grape harvest. The weather was ideal. The sunshine poured down on the vineyards, the countryside rang with the singing and laughing of the grape gatherers; yet Norbury looked very glum, and said openly that but for his guests he would not have been able to carry on. Only Mrs. Norbury, apparently unruffled as ever, cheery as ever, saw to the housekeeping with undiminished efficiency.

"If Mrs. Norbury feels so cheerful, I needn't be in a hurry to pay last month's accounts," Rackstraw said to his sister.

"Mother left you the money to settle for her," said Florence with a sudden frown. "Where's the receipt? I'm writing to her. I'll enclose it."

Mrs. Rackstraw had decided to go to a married daughter in Rhodesia who had had a bad accident and was stranded with no one but a couple of children to help her. It was not money but physical help that was needed. The mother had left over a week ago. Florence had refused to accompany her. She had a tiny income of her own, and the expenses here at the farm were low enough to let her live on it without working. She was by profession a librarian, and had worked as such in South Africa, where she was born.

"I'm writing to her, too. I'll send it." Her brother spoke shortly.

"I don't believe you've paid up yet. Mother ought to have given the money to me," Florence said in her most superior tone.

"You'd have forgotten to settle, in your new campaign against Inskipp," he retorted.

"My new campaign?" she asked loftily, arranging her hair.

"My dear girl, I've known you for over thirty years, remember! Those letters to that old witch in Rennes, Mademoiselle—what was her name—the housekeeper who used to be at that awful boarding-house in Paris when we were there. Don't you suppose I know you're up to something? And something which will pay Inskipp out?"

There was a short silence, while Florence chose a walking stick. She was off for a long scramble.

"Whatever you're at, has slowed up his output," Rackstraw said, lighting a cigarette.

She smiled a slow, very unpleasant smile. By Jove, Flo was plain, Rackstraw thought as he caught it. How on earth she ever expected to marry—

"He'll be writing better than ever soon," she promised in a curiously amused voice.

"I didn't say anything about its quality—quantity, too, counts. As a matter of fact, in the last scene of his he got the love-talk far better than in his opening one."

"Well, there you are!" said Florence, laughing a little under her breath.

"What can you have done that makes him look as

though he had been left a million?" persisted her brother. "And who is this friend of his called Mireille?"

"How should I know? Mireille? . . . Sounds a fancy name," she said innocently.

He gave her a suspicious look, but she began to sing in her hard, nasal voice, and led the way through the garden. She and Blythe were walking over to Castillon. Rackstraw was off for Menton, there to be rowed out to the *Baousse Rousse*, the famous Red Cliffs just over the Italian border where fifty thousand years ago paleolithic man lived—in bodily shape very much like his descendants, where the women wore shell bracelet jewellery very much such as can be bought at the local fairs.

The other two might join him later on, and all three come home together, or they might not get so far. Rackstraw never waited for any one.

Since Inskipp's resolute withdrawal, Florence had turned her attention to Blythe, with what success it was hard to say. Certainly Edna Blythe seemed pleased. Edna was an indolent person who spent long hours extended in a deck chair in the garden.

Whenever visitors came in for a drink, and they were fairly frequent these fine days, and she was out in the garden, she would envelope herself in a *Times* until the visitors had been shown to their rooms. Once, Inskipp happened to pick up her paper after it had been serving her for some time as a screen, and was amused to find its centre neatly pierced by a large pinhole. So that wrapped-up aspect concealed quite a good observation hole; but he dropped the paper again without giving the matter a second thought.

Blythe could be heard now calling: "Miss Rackstraw! Miss Rackstraw!"

His sister looked up and chaffed them as they set out, lunch in their shoulder-bags, stout sticks in their hands. Florence laughed back at her, and waved her hand to Inskipp up in his window.

He promptly sat down and started a letter to Madame de Pra far away in Rennes. A very humble letter, asking her if she could let him have a photograph of herself. He did not say that he had seen those in Florence's possession, but he did say how much he would like to have a picture of the writer of the enchanting notes which were his greatest joy in life. It took him quite half an hour to write, and he posted it in the nearest letter-box to the farm.

It was while walking back that he caught sight of some one—a man—waving and shouting and running. Inskipp waited. A minute later he saw that the man was Blythe. He hurried to meet him.

"It's Miss Rackstraw!" called Blythe, as soon as he got within talking range. "We must get something to carry her on—"

"What's happened?"

Then as Blythe, who looked very pale, did not reply, Inskipp went on: "Has she hurt herself?"

"She's dead." Blythe spoke in a tone as though overwhelmed by the calamity. He looked ghastly. "I'll tell you all about it in a moment. . . . As soon as I've seen Edna. . . . When I get my breath. . . . Back at the farm. . . ." He seemed uncertain where to tell it.

The two, without another word, hurried to the house. There they met Norbury mending the front gate. Blythe grasped his arm.

"Get a stretcher of some sort. Miss Rackstraw slipped off a rock, and is lying dead in a valley near here. Where's Edna?"

"Hold on a moment," said Norbury. "One at a time. Miss Rackstraw slipped? Where? How? But you need a whisky and soda."

Blythe did. Drinking it, he pulled himself together. They were walking in single file, he said, Miss Rackstraw leading, along a narrow ledge of rock, when suddenly a huge roar sounded behind them—a roar like nothing on earth, said Blythe. Startled, Miss Rackstraw missed her footing. She plunged over the ledge before Blythe or the man who was leading a baboon by a strap, and who had sat down to rest by the roadside, could put a hand out to grasp her. Blythe had clambered down after her and found her quite dead with a broken neck, as well as broken back.

"Good God!" muttered Norbury. "What a shocking accident! What became of the man and the beast?"

"I told him to wait by the body. The baboon was on its way to the Chateau Grimaldi, of course."

"I suppose you stopped at the *Commissariat de Police* to tell them about it? It was on your way here," Norbury said, hurrying back with them to the outbuildings.

Blythe had not. He seemed to have no idea where the Castellar police station was.

Norbury shook his head again, and said that they must go there at once. The police would attend to bringing up the body and getting into touch with the man who had the ape. "I suppose you can describe him?"

Blythe said that he was afraid not, beyond that he was middle aged, very dirty, dressed in innumerable garments all more or less ragged, and that the baboon was a big one.

Norbury pursed his lips over this, and again said that the only thing to do was to start at once for the police.

"I want a word with my sister first." Blythe made for the stairs.

"My dear fellow," said Norbury in his most peremptory manner, "you mustn't wait a moment! You must let the police know at once!"

"I must tell Edna!" said Blythe in a dogged tone. "She was a great friend of Miss Rackstraw. I want her to be prepared. The shock, you know—"

But Miss Blythe was not at the farm, and Norbury peremptorily refused to let Blythe try to find her outside. He dragged him almost by force to his car. Inskipp was genuinely shocked at the news, but then came the thought that now the two photographs of Mireille were ownerless. He knew the drawer where Florence kept them. As soon as Norbury and Blythe were off he would take them out into his own keeping.

But how dilatory Blythe was! When he finally got into the car he still looked strangely disturbed, Inskipp thought.

"Got your passport?" asked Norbury.

Blythe shook his head. "I haven't the faintest idea where it is. Besides, it's Miss Rackstraw, not me, who's been killed."

Norbury said no more; he drove away quickly. Inskipp slipped up to Florence's room and opened a certain drawer—it had no lock on it; nothing at the farm had a lock on it—and found the precious pictures. Slipping them into his pocket, he went on to his own room and put them safely away.

CHAPTER 4: MISS BLYTHE TAKES THE NEWS ODDLY

As Inskipp locked the portraits into his suitcase until such time as he could get frames worthy of them, he saw Edna Blythe coming through the gate, looking her usual indifferent self.

Inskipp hailed her and asked if he might have a word with her. She seemed startled, but she was easily startled, as he had noticed.

"It's about Miss Rackstraw," he called when she was inside, and Edna's face lost its look of interest.

"There's been an accident," Inskipp said. "Blythe wanted to find you, but Norbury thought the police should be told at once. Miss Rackstraw . . ." He told her what Blythe had told him. Blythe had spoken of the friendship between the two young women, a friendship of which Inskipp had seen no trace, but to his surprise Edna Blythe now turned an ashen face to his.

"My brother was with her?" she said in a curious, toneless voice and sank into a chair. "You're quite sure he didn't make a mistake? I mean, I suppose she really was dead—not just stunned?"

"He said that there was no question but that she was killed outright, that neck and spine were both broken by her fall. There are some nasty places in the gorges around here," Inskipp added. Then he stopped, for Edna's face looked as though she were on the point of fainting. He started towards her, but she waved him back and ran up the stairs to her own rooms. The Blythes had a wing to themselves. Inskipp took a few turns outside on the cement path. He could not understand Edna Blythe's way of taking the accident to Florence Rackstraw. It looked, it really looked, as though she suspected that Florence had met her death in some other way than as Blythe reported it to have happened. It seemed a preposterous notion, but turning it over now in his mind, he recollected an occasion, a week or so back, when he had come on the two of them in a chestnut wood evidently disagreeing about something. Richard Blythe had moved away just as Inskipp saw the two, and for a second, as she looked after him before she caught sight of Inskipp, the latter had fancied that he had seen the look of a trapped animal on Edna Blythe's face. He had told himself at the time that the shadows of the shifting branches were responsible for the fancy. He was not so sure now. It was a horrid thought. Inskipp was far more than good natured, he had a really kind heart, and that odd impression of the woods, added to the way in which Edna Blythe had just taken the death of Florence while out with her brother, disturbed him. Her brother. . . . Elsie Cameron had never liked Blythe. . . .

She and Mrs. Norbury were both still out. Edna Blythe and he were alone in the farm for the moment. He went to the foot of the stairs leading to her balcony, but when she ran down to him, it was from the stairs leading to his and the Rackstraws' rooms that she came, her suitcase in her hand.

"I went into Florence's room just for a moment," she said, answering his look. Her face flushed. "Florence asked me to see to something for her in Nice. And it must be done at once." She spoke hurriedly, her words tumbling over each other. As a rule Edna had a drawl. She actually bit her lip for a second as she faced him.

"I wonder—"she began. "Mr. Inskipp, I wonder"—her face was scarlet by now—" I wonder if you could let me have as much as—say—five hundred francs. I have hardly any French money."

As it happened, Inskipp had brought from Menton the last time that he was there the equivalent of fifty pounds in francs.

"It's just for the moment—my brother, of course, will repay it at once. I shan't get to Nice till too late for the banks," she murmured.

Inskipp assured her that he would get her the money. She thanked him tremulously.

"And please telephone for me to the Castellar Inn. I'm so upset I can't seem to remember my French. I want a car to take me down—at once!" Her teeth were actually chattering.

Inskipp telephoned immediately. He was told that Miss Blythe could have the Ford, but that there was no one to drive her.

"I'll drive myself. I don't mind. I'll be there at once. Tell him to be sure that there's plenty of petrol."

Inskipp could not offer to take her, for, not much of a driver at any time, he could not drive a Ford at all.

He handed her the notes and received a very grateful stammered word of thanks. Then unexpectedly she sat down at a table and began to write a short note. To her brother, she said. Meanwhile he picked up her suitcase and carried it out to the farm gates. She followed in a moment. She struck him as hardly conscious of where she was going, so long as she was making for Nice—or was that but a pretext to get away from the farm? He thought the latter, as the two now hurried on to the inn together. Some terror seemed to be urging her.

When the Ford was ready she jumped into the driving-seat, told the inn-keeper that she would not forget about the rule of the road in France, hurriedly shook hands with Inskipp, and said that she had written a line to her brother about the five hundred francs, which would he please hand him. She produced an envelope with *Richard Blythe* scribbled in pencil on it. "I'll leave it in his room," Inskipp promised.

She had her finger on the starter, but she took it away. "Not on any account!" she said earnestly, and again with that look of fear in her eyes: "*I* could have done that! Please hand it to him yourself."

She waited for his "Certainly, since you prefer it!" before she set the car in motion.

With her eyes fixed on the road ahead of her, Miss Blythe was out of sight in a few minutes.

She left Inskipp thoroughly uneasy. Back at the farm, he met Mrs. Norbury and Elsie, who heard the news with shocked horror. They, at any rate, did not look or act as though the fact that Richard Blythe had been alone with the dead girl had any terrible significance. On the contrary, Mrs. Norbury spoke of how great a shock it must have been for him.

As for Mrs. Rackstraw, she dreaded to think, she said, what a blow Florence's death would-be to her. And unfortunately the brother, being at the Red Caves, might not, she supposed, be home till late that night. "I suppose Mr. Blythe told his sister before my husband hurried him off?" she asked.

Inskipp said that Miss Blythe knew of the tragedy, and had at once gone to Nice on some errand of Florence Rackstraw's. He said nothing of the extraordinary emotion which she had shown.

Three hours passed before Norbury and Blythe returned. As Mrs. Norbury thought, the dead body of Florence had been taken to the village mortuary. She and Elsie went at once to the place to find it being transformed into a sort of chapel by the kindly people, who have that respect for death characteristic of their race, who see in it a promotion, rather than a mark of bondage.

"Luckily we belong to what is known as *Friends of the Police*," Norbury said with a grin. "It was my wife's doing that we joined, when we first took the farm. It's a small enough subscription when one finds what red tape it saves one from. I told you you ought to take your passport with you, Blythe!"

"But that would have meant a delay to find it," Blythe pointed out. "You went with me—that was enough."

"It wouldn't have been if we hadn't been *Amicales*,"

Norbury told him. "You've no idea how many forms have to be filled in in a matter of this kind."

"Were the police troublesome?" Inskipp asked.

"At first they were inclined to be a bit stuffy," Norbury replied. "But when they heard about the baboon, they knew that Professor Voronoff had a *'Permis'* to have another taken to his Chateau, and Blythe's account of it tallied. Very luckily, too, the man and it were rounded up at Mortola within half an hour. Fortunately the day is dry and the road showed the ape's prints as well as the marks of poor Miss Rackstraw's shoes where they slipped over the edge, so that there was no mistaking what had happened. But now, about Rackstraw at the Red Caves, how on earth are we to reach him? The police have learnt that he has already left the place, so there's nothing for it but to tell him when he gets here.

The Norburys were called away, and Inskipp promptly seized the opportunity to hand Blythe the letter from his sister.

Blythe read the few lines with a frown on his face. He was still frowning as he thanked the other for lending his sister the money. He did not look pleased, Inskipp saw, and the fact added to those doubts roused by Edna's manner.

The telephone rang. It was from Nice. From Miss Blythe, who was asking for her brother.

After a few minutes' listening to what she had to say at her end of the wire, Blythe told her that there would be no autopsy—that the police considered the tragedy to be quite simple and straight-forward. He went on to say that he had her letter, and would settle with Inskipp whom he had just thanked for his most opportune help. That done, he hung up, and went to change and have a bath, for the ravine had left its marks on him.

Norbury came in then. His wife had to hurry away on some household matter, but he poured out a glass of whisky and soda for himself. "Talking is thirsty work— especially talking to the police. Then, too, Blythe—" He paused to make sure that the door was shut before adding: "His nerves were in tatters. He took that poor girl's death uncommonly hard."

Quite unconsciously Norbury's tone suggested his surprise at such a display of emotion on Blythe's part. "I was afraid at one time that the police might think he was taking it too hard, and once the French Johnnies get that idea in their heads they can be very tiresome. Fortunately for Blythe, the place bore out his story in every detail. Personally I hardly know Miss Rackstraw. You and she were rather by way of being friends, weren't you?"

"Yes, she had some sterling virtues," said Inskipp warmly. He did not add that having Mireille de Pra as a friend was the chief among them.

Norbury and he now went up to Rackstraw's room, and tried to find the mother's address. But apparently Rackstraw had no note of it, and finally Inskipp went on to his own room.

He was rather surprised when, sometime later, Blythe slipped in and closed the door carefully behind himself. First of all, Blythe returned to him the five hundred francs lent to Edna, and then he added, with a very poor attempt at casualness— "By the way, Inskipp, do you mind my asking you not to do it again? I mean, lend my sister money. I'm no end grateful as things happened, but even so, I ask you not to do it a second time."

Inskipp stared.

"The fact is," said Blythe awkwardly, "the fact is, that Edna is rather addicted to gambling. That's between ourselves strictly, of course. She's doing her best not to play again, but that's why she never goes down to Menton with the rest of you, and for her sake I cut it out too. So— well—should she ever ask you to let her have any money again, just have a word with me first, will you?"

He waited till Inskipp, very startled, said that Blythe could rely on him not to lend money again to Miss Blythe, then he hurried off as the telephone bell began to ring down below.

So Edna Blythe was a gambler—or had been one of those unfortunate people. But nothing told him by Blythe just now would explain the real fear in her face and voice when she learnt that her brother had been alone with the girl who had met her death —Inskipp went over in his mind every detail of his talk with Edna when she asked him for the loan of the money—though it did explain her and her brother's prolonged stay at the farm, and their refusal ever to go down into Menton.

Going to the big sitting-room used by all the guests as a lounge, he learnt that Edna Blythe had telephoned to say that she had already started back for the farm. So she was not spending the evening at any casino. Curious . . . Blythe must have been very urgent on the matter. Or had her own good sense triumphed?

His thoughts turned to Mireille. She must be told, of course, but it would be a dreadful shock to her. By this time, he and she wrote to each other as implicit lovers. He had finally made no secret of his hope that, once her divorce was secured, they could stand affianced before their world; and Mireille had written him a most touching little note that never left him, confessing that she asked nothing better of life than that this should happen, that his letters had completely won her heart.

Miss Blythe got back late that night, and seemed delighted to be once more at the Chevre d'Or. In reply to Mrs. Norbury's questions as to what commission of Florence Rackstraw's had taken her so hurriedly to Nice, she only shook her head, and said that she was pledged to secrecy.

The next day, Rackstraw was still absent, very much to Norbury's vexation, for a note had come from the police requesting some one from the farm to go down to the British Consulate at Nice, and there explain just what had happened. The police had sent in their report, but, if the Consul thought fit, he might want an independent investigation made.

Norbury could not possibly leave, and Blythe had, he said, developed a throat overnight which prevented his using his voice.

Inskipp volunteered to go down and see the Consul at Nice, for he wanted to buy the most gorgeous frames that he could find there for the two portraits of Mireille. Mrs. Norbury thought that since her husband could not go, she ought to. So finally it ended in Mrs. Norbury, Elsie, and Inskipp going down together, while Edna Blythe insisted on her brother going to bed and letting her stir him up a linseed poultice.

Mrs. Norbury had begged her husband at breakfast to look again for Mrs. Rackstraw's address. But it was not until the car was almost at the gate that Norbury came down, waving a letter in his hand.

"Here's a note I found on Miss Rackstraw's mantel. In it is her mother's address in Bulawayo, or just outside it."

A cable was immediately telephoned. A long cable breaking the dreadful news.

At the British Consulate in Nice, they found that the French report had been so detailed that, after a few signed statements, the matter was at an end, as far as inquiries went. But the Consul wanted Florence Rackstraw's passport to be returned for cancellation.

"I think she had it with her," Mrs. Norbury explained. "We can't find it anywhere among her things, I feel sure it must have slipped out of her bag when she fell, and is lost somewhere among the undergrowth, but I'll look again for it when I get back to the farm."

On their return, Blythe's tonsilitis attack seemed to be very much better, so much so that he would be up and about on the next day, his sister thought.

"Funny, the way it's taken him!" said Norbury to his wife when they were alone. "I believe that throat of his was merely to get out of going with you."

Mrs. Norbury looked incredulous for a moment, then she said thoughtfully, "That seems rather far-fetched. I mean, that Miss Blythe would lend herself to any acting.

But the Blythes are rather funny—don't you think so, Frank?"

He had picked up a pile of French notes from the dressing-table. "These are from the Blythes? Wonder why he never pays with a cheque? Is that what you mean by funny?"

"I was thinking of the fact that neither of them ever get any letters." His wife spoke under her breath.

"They go down to Menton for them, so he says, and get them from Cook's, or from Barclay's bank."

"There are never any envelopes thrown away in their paper basket by either of them. Even Sabe has spoken of it."

"They are our salvation this bad year," was Norbury's only answer.

"All her underwear and all her clothes were bought at Menton," went on Mrs. Norbury. "The last place where one would buy an outfit, if one could help oneself, with Nice so close to us." She stopped, for Norbury's face showed clearly that he did not want to hear any gossip about the Blyths, the most profitable guests at the farm.

CHAPTER 5: INSKIPP DECIDES TO RETURN TO ENGLAND

Rackstraw arrived early next morning. He had been up in the hills, and so had missed the messages to him that the police had sent out.

In a couple of days it was, Inskipp thought, as though the sea had closed over the ugly, lanky figure of Florence Rackstraw, or as though she had never been, so little difference did her death seem to make in the life at the farm. He had to wait some time for a letter from Mireille; she wrote in great grief at the loss of her friend and then went on to tell him that she had been hurt in a car accident and that her arm had had to be set in plaster, though her fingers were free. She had no portrait to send him, she wrote, but would have one taken as soon as her arm was free again, and would send him a copy. The note was brief, as holding a pen under such circumstances was very difficult. She wrote that she hoped he could read her altered writing. But her next letter was typewritten. Mireille said that she had bought a typewriter, as the doctor told her that a compound fracture of the upper arm— which, it seemed, was what she had had—was often long in healing. Mireille wrote that she had told them to take all the time that was necessary, rather than let her arm be shortened, or stiffened. They had assured her that that could not happen, if she was patient. And again she spoke of what a loss the death of Florence was to her.

Inskipp was beside himself at the thought of her suffering, though she wrote that she was being wonderfully nursed by the nuns. As for her coming to the farm, she agreed that she could still come, but not for some time as the slightest jar might injure her arm beyond repair.

Inskipp forced himself to be content with her letters, and they were enchanting. Gay—sweet—and humorous by turns. But he found it hard to wait. He thought of coming to Brittany himself, but when he suggested this to Mireille, she wrote very definitely against it. Gossip would at once learn of his presence and of their friendship—and their hopes. And the knowledge would be used by the de Pra family to put yet another obstacle in the path of the divorce, which they were contesting so obstinately.

Autumn turned to winter, Christmas came and went, a gay festival, with circular loaves carried like wreaths hanging on the arm to be blessed at midnight mass on Christmas Eve, with saucers of growing wheat set at the corners of the tables, which had been set to soak on the festival of St. Barbara and which were now hand-high little tufts of green tied about with scarlet ribbon. Rackstraw and Inskipp were deep in their work which was practically finished. Rackstraw was going home shortly to find a producer, but as yet he had made no move. The Blythes spoke of leaving about the same time, but they too lingered. As for the Norburys, they seemed to have turned the corner at last, and showed cheerful faces as they went about the place. So had Inskipp up to these last days, but now, every twenty-four hours marked an added gloom. Rackstraw happened to come on him pacing his room one afternoon.

"I wonder if you could let me have—" he began. Inskipp made a gesture of negation which for him, was quite violent.

"I shall be able to pay back every farthing when I get home, apart from my share of the film," began Rackstraw huffily, but again Inskipp did not let him finish.

"I'm afraid I must ask you to do it before you leave. I'm sorry, but are you aware, Rackstraw, that you've borrowed close on fifty pounds from first to last?"

"Have I really? Well; as soon as I get home you shall

have it back—and interest too, if you like."

"I'm in a hole myself," said Inskipp, "or I shouldn't have to hound you for the money. I invested pretty nearly everything I own in Waverly Shipping bonds. They've become unsaleable, since Lord Waverly committed suicide last week."

"Did you put everything into one basket? My dear chap, how foolish! You should never do that, you know. Spread your risks. That's the point in—"

"The point is, that I want that money returned to me before you leave here," said Inskipp firmly. "I'm sorry, but I must have it."

"Well, I'll see what I can do," promised Rackstraw graciously, as though he were helping the other out with a loan. "I'll see what I can do."

Inskipp with a nod, let the matter rest there for the moment. He was indeed hard pressed, and his face grew careworn as he stood turning over what he had best do. Some sort of reconstruction scheme would certainly be put forward by the Receiver, and in his opinion the shares had not been overvalued at the price at which he had bought them. Given time, he believed that a good deal, if not all, of his money might yet be saved. But what was he to do in the meantime? There was no help for it, he must call in every outstanding farthing belonging to him, and return to England.

The trouble was that in the middle of November, Mireille had written asking him for a loan to help her get her divorce. She had explained that under the will of a French aunt, she would inherit the equivalent of around three thousand pounds, but only when de Pra was dead, or divorced by her. The aunt in question had so much disliked the marriage. She had sent Inskipp a copy of her aunt's will, and the name of her solicitor who lived at Clermont Ferrand, and added that she would need about seven hundred pounds at least, that the solicitor in question had offered to lend her the money, but at such extortionate interest that she was very unwilling to accept his offer.

Inskipp had written to the man, and had had a letter from him. Inskipp had wanted to know whether there was any doubt about the divorce being ultimately obtainable. The reply had been entirely reassuring. The avocat had explained, however, that it might cost nearer a thousand than seven hundred pounds, as very expert medical opinions on the question of Mr. de Pra's sanity and impossibility of his condition improving would have to be obtained. He had lived a long time in Indo-China, this would mean extra expense. Maitre Francois added that he could easily raise the sum, but that the client who was prepared to advance it insisted on the high interest to which Madame de Pra objected.

Inskipp thought of going to Clermont-Ferrand, but the journey from Menton was difficult and long, with many changes. Nor would he, a stranger, be able to rely on his judgment of the character of this Maitre Francois. He must get some information about him from a reliable source. And then he remembered that at the Menton branch of the English Bank, the manager had once spoken of knowing Auvergne well. Clermont-Ferrand is the capital of Auvergne.

He went down to Menton, and cashed a note at the bank in question, waiting about until he caught sight of the manager. Then he stepped forward.

Could the manager spare him a few minutes in private? A most obliging man promptly took him into his own room and offered him a chair.

Inskipp explained that he had been given the name of a Maitre Francois, as that of a good avocat of Clermont-Ferrand. Could the manager tell him what was his reputation.

The manager promptly told Inskipp that his affairs could be in no better hands, especially if they belonged to what he might call the family type. "I don't know him personally, but every one in Auvergne knows his name. He rather specialises in divorce cases, but by no means entirely. I hear he is being very much pressed to go into politics. You will be lucky if he takes on any new business."

"Is he well-to-do? Frankly, it's a question of a lady placing rather a large sum of money in his hands to be applied to—er—legal work."

"My dear sir, a Frenchman doesn't think of entering politics if he is not well-to-do! Maitre Francois is considered a rich man, and comes of a very wealthy Clermont-Ferrand family. He belongs to what they call the *noblesse de robe*."

Inskipp thanked the manager and left. The next post carried a letter to Mireille saying that he could let her have the money without, of course, any interest. Should he send his cheque to her, or to Maitre Francois? He had made it out, he wrote, for a thousand pounds, the surplus to be retained temporarily by the solicitor for unexpected emergencies.

She had written him a most grateful note, asking him to send the money to Maitre Francois who would draw up the proper papers for it to rank as a first charge on her legacy from her aunt. She did not want it sent by cheque, however, as it would so remain entered on his books. Under the circumstances, she thought the money had best be sent in 1,000-franc notes.

Inskipp thought it over, and decided that her caution was justified.

The pound was exactly a hundred francs at the moment, so that a very small packet of the thin, beautiful, French notes made up the equivalent of the sum wanted. Inskipp obtained them at the bank in Menton against his cheque, and, for additional safety in the post, had the manager make a note of their numbers.

Maitre Francois duly acknowledged the notes, enclosed some papers for Inskipp to sign, and said that the figure set was an outside estimate which he hoped not to have to reach.

Mireille wrote to Inskipp scolding him tenderly for his

generosity. She herself was living very cheaply at the convent, and would be at still less expense in the future, as the time had now come for her yearly round of inescapable family visits to begin. Inskipp was to continue to send all his letters as, at her request, he had done the last ones to her, care of Maitre Francois. Otherwise, Mireille wrote, she and he could not correspond at all. The idea of her receiving a letter in an unknown handwriting—a man's too—without reading it aloud, was unthinkable to her family circle. As for her arm—it was healing very well, but she still could not hold anything small, such as a needle, or even a pen, in her fingers without her hand aching badly. Her relations always went to one or other of the many French spas and were already discussing which would be best for her arm. No, she could not get away to *La Chevre d'Or* yet. But once her three months' duty round was over, she could come—and come without rousing comment, and be there for the spring parade of Provence.

When the blow of his almost unsaleable shares fell on him, Inskipp thought it over, thinking for two people, himself and his future wife, Mireille— for they were by now definitely engaged—and it seemed to him that there was but one thing to do. Mireille must borrow from her solicitor the equivalent of the thousand pounds which he had lent her; and he—Inskipp—would take back his own loan and pay the ten per cent interest asked by the solicitor's client. It could not be much longer now before the divorce went through—another three months at most, thought the Clermont man, and then the money could be repaid from the legacy coming to Mireille. As for himself, Inskipp believed that if he went and had a personal interview, his own old Stock Exchange firm, who happened to have just lost a partner, might let him come in again with his depreciated shares as his investment and, since he was returning to the House, he could arrange to be let off the purchase price of his seat, or at any rate have it lessened to a sum which he could raise.

Meanwhile, with the return of the thousand by Mireille he could live, and as his income from the firm he intended to join would, after the first year, be quite adequate, he and Mireille could start life together in comfort if not in luxury. But he must first, for both their sakes, get back his loan—and he wrote a very businesslike note to Mireille, setting it all out clearly.

He had, in return, one of the most enchanting letters which he had yet had. Inskipp read it with tears in his eyes. His heart was very tender towards the lovely creature who had come into his life, "lovely within as without," he murmured, as he put the letter away. For the rest, he was glad that he had the photographs of her that she had given to Florence Rackstraw, for there were no photographers near the convent, and, though Mireille wrote every now and then that she would have her portrait taken, she had very little time for long outings. He had let her guess almost at once by some phrase of hers that he had, or had seen, her portrait, and she more than once wrote as though that should content him until they should meet. Inskipp with some misgivings, had finally sent her one of his that he had taken for the purpose in Menton, and she had said that he looked just as she had thought that he would look. A sentence which made him laugh a little wryly, and put aside in his memory as something with which to tease her, when they really should talk together. . . . When he should hear her voice. . . . Florence said that she had the most beautiful voice that she had ever heard, and Inskipp loved a sweet voice.

The reply from the solicitor at Clermont, as Inskipp called the town to himself, was slow in coming. Maitre Francois pointed out that it might take him some time to find any one willing to lend the necessary amount needed by Madame de Pra, as the client who had proposed it before had been drowned in one of the recent floods which had turned the surrounding plains into lakes. He did not despair, he said, of ultimately finding a lender, but, just at the moment money was very tight. That he did not think the loan an impossibility, was the great thing, Inskipp decided, for Francois had struck him from his letters as a man who would be ultra cautious in money matters. He probably was equally cautious in his promises. But there would be no more loans to Rackstraw. Both he and Inskipp believed that they ought to sell the scenario for a good figure. Rackstraw, who had quite a fair knowledge of such things, talked of an out and out sale for four thousand pounds. Still, there must be no more loans. . . .

Having given Rackstraw his ultimatum as it were, Inskipp went for a slow walk and on his return he looked around for Norbury. He might as well know that his— Inskipp's—stay was drawing to a close. He came on him sitting in the hot sunlight against an old wall entering the weights of basket of oranges as they were called after him.

Inskipp told him that he must shortly go home. At the moment he could not give the exact date.

"Any complaints?" Norbury asked.

Inskipp said that he had been extremely comfortable. It was necessity, not choice, that was making him leave.

"I may have to go home very shortly myself, though it is January," said Norbury now. We might go together. When my wife and I were in Marseilles in November, doing the farm's annual purchases, we heard of a man in London who wanted to act as an agent for Riviera produce. Honey and *raisine* especially. I've had his position looked into, and been corresponding with him, and now the deal is ready to go through. The sooner the better, but I won't close without having seen him."

CHAPTER 6: SOME OLD NEWSPAPERS FURNISH INTERESTING READING

It was sometime in the late afternoon that Inskipp drew up his plans more definitely. In reply to another letter of his to Maitre Francois, that gentleman had written that he had now found a client who would make Madame de Pra a loan on her aunt's legacy. It was difficult to say what displeased Inskipp about the note. An absence of precision, perhaps. It looked to him as though Maitre Francois were more concerned about running up a big bill of costs than about securing the loan. That seemed odd in a man of his reputation. . . . The whole letter, however, seemed odd to him, though he could not put his finger on the exact reason for the feeling. He decided that he would stop over at Clermont long enough to interview the maitre. And he decided also that he would not give him any preliminary warning.

The man's letters hitherto had impressed him very favourably. He wrote very fluent English. If he spoke the language as well as he wrote it, they should soon be able to understand each other. Inskipp only hoped profoundly that the tone he detected in the last letter did not mean that the lawyer was not as certain now about securing a divorce for Mireille as he had seemed before.

Had something unforeseen happened? Had some new law been passed? Or was one about to be passed? The mere possibility weighed on Inskipp profoundly. But he hoped soon to have his mind set at rest. He found that Rackstraw was perfectly willing to leave for England in a week's time, provided they went by train and boat. That arranged, Inskipp went again in search of Norbury.

He found him in one of his barns, with a big stand of pears and a pile of old newspapers. Each pear was to be wrapped afresh before being laid back again on its tray. At the moment Norbury was not working. He was lying on his stomach on a spread-out paper apparently engrossed in reading its contents.

At the sound of Inskipp's steps, Norbury promptly rolled over so as to completely cover the paper. Then he looked up.

"Hard at work, I see," said Inskipp, grinning. "I heard you say that there's nothing like a glass of Castellar to make you feel energetic."

"I said that it made one work like a nigger," corrected Norbury, getting up, "and it does!"

Norbury was putting together some sheets of the many papers scattered around him. Evidently he had been spending some time in reading. He now held one out to Inskipp with the odd words, "You're a discreet chap; do you recognise that woman's face?"

Inskipp did not. He was never a keen observer.

"How about this one—same woman—but I've altered it a little?" Norbury passed him another paper, folded so that another portrait of the same face showed. The face had had slanting eyebrows pencilled in by Norbury, and instead of the neat roll of long hair on the back of the neck that showed in the picture, he had drawn straight, shingled hair hanging on each side of the face.

"Why, it's Miss Blythe to the life!" Inskipp said with a laugh.

But Norbury did not laugh. He glanced at the little window above them. It was shut.

"Look here, Inskipp, I can rely on that discretion of yours—absolutely?"

"You can. But why?"

"Have a look at the name below the picture."

Puzzled, Inskipp opened up the paper. He read aloud:

"'Mrs. Whin-Browning getting into her car.' Mrs. Whin-Browning!" he repeated in a tone of stupefaction.

Then he studied the altered face again.

"It's certainly awfully like Miss Blythe, but I suppose

altering a face like that, one might make all sorts of likenesses—"

"I haven't altered it except as Miss Blythe has done," said Norbury meaningly. "*I* didn't change the eyebrows and darken the hair."

"Good God!" came from Inskipp, who was now staring as though hypnotised at the portrait. "You think—it's not possible!"

"Look at this," said Norbury, pulling out another sheet. It showed a young man in flannels.

"That's Blythe! said Inskipp instantly, "and a jolly good picture of him too! He stopped as he read the words below the snapshot.

"Just so," said Norbury meaningly. "'Hector Whin-Browning playing cricket.' He was the younger brother of the one who died. He didn't appear in the case at all, as he was in Paris at the time. Well, I don't think there's much doubt who the two Blythes really are."

Inskipp nodded in silence.

About a year ago, a London barrister named Ambrose Whin-Browning had died from influenza, it was thought. A couple of weeks later his sister, who lived with him and his wife, died also. This time there was an autopsy, which was promptly followed by the exhumation of the brother's body. Both deaths were proved to have been the results of arsenical poisoning.

The case had been an amazing one. It had shaken all England, though it had only progressed as far as the inquest stage, for the coroner, who was also a solicitor, had made the most of his out-of-date powers, and had conducted it as far as possible as a trial of Mrs. Whin-Browning for the murder of her husband and of her sister-in-law.

The third day of the inquest had been a Saturday. In the afternoon, Edna Whin-Browning left her home in Brighton where the two deaths had occurred, and had gone for a swim. She never returned. Her clothes were found close to a very dangerous cave, one with a tremendous out-current, but the police believed that she had made her way abroad.

The inquest had continued on the Monday without her, and had finished on the Wednesday in a verdict of murder against Mrs. Whin-Browning on both counts.

For a month the papers had been filled with portraits of her, accounts of her past life—which proved to be disappointingly blameless—and speculations on whether she had been drowned or not; and if so, whether it had been accident or suicide.

There was a silence—on Inskipp's part, of sheer stupefaction as he studied the picture again.

"It certainly is her. Her face is much thinner—she's altered the shape of her eyebrows, and she's cut her hair short. I rather thought she was innocent, only lost her nerve, and fled."

"So did I!" came from Norbury. "And I'm still convinced that she is innocent. My belief was, and is, that her companion, the young woman's name was Marsh, I think—was in love with Whin-Browning, that he got tired of her, and that Miss Marsh did for him in revenge. And, because she suspected, or saw, something, the sister had to go too. Evidently the brother thinks his sister-in-law— our Miss Blythe—innocent. Or he wouldn't be standing by her. Without him, I don't see how she could keep afloat. If innocent, she wouldn't have made any arrangements about her money." There followed another silence.

"Her running away was what turned the scales against her in most people's opinion," said Inskipp. He had had no time for papers himself at the time of the inquest except financial ones, but no one had talked of much else for a fortnight.

"What turned the scales against her was the spiteful evidence of the companion, Miss Marsh. The person who I believe to've done the poisoning. As to getting away—only thing to do, in my opinion. She was for it, if she had stayed!" said Norbury, getting up.

"How did you come on these?"

"The British Club at Menton sent them with a cart-load of others. I always buy their thrown-out newspapers. It was mere chance, as I was cutting them into squares, that the likeness struck me, and then I saw that one of the brother—of Blythe—and knew!"

"And do you also know, what are you going to do?" asked Inskipp.

"Nothing," Norbury replied with conviction, "unless keeping silence is doing something. She's greatly to be pitied," he went on after a moment. "A wealthy woman—turned into an outcast."

"Wealthy?" Inskipp asked. An idea had struck him.

"Very. The coroner made a lot of capital out of the fact that each death was tremendously to her advantage. Her husband had left everything to her, except a large bequest to his sister—he only had the one—which, if the latter died unmarried before his wife, was to go to the wife. Mrs. Whin-Browning had had no settlements made on her when she married."

"So that, before the casualties, the lady hadn't much money?"

"Not a penny piece, except as her husband allowed it to her. The coroner made a lot of that too. She must have around eighty thousand now—which she can't touch." Norbury pulled the stack of papers towards himself and began to look them over. Remember, I have your word to keep this discovery of mine to yourself! I shall burn these papers."

"May I keep them for a bit? An idea has just struck me." Inskipp's face was alight. "If she's innocent—"

"Oh, she is! I'll stake the farm on that!"

"If I agree with you, when I've carefully gone through them again, I might offer my services to Mrs. Whin—"

Norbury's finger stopped him. "I think we'd better not use that name!"

"Quite right!—To Miss Blythe. If I do offer to help her, and if she thinks that amateur help can be any good to her, I might see what can be done when I get back to

England. I'm afraid I should have to ask a payment."

"Of course, you must ask a good one. It's worth it," Norbury said promptly.

"I might suggest five hundred," said Inskipp.

"Half down; the remainder if I succeed. I shouldn't be able to devote my time to it otherwise, and I should like immensely to undertake it—"

"So should I, if I could spare the time," said Norbury, " but I can't. This farm takes all my time. And if I do start an agency in London to sell Riviera produce, that will mean no end of book-keeping. As to the newspapers— take them by all means. As many as you want—but keep them locked away very carefully. It's life or death to that poor woman."

"I certainly will, but I had to tell you of what's in my mind," said Inskipp, "as I had promised you to say nothing about what you were telling me."

"That only applies to the world in general—and here at the farm in particular."

Norbury and Inskipp together weeded out the papers that dealt with the Whin-Browning case, and then, leaving Norbury to get on with his fruit, Inskipp stepped out into the sunshine. Going round the other side of the wing, he almost fell over Rackstraw lying in the shade of the wall just under the window of the room where he and Norbury had been talking. Fortunately, Rackstraw's naps were known for their heaviness. Lying on his back, his mouth open, he looked the picture of slumber. Inskipp stepped across him, and made his way to his own room.

The terror which he had read in Edna Blythe's face when she heard that Florence Rackstraw had fallen and been killed when alone with Blythe . . . her flight—for it had been that—to Nice. . . . He saw that probably what had frightened her was the police inquiry which Florence's death might entail. Very likely the letter that he was to hand Blythe and not leave in his room for him, referred to this. The passports of herself and Blythe would be in their real names. Norbury let his guests fill in their own "arrival papers." That, Inskipp saw, was probably the reasons why the brother and sister had stayed, and intended to stay, on at the farm. Blythe, too, had not shown his to the police, and had not gone down to the British Consulate at Nice. All Miss Blythe's dislike of strangers was explained now, as well as her own and her brother's withdrawal, as much as possible, from their fellow guests.

Inskipp went carefully through the papers. Then he locked them away in his suitcase, and sat on thinking. He was not satisfied. He was not so sure of the woman's innocence as he had been before he had read all the facts. He wanted to be. He would like to help her—if she were innocent.

It occurred to him that he had a means of testing that innocence. If he offered to go to England to rehabilitate Mrs. Whin-Browning, and if she agreed to his terms— that, Inskipp decided, would prove her to be, as Norbury maintained, only unfortunate —not guilty.

Inskipp ran lightly up the stairs to the sitting-room of the so-called brother and sister which was in the west wing.

Inskipp closed the door carefully behind him. "Forgive my bursting in on you like this," he said as he did so. "I want to talk to you two—quite frankly—if I may."

He did not dare give himself time to think.

"Sit down," said Blythe, and something in his tone suggested a man who might not be quite so easy -going as his face looked. As for Miss Blythe, she turned quite pale.

"I am going back to England shortly, and I wondered whether, while there, I might not be able to serve you, Miss Blythe."

She stared at him, too taken by surprise to speak—or too frightened.

"I'm going to England shortly," said Blythe in a level tone, "so that I don't see—"

"You might be handicapped—Mr. Whin-Browning," said Inskipp in a whisper, coming very close to him. "I should be quite free to get things cleared up without any one suspecting that there was a connection between us."

There followed a moment of absolute silence. Miss Blythe had leapt to her feet and stood now staring at his face. He turned so that she could see it clearly. As for Blythe, he had stepped back, but his fists had clenched. There was a very ugly look on his features.

"Suppose you let me talk to Miss Blythe first, by ourselves," suggested Inskipp. "If she accepts the offer of my help, then we three will go into the matter together. If she declines, then the whole affair will be instantly buried."

For an instant, their eyes met. In hers was a look of agonised hope. Only an innocent woman, Inskipp believed, could look like that at such a moment, and he felt sure of his ground.

Blythe came closer, the veins on his neck and temples were swollen, but his face was now paler than his sister-in-law's.

"My name is Blythe, and I'll thank you to remember it!" he said icily. "As for any help—we need no proffered services."

Standing behind him, but a little to one side, Inskipp caught a warning, and yet an imploring look, from Miss Blythe. It only lasted for a second, then she looked down at her tightly-clasped hands.

"I don't see how you are going to prevent my talking to your sister alone," Inskipp said, facing up to Blythe. He did not like the look on the man's face at all. "Unless you mean that you consider her your prisoner"

Blythe took a step towards him and for a moment Inskipp thought that there was going to be a rough house. But after standing for a second, almost shoulder to shoulder, Blythe turned away to the woman.

"What do *you* say?" he asked in a surly tone.

"I want to hear what Mr. Inskipp proposes," Miss Blythe said with composure. "If you will go for a walk for an hour, that would give us plenty of time to thrash the question out, and have something definite to tell you on your return."

"You're a fool, Edna!" said Blythe in a warning tone, "the only thing to do now, is to lock this busybody up where he can't do any harm, and get away— over into Italy, and through it into that other place I know of—"

"No," Edna said firmly, "the offer was made to *me,* concerns *me,* I want to hear what Mr. Inskipp has to say. I want an hour to talk it over."

"Do you, by God!" The words were a snarl. "He'll have to settle with me, remember."

She turned to him with a smile.

"Of course he will. Naturally he will. Now leave us here for an hour. Unless you want us to go for a walk—"

"No," said Blythe very ungraciously, "this is the safest place for a private talk. I'm off. For exactly sixty minutes."

Blythe stamped heavily down the wooden stairs.

Edna stood listening intently, she went to the window to watch his burly figure making off by the maize plantations, then she turned, her face all white and quivering.

CHAPTER 7: INSKIPP UNDERTAKES A COMMISSION

"And now, Mr. Inskipp, what is it exactly that you have to say to me?"

Edna Blythe sat down on a very hard, stiff, sofa and motioned him to sit beside her. Her face was more composed, but she was still trembling.

"First of all, I want you to feel certain that I come as a friend," he said awkwardly. "I know who you are, and I realise what a hole you are in. I realise, too, that, however much he wants to help you, Blythe must be handicapped by his relationship to you—and by his name. He can hardly work at clearing you without attracting attention. Whereas I, a complete stranger--"

"How did you learn about me?" she asked in a whisper.

"Some old papers—which I have safely locked away in my room."

"Portraits?" she whispered.

"Especially that of your brother-in-law," he agreed.

"And—does any one else know?" She could hardly get the words out. Looking into her face of terror, Inskipp evaded a truthful reply. "I've not shown them to any one. I've locked them up securely."

"Oh, thank you!" she breathed, too agitated to notice that he had not really answered her.

"I am convinced of your innocence," he went on, under his breath, "I would like to help you. I have no special qualifications beyond my goodwill. I used to be on the Stock Exchange. But, as I see it, any help is worth your accepting."

"Any real, honest help—yes," she said in a sort of

gasp.

"That at least I can offer," he said, looking full at her. "Real and honest. I suggest an agreement, since I'm too poor just now to work for the love of it— as I would gladly do."

He named his proposed terms. He wanted to get this part over early. He did not want her to thank him for his chivalry, and then have to speak of money.

She said nothing for a moment.

"If you think two hundred and fifty too steep to pay down straight away— " he began awkwardly—

Suddenly he realised that she was crying. At first gently, then almost wildly.

He waited for her to grow calmer. Finally she turned to him, wiping the tears off her cheeks.

"If you knew what your offer means! What despair I've been in. How helpless!" She struggled for composure.

"You accept it?"

"With a deeper gratitude than I can say! You see, Hector—"She put a hand out as though to ward off a danger. "I thought I had no one else," she whispered. "He wants me to marry him. I daren't refuse. And yet—"

"You don't love him?"

"Even if I loved him, I wouldn't marry him. I wouldn't condemn myself to remain Mrs. Whin-Browning all the rest of my life. But as it is, I—" she drew a swift, sobbing breath, "I haven't been able to talk to any one. I must speak to you—once! I didn't love my husband. The coroner knew that from that odious Marsh woman. My solicitor had learnt that he was going to come out with that when the inquest opened again—on Monday."

This was news to Inskipp.

"I *can't* marry Hector," she jumped to her feet. "The very look of him—he's like his brother—his mere presence in the room—I've been thinking lately that I should have to kill myself to end it," she went on in a rush of emotion.

"He loves you?" Inskipp asked. He had to know where

he stood.

"Yes. He helped me to escape. Nothing can alter the gratitude I ought to feel for him for that, you may say, but he has altered it—swept it all away. He will only help to prove me innocent if I marry him. I have put him off— asked for time— but I thought I should have to give in— or take the only way out."

"Can he clear you? I mean, does he know any one, definite, fact which would do this?"

She shook her head sadly.

"No. But like you—like any one who would try to help me—he would have to see where he could catch Miss Marsh out. For she was the poisoner, Mr. Inskipp. And there must be some trace of it. Poison can't be bought without signing books— without people knowing about it—"

"And Hector Whin-Browning has insisted on marriage in return for saving you?" It was an infernal bargain, Inskipp thought.

She nodded.

"But surely you could have got out of it," he went on. "I mean, no one would have blamed you if you had promised him, and then thrown him over? Besides, what about your names leaking out? If you were married under false names, and each knew it, the marriage wouldn't be valid. You would be free."

"That was my first hope," she said, but with a stricken face, "but he warned me he wouldn't set to work until a month after the marriage. But, if you can let me do without him altogether—"a look of rejoicing swept for an instant over her face.

"I will do my best," he said firmly.

"Lately he's beginning to realise that he can't stir to help me himself without leading them eventually to my hiding-place and bringing himself under suspicion of being an accessory after the fact. And that's a point that I hope you have thought over, Mr. Inskipp"—she bent closer towards him—"should you fail, should you be unable to clear me—you may get into dreadful trouble yourself for concealing my whereabouts."

Inskipp was well aware of such a danger, but he thought it a remote one. Even if he failed to clear Mrs. Whin-Browning, he did not expect to be suspected of knowing her hiding-place.

"Would Blythe give me away?" Inskipp asked promptly.

"Not unless he thought that I might not be going to marry him. In that case he might act on some impulse."

"I wonder if it would relieve matters if he knew, in confidence, that I am looking forward to my own marriage? This is her photograph—" Inskipp took out a portrait from an inner pocket which brought an exclamation of admiration from Edna.

"But how beautiful—how absolutely beautiful! Who is she?"

Inskipp pocketed the photograph again. "Her name is Mireille. The engagement is really a secret," he said, "and there are family reasons why it must stay so for the present—unfortunately. I only produced her picture to show you that you need not be afraid of sentimental complications. This is a purely business venture on my part. Now will you tell me your own story of what happened—"

"Certainly. But first, the money—do you mind letting Hector think that you are only to be paid afterwards?" she asked, flushing deeply. "I have to act as though I have none. I have plenty—in English notes, but I had sworn to myself to keep it till it could be used to definitely free me. My solicitor had me send for all my available balance at my bank after the first day of the inquest. He was afraid that things might be difficult."

"Did he help you to get away?" Inskipp asked impulsively.

"I promised never to tell how I was got out of England," she replied to that. "But the point is, that I left with plenty of English money—in a screw-topped bottle," she added with a laugh.

So she *had* swum to safety.

"Hector has paid for both of us ever since. He is very well off. He likes to think me entirely helpless, and I soon saw that the time might come when I would need every farthing I managed to get away with."

"Why didn't you try to escape? Leave him? If he's such a tyrant?"

"He told me that he would set the police immediately on my trail," she said under her breath. "And he would, too! That's the danger. If you want to help me, you will have to be very careful. You will have to be careful of him, I mean, as well as of the police."

"But surely he wants to save you from this dreadful position—to clear you—" Inskipp's generous heart was aghast.

"He does. But he had hoped to do it on his own terms, though I think he's just beginning to realise that that may be impossible."

There was a silence for a moment.

"When that accident happened to Miss Rackstraw—" he began tentatively.

Edna interrupted him impulsively. "I was terrified. So was he! An inquiry into her death might have meant our discovery. I hadn't even a passport then that I could show. I mean," she looked uneasy, "I mean my own passport is so dangerous. I thought I should go out of my mind with the terror of what might be ahead of me! That was why I rushed down to Nice. I've been angry with myself ever since, that I didn't go farther— get away, that I returned to the farm. But now— now—there's a chance of being really set free from this dreadful, everlasting hiding, this perpetual fear!"

"What about the casinos?" he asked suddenly. "How do you manage, if you want to play?"

She stared in what appeared to be honest surprise. "*I* never play. My husband used to. But he lost so much, that it cured me of any liking for gambling."

So Blythe had not been telling the truth. He had only wanted to make sure that Edna should not have the means to run away! It was a horrid idea.

The two of them drew up a simple contract. Hector Whin-Browning would insist on what would be called by that name, but this private one acknowledged the payment to Inskipp of two hundred and fifty pounds, with the promise of another equal amount if, and when, Mrs. Whin-Browning could return to England without any danger of arrest.

Inskipp had wondered whether she would be willing to accept him on his own terms. For all she could tell, this might be just the first edge of blackmail. He might have no intention of doing anything whatever for the money.

He said as much to her, putting it quite bluntly.

She gave him a tragic look. "I have to chance that," she said sombrely.

"But then—I have to chance so much more than that. I have to chance my neck." She said the last words slowly and with an irrepressible shiver. And he felt his own scalp tingle. "If you don't succeed—" she broke off. And then pulled herself together. "But I feel sure that you will! I am innocent. So some one else must be guilty. I never have believed in these detective stories which make all sorts of complications twist around a crime. It's so untrue to life. I don't think that you, or any one with brains, who would make the effort, couldn't clear up any crime in a couple of days. Here, it's a question of a very few people who could have done it—I'm out of it. That leaves really only Miss Marsh as the suspect. Concentrate on her, and you can't go wrong."

Inskipp felt that there was something in this advice.

"I suppose your solicitor would have done that, if it had come to a trial?—I mean, have concentrated on your companion, Miss Marsh?"

"He thought me guilty," she said wearily. "The only one who really believed in me was Hector—and the servants. It might pay you to question them about those days. One of them, my parlourmaid, Ada Greenlee, has a situation in Dover, I believe. You might try her first."

Hector Whin-Browning—or Richard Blythe as he signed himself, came back now, and within a minute, Edna had managed to pass on to him the news that Inskipp was engaged to be married, though, since her family objected to the match, the engagement was a secret one. At that Blythe thawed. After a few words of congratulation to Inskipp and the latter's reply, he was shown a glimpse of the photograph. He seemed about to ask a question, but instead he began to draft the contract, with the look of a man who has no thoughts to spare on nonessentials.

Then the three of them went over the case again very thoroughly, and Inskipp, primed with a mass of notes which he took as they talked, felt that with these, added to the newspaper clippings, he ought to be able to help Edna. He, too, agreed that the criminal could only be Miss Marsh, and that very likely an inquiry into her past would soon yield some helpful results.

The parlourmaid, if still in Dover, might help. The coroner had believed that she had some spiteful tale about the companion which she wanted to air, and which he intended should not be told; but Edna thought that Ada Greenlee, who was very truthful, might be of the greatest use to Inskipp. She corresponded occasionally with her solicitor, and she would get the address and send it on to him.

"You are going to England anyway," said Blythe finally, "on your own affairs you told us. I ought to go too. I must show myself soon for a couple of weeks. We might go together, as far as Dover at any rate. Though, you will, of course, call on me in town to hear what I have to tell you about the two deaths—"

"But you haven't anything to say—you weren't in England!" protested Edna Blythe.

"Inskipp will call on me to learn that I have nothing to tell him," insisted Blythe, "in that way we shall meet at my club. After that, while I'm in town, I should expect to keep in touch with him, and hear how he is getting on, for he will be looking into the case for me. After all, Edna, though Ambrose and I didn't hit it off extra well, I assure you I'm more than interested in clearing up his murder."

"I can't stay here alone," Edna said to that. "If you two go to England, I think I might venture—must venture—to get nearer to home."

But Blythe would not hear of it, and Inskipp, too, begged her to stay in this out-of-the-way place where no questions would be asked about her. Inskipp hoped that it would not be for long, that a very few weeks might let them send for her to join them, but until they should send word, she must not jeopardise her life.

When he left the two, he saw Norbury in a shed wheeling his wire trays into a dark, airy corner. A glance from him, and Inskipp whispered, "Terms agreed. I'm to get to work," before he passed on. In his own room, he paced up and down, turning over the facts as far as he knew them. He was learning them by heart as though for an examination. Names, places, and hours that mattered. It was, as Edna Blyth had said, a seemingly simple case. The only two possible criminals seemed to be herself, or her companion, Miss Marsh.

And yet, his first glow over, Inskipp was struck with the insufficiency of motive in the latter's case. Even assuming, as so many did, as apparently Edna Blythe knew, that there had been a love affair between husband and companion, nothing fresh had arisen to account for murder.

And then an idea occurred to him. Had Whin-Browning made a new will? Was Miss Marsh's name in it? Had he been poisoned because he had threatened to destroy this second will? Had he managed to do it, and had the poisoner slipped up on the crime?

Inskipp decided that he would investigate along that line first of all. That decided, he switched his mind to his own affairs. The two hundred and fifty pounds would be very useful. He would spend as little as possible on himself, and be as careful of the money as he could. Inskipp knew many a cheap place in London, or at least he knew where to find them. He might not need to look them up. Only after his talk with Maitre Francois at Clermont would he know just where he stood, and how much likelihood there was of a speedy loan to Mireille, which would free his own, urgently needed, thousand pounds.

He had a talk with Edna the next day, when he chanced on her alone in a sunny spot. He did not mention the possibility of a second will, but he spoke of hoping to see Miss Marsh on his arrival in London. She had a sister employed in the post office, and through her he ought to be able to find where she was now staying. I shall write and ask for an interview. I shall pose to her as a mere acquaintance of Blythe's writing up the case," he added.

"But the danger of going directly to her?" Edna protested. "Oh, Mr. Inskipp, the real, personal, danger! Once a poisoner, you know! I think you ought to proceed more carefully—more subtly, if I may say so. Find out all you can of her past life, yes—but don't for goodness' sake go directly to her!"

Inskipp told himself that it was charming of her to care for his safety so keenly, but he was conscious that he would have preferred a vigorous assent. Somehow such solicitude—in a woman in her desperate case—she must have a very unselfish nature—very! Of course, obviously, she could not be afraid of anything he might learn from the one-time companion—she could not be hiding anything from him. No woman in her position would be so mad; and Inskipp had learnt to have a great respect for Miss Blythe's brains these last hours. No foolish woman could have kept to the point as she had done in their talk. No, no, he told himself, as he left her under her umbrella, the cigales chirping all around her, she was merely too sensitive.

Women were like that. There was Mireille first and

foremost, who never seemed to think of herself. And here was poor Mrs. Whin-Browning. . . . Inskipp determined to do all that was humanly possible to set her free from her dreadful position.

CHAPTER 8: INSKIPP GOES TO DOVER

There was quite a party from *La Chevre d'Or* starting off for England together. Elsie Cameron went, too. She was going first to Aries and then on to Cassis—that haunt of the artist in Provence. There was nothing to detain her at the farm. Her sketches were finished, and finished also was any chance she might ever have had of being more to Inskipp than the merest of acquaintances. For weeks she had hoped—then half hoped—then almost hoped. Now there was certainty. From Cassis she was returning to her home in Perth, and it would be years before she would see Menton and its valleys again.

Inskipp only told the others of his proposed stop at Clermont-Ferrand when they were getting their tickets in Menton on the Friday afternoon of their departure. Blythe had anyway wanted to stay over the Saturday in Paris. Rackstraw had an appointment for early Monday morning with one of what he called his "film magnates," a man who lived just outside Dover. He wanted Inskipp to accompany him, and the latter saw no reason why this should not be possible. By leaving the Menton-Paris train at night, Inskipp could be in Clermont before eight the next morning. And, should all be well, he expected to go on to Paris by the half-past two express in the afternoon.

They talked the time-table over at Cook's, bought their tickets, and drove on up the charming gardens to the little station above them.

Inskipp wondered what would have happened before he saw this scene again. Edna Blythe would, he hoped, be set free from her really horrible impasse. And he himself might be in a vastly different position. It was even possible that he might not come back alone, that beside him might be a lovely girl . . . if all went well, Menton would make a charming stop on a honeymoon—

"Inskipp, Inskipp!" came Laroche's voice in half-real, half-mocking concern, as the car stopped at the station. The Frenchman was seeing them off. "You look again as though you had seen the Golden Goat! Remember, whoever sees him will never afterwards be content. He will always want something he cannot have."

"But what *I* want I'm going to get!" laughed Inskipp as he got out and turned his attention to his luggage. Mrs. Norbury and Edna Blythe had not come with the Frenchman. The former had caught a chill, and the latter had told Inskipp sadly that she could not bear to see them leaving for home and be condemned to stay behind. At last the Ventimiglia-Marseilles-Paris express was signalled. They took their seats, Laroche swung his hat gaily, and the train steamed out on a far more momentous journey than most of the people on her suspected.

Marseilles was reached at a little after ten at night, and there Inskipp said good-bye to a very cool and distant Elsie, promised the others not to overstay his time, and got out. His train to Clermont-Ferrand left in two hours. In it he found an empty carriage, and promptly went to sleep till half-past seven saw him getting his things together at his destination. He had been passing through a quite pretty agricultural countryside—chiefly dairy farms—and now, at the foot of the true volcanic outline of the Puy de Dome, he saw a very straggly, uninteresting-looking town lying before him. Inskipp had a long and thorough breakfast, and then went for a walk to kill time till it should be ten o'clock.

Clermont—and Ferrand, too—the older capital joined on to it—had nothing to offer Inskipp. Passing a bank which was just opening, he saw that it was a branch of one he knew by name. He was very tired of walking about. It occurred to him that he might put in a few minutes asking still another authority about the reputation of the man whom he wanted to see. He cashed a traveller's cheque and asked for the "directeur," who happened to be just coming in. To him he put very much the same questions as he had to Mr. Squires, and received as absolute an assurance of Maitre Francois' standing.

"If he told you that he was arranging—say a loan—do you think he can be relied on—as to time, I mean? It's a rather important affair."

"If our Maitre Francois told you that the affair would be completed in a given time—you can rely on his limit absolutely. He has the reputation of always being very cautious about his promises, but of keeping them to the letter—and to the minute. He has some very big families among his clients. We are very proud of our Maitre Francois, I assure you!"

Inskipp reached for his hat, and felt that he had been a fool to worry. He almost regretted that he had taken the time—and spent the money—on his trip here. Outside of the bank he made his way to the Rue Jaude. Its appearance surprised him. Had he come straight here without having had any information about the lawyer, he would not have expected to find a local celebrity installed in it. Half-way down the tumble-down street a man was leaning against the wall glancing at some advertisement hoardings. The house appeared to be the one for which Inskipp was searching. The man moved. Inskipp then saw that his back had hidden a brass sign on which were the words: *Maitre Francois du Barreau de Clermont-Ferrand.*

The door was standing open. He stepped inside, and the man who had been outside immediately followed him.

"You wish to see Maitre Francois? You have a rendezvous?" he asked.

Inskipp said that he had no appointment, but that he wanted a word with the lawyer all the same. He gave his name, and added that he was a client of Maitre Francois.

"In that case . . ." said the man courteously, and

opened a door leading into a large room. He excused himself for a moment as he shut it.

The outside of the house had seemed to suit the slummy street, so had the passage, but Inskipp had never stood in a handsomer room than this. Nor one in which money proclaimed its presence more clearly. The carpet was wonderful—he did not know how wonderful, for its softly-coloured wreaths of flowers had been woven at Aubusson. Old tapestries in black frames covered the walls. The furniture was of "white" walnut, very beautifully carved. The large arm-chairs were of dun-coloured leather. Two superb bronzes stood on tables. As for the door into another room beyond, it and the skirting boards were gilded—a soft, almost matt gilding.

He took a chair and told himself in future never to judge a French house by its outside.

The man whom he had seen before came in. He introduced himself as Maitre Francois' head clerk, by name Oreille, and went on to say that the Maitre was away—pleading a very important case at the St. Etienne Assizes—and might not be back for days. Monsieur Oreille repeated his regrets, and offered Inskipp a box of cigars which matched the sumptuousness of the room. Yet Inskipp wondered at the rims of the nails which held out the box. They did not look as though they had been cleaned for years, and there was a touch of gilding about one of them that looked as though Monsieur Oreille, like an animal, kept his nails trimmed by scratching the woodwork.

He took one of the cigars, and found it better than his dreams. He asked Oreille if he knew about his—Inskipp's—business, and was told that the head clerk knew nothing beyond the name. Maitre Francois always kept his clients' affairs strictly to himself. They chatted a little longer, and then Inskipp took his leave. Oreille went to the door with him, talking volubly. So volubly that Inskipp did not notice that over the brass plate now hung two of the hoardings announcing coming sales of property at which Oreille had been gazing when Inskipp had arrived.

As he walked away, Inskipp again told himself that he would be a fool to worry further, that he had been a fool to have worried at all. He must be patient and wait for Maitre Francois to arrange the loan in his own time. The Frenchman had written that he hoped to have the money very shortly. Inskipp must rest content with that.

Finally his train came in, and he was able to go on to Paris. It was only when the train had started that he remembered that he had not given Maitre Francois— through his head clerk—the address in Dover which would find him from to-morrow—Sunday—night, till at least Wednesday night, possibly longer. Rackstraw's hopes of interesting his film friend in Haroun might mean a longish stay, and his own inquiries for and of Mrs. Whin-Browning's one-time parlourmaid might mean that he would have to be some days in the old port. He hurriedly scribbled a few lines at the first stop—St. Germain des Fosses—and gave his address as "The Lord Bishop Hotel, Dover." He posted his letter in the St. Germain station just five minutes before the next collection.

Next morning he proudly showed himself at the Paris breakfast-table as a man of his word, and the four of them took the midday boat train for Calais. On the train Inskipp, for the first time since they had left the farm, had a chance for a talk alone with Blythe.

They settled themselves in an empty compartment, and Blythe, at Inskipp's suggestion, told him about the home life of the Whin-Brownings. He had been talking some time when he let a word drop about Edna's mother, which surprised his hearer.

"Mrs. Whin-Browning's mother? Is she alive?" Inskipp asked.

Blythe hesitated for a moment. Then: "Oh, certainly. Certainly. But now about my brother's will"

But Inskipp was curious. He learnt that Edna's

maiden name had been Thompson, and that her father had been in the War Office.

"I ought to get in touch with her mother," Inskipp said promptly.

"What on earth for? She's only interested in cats. She liked my brother, poor Ambrose, but she rarely visited him and Edna. She knows nothing of their home life—"

"I might find her of use," Inskipp persisted. "Where does she live?"

"The last I heard of her she was somewhere in Egypt—Luxor, I fancy." Blythe spoke vaguely, but there was a look about the mouth that Inskipp by now knew meant vexation, and, on Rackstraw looking in, the two went back with him for Bridge.

It was during the first rubber that Inskipp, while dummy, idly looked through some magazines and weeklies bought in Paris. In a *Looker-on* a name below a photograph caught his eye: "Mrs. Thompson, judging at the Cirencester Cat Show."

He re-called how, some time ago, Florence Rackstraw had queried the pronunciation of *Cirencester*, and how Edna Blythe had said, "*Sister*," without thinking, and very definitely. The paper went on to say that Mrs. Thompson was herself an owner of some fine tortoise shells she bred at her home, Newburn Cottage, Cirencester, which she hoped to exhibit at the coming cat show at the Crystal Palace.

Inskipp noted the address. More, he got a letter pad out of his suitcase and, later on, wrote to Mrs. Thompson. He wanted, he said, to buy a tortoise-shell cat, and asked her to reply to the Lord Bishop Hotel at Dover.

He had been intrigued by the effort of Blythe to keep him from getting into touch with Edna's mother.

CHAPTER 9: THE PARTY OF FOUR BREAK UP

In the Customs Shed at Calais, Inskipp's letter to Mrs. Thompson fell out on the floor. Luckily Blythe, though standing next to him, did not seem to see it, for it fell face up, and a moment later Inskipp retrieved the envelope, to post it later in Dover on his arrival.

It was a very bad crossing, but the effects of a short bout of sea-sickness are very quickly over, and when they found that there would be no difficulty about getting rooms at the Lord Bishop Hotel, Blythe ordered cocktails of unusual magnificence.

Inskipp asked whether there were any letters for him. In return, a square, unmistakable "foreign" looking envelope was handed him. It had just that moment arrived, and was from Clermont-Ferrand. In one corner it was marked *Par'Avion*.

A premonition came to Inskipp as he took it. A certainty of some bad news. Tearing it open, he found that his own letter, written on the train and posted in St. Germain des Fosses, had been returned to him. The covering letter was in French. It was signed Andre Francois. Must be a relative, Inskipp thought. A son, probably, for lus other letters had been signed simply—A. Francois. He settled himself down to read, and when he did so he felt stunned. The letter ran in French:

"Monsieur,—I am returning to you a letter which was opened by my secretary just now, as it seemed intended for me. But the contents show that there is a mistake. Your name is not known to me. We have never corresponded.

*So why send me your address? And yet there
is no other lawyer of my name in Clermont-
Ferrand. I'm at a loss to understand how a
mistake has arisen, in which my name seems to
be involved—for evidently your letter is but part
of a correspondence. I hope this will reach you
by air-post to-morrow, Sunday, and I shall much
appreciate an explanation of what I find very
incomprehensible.*
"*Agreez, Monsieur, etc.,*
"*Andre Francois*
"*(de la Barre de Clermont-Ferrand).*"

The paper was of a very expensive quality, and had an
address engraved in one corner. An address in the Place
de Jaude. *Place* de Jaude, not Rue Jaude.

Inskipp felt like a man in a nightmare.

Blythe came across to him. "I hope there's nothing
wrong," he said in a tone of real concern, but speaking
very guardedly. "You look as if you'd had a jolt. Nothing
to do with—her?"

Inskipp shook his head. "No, no. It's a financial
affair," he muttered thickly. It was raining hard, or he
would have stepped out for a walk. As it was, he went in
to the writing-room, which happened to be deserted, and
read the letter through again and yet again.

What had happened? To whom had Mireille been led
to confide her case? To whom had he sent that thousand
pounds in French notes? Obviously the Maitre Francois,
whose praises had been sung by two bank managers, was
not the A. Francois whose gorgeous office in the dingy
house in the obscure little street had been visited by him
yesterday morning. By bad luck—Inskipp called it his
stupidity and carelessness—he had not mentioned the
address where lived the Maitre Francois, about whom he
was inquiring. And there was only one avocat of that
name!

Inskipp set his teeth.

Mireille's divorce! No wonder it had dragged!

Inskipp sat a long time in that writing-room. He finally decided that as soon as possible to-morrow, Monday morning, he would put through a long-distance call to the Maitre Francois who had written to him, explain how things were, and take his advice. Inskipp was quite sure that the famous avocat would take energetic steps to sift the matter. And it needed sifting.

That decided, he got up and made for his room. Inskipp had been on the Stock Exchange, and had been in his own way something of a speculator. He had learnt then to do what Napoleon once described himself as doing—that was, to shut in the drawers of his mind, closing within them anything that worried him. He now resolutely closed in the drawer which held the name of Francois of Clermont- Ferrand, and began to tidy himself up for dinner. He was helped by the fact that the affair was too bad—too inexplicable—to tempt him to think it over. The many letters exchanged between himself and the other—their importance—the slum of a street—the gorgeous office—he closed that drawer with a bang and turned his mind to more ordinary affairs—affairs which could be understood.

The four men had not arranged to meet at breakfast on Monday morning, and when Norbury looked through the lounges at one o'clock there was only Rackstraw who beckoned to him.

"Inskipp must have gone up to London with Blythe after all," he said. "He asks me, in this, to settle his bill here for him. Pretty cool, I must say. He could have borrowed from Blythe. However, that's the worst of being good natured. I'm always being put upon. Shall we lunch now?"

"Inskipp didn't go with Blythe," said Norbury, leading the way to a table in the window. "Blythe asked me to say good-bye to Inskipp for him, as he wasn't in his room."

Rackstraw held out the note.

It ran, in pencil,

"I have had to go to London by early train.
Please settle my bill and send my things to
Cumberland Hotel, W.2 as soon as possible.
Make any arrangements you like about Haroun.
I shall accept them as best possible. Will let you
have P.A. if you think necessary. Shall be
exceedingly busy for some weeks.—Inskipp."

"How did you get this?" Norbury asked, handing it back.

"It was in the pigeon-hole for my room. Hall porter didn't know it was there until just now."

"Have you sent on his things?"

"Why, I only got the message when I came in just now! Dashed inconvenient it happens to be, too. I haven't any more spare cash than I need to take me back to your farm. I'm returning at once," he added in response to Norbury's inquiring look. "By the evening boat. I've landed a commission for a film scenario after my own heart. A talking film, of course." And Rackstraw went on to tell of his interview this morning with the Film King as he called him, and of the latter's total lack of interest in Haroun. "But," he went on excitedly, "he was awfully struck with what I chanced to tell him of the Red Caves. He saw at once that a film of paleolithic life in them—as I outlined it—might be worked up into something really good. And after a bit—just at the end— what do you suppose he did?"

"What?" Norbury asked obligingly.

"Asked whether I would take it on. Write a scenario— a talking one, of course—called the Baoussi Roussd, and before you could say Jack Robinson he had one of his secretaries in, and we drew up and signed an agreement. How's that for a morning's work, eh?"

"And what about Inskipp—where's he in it?"

"Nowhere," replied Rackstraw with brevity. "Haroun

is an absolute washout. I knew it, of course, but I'm a good-natured bloke. I didn't want to dash Inskipp's hopes. But he's going to London. He's there by now—like Blythe. He won't give the matter a second thought. Nothing like Town to get one out of a rut, eh? But as soon as I've sent off his things—I'll telephone to Carter Paterson to call for his suitcase—I'll see about a ticket back to the farm."

Rackstraw went on to say that he should stay at the *Chevre d'Or* until he finished his new scenario —a matter of three months, possibly.

Norbury suggested their both returning together, as he would not be long in town, but Rackstraw that he wanted to leave at once—to-night. He was itching to set to work, he said.

He charged Norbury when in town to see Inskipp and explain what had happened about the film, but the latter refused point-blank. Rackstraw must break his own news to Inskipp, for Norbury told him plainly that the latter might think himself

very badly used.

Rackstraw frothed up at that, but Norbury was making a list of purchases for this afternoon, and the indignation was wasted.

After lunch, Norbury hung about for a moment. He did not believe that Rackstraw, left to himself, would settle Inskipp's bill.

"Look here," he said suddenly, "I must leave now, or I shall miss my train. You spoke of being short of cash at the moment—well, here's a pound for Inskipp's bill. It won't be more—as Blythe had our dinners put on his account. If you'll settle for that now—you might forget it later in the rush of getting off—I'll charge it to him when I hear from him. He expects to be back at the farm with his sister in a couple of months or so."

"Excellent idea!" said Rackstraw. "Of course it's quite simple for you. I never mind lending money, but I hate to dun for it afterwards." He actually got up and strolled to the cashier's desk, though it must be admitted that

Norbury waited for him to do so, and before Norbury had moved away Rackstraw held the receipt for Inskipp's room.

"What about the gentleman's luggage, sir?" asked the clerk.

"Carter Paterson is calling for that," said Rackstraw, making for the lift.

Once Norbury's train was off, Rackstraw busied himself with his own preparations for a quick return to *La Chevre d'Or*. He might have waited for the other without much inconvenience, for, as he had anticipated, Norbury arranged matters very easily with the man who was to act as his agent. So easily, that, after some shopping, he crossed in the next day's Folkestone-Boulogne boat.

Mrs. Norbury was down at the farm gates to greet her husband. "Miss Blythe has gone into the hills for a weekend. She has kept on her room, of course, and told me not to worry, however long she might stay away. I had no idea you would be back so swiftly. It hardly seems worth while to have gone."

"Nothing like a personal inspection," said Norbury to that. "It was well worth the journey to have a clear idea of the man at the other end. I want to plant some more *greffes*, and some new peaches, and put down some more strawberry beds."

They went into the details together. Mrs. Norbury was not very delighted. All this meant heavy expenses, and that meant worry to her careful nature, which her husband called stingy when he was angry, though as a rule he valued that trait more than some others of hers.

CHAPTER 10: A DEAD TRAMP IS CLAIMED BY TWO WOMEN

Chief Inspector Pointer was wanted in the office of the Assistant Commissioner of New Scotland Yard. Pointer was a tall, spare, bronzed man, with a grave but pleasant face, about which the only noticeable thing were the eyes. Their glance, inscrutable though it was, suggested power and personality.

"Solomon had to decide between a baby and two women who claimed it, didn't he?" was the unexpected beginning of his chief. "Well, when you take these papers down to Dover, Pointer, I want you to settle between two women who each claims a dead body as that of her husband."

Pointer waited.

"One woman is a local charwoman, the other lives in Canada, but belongs by birth to a fairly well-known Kentish family. You're to decide who is to have the honour of burying a tramp."

Still Pointer waited.

"A tramp found dead in a shelter on the cliffs last Monday morning. Day before yesterday. Found murdered, I should say, or manslaughtered. First sandbagged, then finished off with something harder, early on Sunday night, says the doctor. Drunken brawl between two down-and-outs, is the local police theory, and, of course, that's all there was to it. So when Mrs. Simpkins, a charwoman, claimed the body early this morning as that of her husband, there was no objection. It never rains but it pours however—as we know here to our cost— and within half an hour, a Mrs. Harding claimed him as her husband, an artist, who had left her some two years ago in Toronto."

"And where do we come in?" asked Pointer.

"Ah!" the A.C. grunted. "Just so! Where? Damned cheek: that's unofficial, but true, none the less. The Dover Chief Constable is, as you may know, very keen on all murder cases being investigated by the Yard. His men don't like it. You know that, too, probably. He's down with 'flu at the moment, and they're getting their own back— in a quite correct way, of course—by foisting this dead tramp on to us. I suppose that technically it is a murder case. But in reality, of course, there's no finding out who slogged who. Privately, as I say, I like their cheek in calling us in on such a case. I should send down a junior, but that you happen to be going with those documents for Sir Arnold."

Sir Arnold Porteous was the Lord Warden, and the papers in question were from the Home Secretary, and very important.

"Find out before you return which lady has the right to the body. It's all there is to do."

Down at Dover the men at the police station were surprised to see Pointer, who went there immediately after a brief interview with Sir Arnold's private secretary.

"Hallo! Hallo! Hallo!" said Superintendent Grayson as he shook hands warmly. "Is the tramp a Balkan monarch in disguise? Otherwise, why the compliment of sending you down here to us?"

Pointer explained about the important papers in his charge which he had just handed over at the Castle.

"Solved the puzzle yet of whose husband the tramp was?" he asked.

"No, we still don't know who he really is, whether Simpkins or Harding. Off-hand, I should say Simpkins, but that an artist can get down on his uppers as well as a man on the dole. His clothes are at the mortuary. If you can call them clothes. He must have spent his nights in the ditches, by the look of them."

Grayson had a guilty air which suggested that the reply to his request for the Yard's assistance had been a bit more than he had bargained for. Evidently the A.C. had been right in his guess at the motive behind it.

"Who found the body?" Pointer asked.

"One of the regular cleaners. It was lying inside the shelter."

"Any signs of a struggle?" Pointer asked.

"None whatever. It was a case clearly of just a couple of nasty blows—one with a sandbag, one with something a deal harder. No weapon has been found, but there was a little pile of sand in the corner by the entrance, which was just enough to fill a sock comfortably. Sand from the seashore just below. It's all quite simple, bar the man's name." Grayson looked apologetically at the other as they stepped inside a small building. He led the way inside to a slab on which lay a body covered with a sheet.

Pointer looked keenly at it when the sheet was lifted. He saw a young man who looked about thirty years old, with a clean-shaven face which wore a look of deep content. It was the face of one who had at last reached a place where all was as he had hoped it might be.

"Death makes a difference in some cases, doesn't it?" murmured the superintendent.

"In *some* cases," Pointer answered. Personally, he did not think that it could have transformed a tramp's face into this. But Grayson had no such ideas. He pulled out his watch.

"Seen enough? I told the Simpkins woman to be at the police station at twelve. It's twenty minutes to that now."

"I'll stay a while longer and have a look at what the man was wearing."

After a word to the mortuary keeper, Grayson left the chief inspector.

Pointer lifted the man's hands. They were unmanicured, but well cared for. They were not swollen or marked in any way. The knuckles were not barked. He looked at the soles of the feet. They were not those of a man who had walked a great deal, and, above all, they were not those of a man who had ever worn ill-fitting shoes or boots in his life. The man had no corns, and the soles were fairly free even from callouses. The nails were trimmed. He looked at the teeth, which were well brushed and in perfect order, while some of the gold fillings looked like very recent work. They bore out the clean-shaven look, and the neat trim of the hair. The body had no marks.

But if it did not look like a tramp's, the same could not be said of the clothes. They were as disreputable a lot as even Pointer had ever seen. There were no underclothes. The cheap shoes, of white canvas, were new, but smeared with mud on top.

Pointer asked if he could use the telephone, and after sending a message, had the clothes made up into a bundle. By the time that this was done under his eye, the policeman for whom he had telephoned appeared and took charge of them.

Back at the station, Pointer had the report of the cleaner who had found the body brought to him. There was also some flashlight photographs of the shed with the body in it. They showed a wooden bench placed diagonally across one of the back corners. The body lay close by. Another photograph showed the small pile of sand.

As the man's belt was missing, and he had no suspenders, the police inclined to the belief that he had carried his money in it, and that the fight had been the result of a quarrel for it.

Pointer handed back the report and photographs and stood a moment thinking. The sunburn on the dead man showed that he had been in the habit of wearing a hat. Where was it? Had it been suspected of also possibly holding whatever it was for which the man had been killed?

But it was the sunburn itself about which Pointer was thinking. There was nothing weather-beaten about the face or the hands. And the hair had the soft feeling which is only the result of care.

The superintendent came in. "Mrs. Simpkins is waiting, and Mrs. Harding has just arrived. By the way, do you really want us to keep those unspeakable garments here in the safe?"

Pointer said that he did.

The superintendent sighed. "Would that we could have them disinfected first. I suppose we mustn't boil them?"

Pointer only shook his head. "They don't need it," he assured the other. "They're as dry and free from vermin as though they had just come out of an oven. In fact, they rather suggest that he has lived in one for months. I told your man to handle them as if they were glass."

"Pretty tattered," agreed Grayson, "and possibly not helped by a tussle at the end."

"He couldn't have been very violent in those clothes," said Pointer, "or they would have fallen in snippets around his feet."

Pointer did not think that the police had grasped that the garments were really extraordinarily brittle.

Grayson looked puzzled. "No oast houses around us. Nor do the clothes smell of hops. And that would be last autumn—"

Pointer did not think that the clothes, any more than the hands, were those of a man who had worked in an oast house. He said as much.

"Those white shoes," he continued, "they have never been out in the rain, yet it rained all Sunday evening."

Grayson nodded. "Agreed. Very stormy evening and night down here. We think he was given a lift by some carman or delivery man who gave him the shoes—as being too small for himself. Or he stole them from outside a shoe shop and put them on inside the shelter, giving whatever he was wearing to whoever was with him— whoever killed him. Any particular line you'd like us to follow up?"

"Yes, I wish your men would search very carefully for a man's umbrella, good make and condition, flung down on the sands, or into the sea, on Sunday night. It won't have been flung far, and the tide was coming in at half-past nine—the hour at which the doctor thinks the man was killed. I would like you to offer a reward of one pound for such an umbrella—found around or below the shelter Monday morning, in case it has been picked up."

"Where does the umbrella come in?" asked Grayson as soon as he had made a note of both the things asked of him. "Whose umbrella? Good make . . . good condition. . . . How do you get that?"

But just then an irate lady whose clothes had been damaged by her neighbour's garden hose demanded an immediate interview with the superintendent.

Twenty minutes later the chief inspector stepped into Grayson's office. Mrs. Harding had just driven away in a taxi—and apparently also in a high temper. Unknown to her the driver of the taxi was an ex-policeman, who had received a signal to keep the station informed of where he drove her. In case her destination should be a railway station, he knew just what to do.

"Well?" asked the superintendent. "What's the result of the Yard's third degree?"

"Mrs. Simpkins has lost fifty pounds, and Mrs. Harding—I shouldn't be surprised if she's lost a husband. But neither of them have the body. Mrs. Harding didn't want it at the last. She agreed that her husband—late or present—has a large circular mark under one knee. She quite forgot to mention it until I reminded her that it was the dead tramp's one mark."

"Lost a husband? What on earth do you mean?" Grayson was bewildered. "Of course we know the tramp had no mark on him. But the first part—"

"I may be wrong about the husband, but it is difficult to see why else Mrs. Harding claimed the body—until she heard that it was a case of murder."

"You mean manslaughter. Tramps often carry a sandbag as other people carry walking-sticks. But let's get it clear. This isn't the Yard, remember, with your

lightning minds. We're yokels—plodders—" Grayson had
a great liking for the chief inspector. "Now, to go back,
and this time in words of one syllable—Mrs. Simpkins
lost fifty pounds. See 'First Statement.' Explain, please."

"She had insured her husband for that amount, and,
being probably more than usually hard up—I should
guess her to be an improvident, cheerful soul—I think
that she saw her way to securing it when she read the
description outside on your hoarding of the tramp found
dead."

"Does she take back her claim to the body?"

"Absolutely. When I showed her it was impossible,"
was Pointer's reply, "for that dead man to have ever
worked in a quarry. Her husband was a quarryman."

"Then what about Mrs. Harding's lost husband? 'Lost
where and how?' See 'Second Statement.' Explain,
please."

"I think she wanted to marry again in a hurry —and
could only do so, naturally, by showing that she was a
widow. For which purpose any corpse would do, which
could be buried under the name of Harding. I fancy she,
too, must have read the description on the hoarding."

"She did. I happened to be coming into the station and
saw her. She had been strolling along, very much the
tourist—the stranger—looking about, when she stopped
and read the account. She stopped so long that I was
quite prepared to see her come in, but she went off then—
to think it over, apparently—and came back about an
hour later to claim the body. And, but for the chance that
there were two of them after it, either of them could have
secured it. There doesn't seem much to go for in the body
of a dead tramp. One doesn't expect competition in that
line. So her motive for claiming the tramp as her late
husband—let alone for making him late—so to speak, is
just to be able to remarry!"

Pointer did not think that Mrs. Harding had anything
to do with the murder. He believed that she had come on
the scene merely for the reason which he had given to the

superintendent—namely, a chance to become a widow whose bereaved status would stand inquiry. For the rest, he believed her to be genuinely indifferent to what had happened to the tramp, and at the last only concerned with not being dragged into unpleasant notoriety in the papers, once he had told her that he believed the tramp to have been murdered. It was then that she had remembered a large mark on her husband's knee.

"Whatever he was in the past—whether Harding was his name or not—those clothes mean that he had become a tramp all right at the end," protested Grayson.

"That man was no tramp, Grayson."

Grayson was sitting very grave and attentive now.

"You think that—do you? Humph. From what? Refined expression on his face, about which Doctor Harris held forth to us?"

Pointer detailed the care of the teeth, of the whole body. "Why, Grayson, if you had run your hand over the hair, you'd have known that that man wasn't a tramp. He has well-groomed hair, and has always worn a hat—a hat with a brim. No, I don't think this is just a case of a slogged tramp. I think we have a cunning crime to deal with—and bring home to the murderer."

If so, Grayson was shocked as he thought by how narrow a margin the crime had escaped detection as such.

"Something took the dead man—as I'll call him —to that shelter on Sunday night," Pointer went on. "You found out that a couple of young people left it empty at seven. It's possible that Y, the murderer, had given X an appointment there. If X went there on an appointment, the fact of a shelter having been chosen suggests a rendezvous. Off-hand, one would guess that the shelter was near where X lived and not near Y's home. It was a beastly evening and night, and living as soft a life as I think X did, he wouldn't be likely to be willing to go far afield in such weather."

"You can't get near those shelters in a car, whereas farther out on the cliffs towards Folkestone are several to which you can almost drive up," threw in Grayson.

"That looks as though X hadn't a car. His hands, too, suggest that he is no driver. But his shoes may have been taken away to prevent the marks on the heel suggesting that. As for the murderer, he would be able to bring the clothes found on the body and take away the ones that X was really wearing in a small suitcase—or in a paper parcel. In which case they were probably sent off at once to some out-of-the-way corner. I don't suppose he was foolish enough to do it, but you might send round an inquiry to any post office open on Sunday night, and ask if any large brown paper parcel was sent off then. Next day, of course, it would be hopeless to trace such a thing."

"X—the murdered man—isn't a local man," said Grayson, coming out of a profound cogitation. "That much I know. But of course—here in Dover!" His tone said that the difficulty of tracing the so-called tramp would be enormous.

"Those clothes won't help," he went on ruminatingly. "They're regular tramp's clothes, whatever X may have been."

"Not a tramp's clothes," said Pointer confidently. "Think of that dryness and the feel of them—dust — sand—wind-driven. I've felt a banner that had been hanging out a long time in the open air in the summer until it was almost falling to pieces, and it felt as these clothes do."

"Oh?" said Grayson dubiously. "But those rags and a banner don't seem to have much in common."

"That's what makes me wonder if they hadn't been taken off a scarecrow," said Pointer, staring at his shoetips.

"By Jiminy!" muttered Grayson, whereby his men, had they been in the room, would have known that he was greatly moved. "By Jiminy, I do believe you've got it!" Then his face fell. "But the dryness of them, and the rain we've had—"

"Scarecrows aren't needed all the year around," said.

Pointer, whose brother was a farmer in the Midlands. "It looks as though, if off a scarecrow, it must have been standing under shelter somewhere—" He broke off. He did not know of any scarecrows so cared for, but he would ask his brother. Besides that, there was something about the feel of those garments—dry dust driven into the very weaving, gritty to the touch, that did not suggest England at all. But who would bring away the clothes off a scarecrow from abroad? Yet the tan of the dead man's face up to the mark of where he had always worn a hat, and of his hands and forearms, also suggested some sunnier place than Britain.

"I want the garments sent to Hendon," he said after a silence. "They may be able to give us a hint as to the fields they stood in—if they are from a scarecrow."

"Are you going to have X's photograph in the papers?" Grayson wanted to know.

Pointer thought that that should be done at once with no mention of the word tramp or of murder, but merely accompanied by a statement to the effect that the police were anxious to find out who the man was who had been found dead last Monday morning in a shelter at Dover, as he had no papers or possessions on him—not even a hat.

"When he was sandbagged he was bareheaded. So says the doctor's report. And so say I, too," Pointer went on.

"Perhaps he was a very polite bloke," suggested Grayson with a grin, "and stood bareheaded to greet the gent with the sandbag."

"And how did they see each other?" asked Pointer.

Grayson bit his lip. That puzzle had quite escaped him. The inside of the shelter would have been pitch dark.

"I think that some one—Y—was waiting inside, crouched down behind the bench." Grayson looked at the photograph of the shelter—"and slogged X when he was comfortably seated?" he finished.

Pointer nodded.

"Then who had the light? As you say, a light of some kind must have been used." Grayson put the photographs away again.

"Yes." Pointer looked thoughtfully at his shoe-tips. "Yes, and the man behind the bench apparently counted on that. A match to light a pipe or a cigarette would hardly have been sufficient— unless the murderer was an expert slogger. It looks as though X, the murdered man, had been asked to bring a torch along—and turn it on as he sat on the bench, possibly under the plea of identifying him by it." And with that Pointer rose.

"And now what?"

"Routine work. The face is not an ordinary type. I may be able to get it identified."

CHAPTER 11: A NAME IS FOUND FOR THE TRAMP

Photographs of the murdered man had been distributed to the press for dissemination. Pointer, armed with two of the clearest—full face and profile —went the round of the hotels, boarding-houses and inns of Dover town and harbour. A plain-clothes man would question the keepers of apartment houses and smaller lodging places, but Pointer was backing his belief that the dead man was used to the good things of life. All this really was what he had called routine work. At the first hotel he drew a total blank, but at the second, the Lord Bishop, the hall porter rather thought he recognised the photograph as that of a young man who had quite recently claimed a letter that had just arrived—a registered letter. The hall porter even remembered that it had come by air from France. He looked through his book. Unfortunately there were several such letters, and he could not be certain of the name or the day—except that it had been some time this last week-end. Saturday, Sunday or Monday. The hall porter could not be more precise, nor more certain. Pointer passed on to the cashier's desk. The chances were even that the dead man had settled his bill on Sunday. Three men had done that and left Sunday afternoon. "Now of the others," Pointer continued, "was there one who didn't settle his own bill, but had it settled for him—on Monday, probably, and I should expect early Monday morning."

The cashier had only come on duty at noon on Monday last, but a gentleman had settled then for a friend. That much the man remembered with certainty, but not the name either of settler or of the bill settled. Pointer looked through the names of those whose accounts had been settled early on Monday and made a note of the names. Then he started the questioning of the housemaids and floor waiters—without success. But one of the Boots, when shown the portraits by Pointer among several others, said that that chap—he laid a finger on the portrait of the dead X—had borrowed his pocket torch last Sunday evening around seven. In reply to Pointer's hope that he had got it back all right, he had not. But as it was a sixpenny one, and as the gentleman in question had "made it all right" with him, he had no cause to complain. The borrower of his torch had come from one of the rooms opening off a side corridor on the third floor where on Sunday he was mending the electric light switches at the time—from ten past seven on to around half-past— an emergency repair. It was because he all but collided with him that the young man had stopped, asked if he was the Boots for that floor, and on his saying that he was, had wondered if he could let him have the loan of a pocket torch, as his own needed a fresh battery. The Boots had one in his kit at the time, and it had promptly changed hands.

"Did he take it on down with him?" Pointer asked.

The Boots thought not. "He stepped back along the corridor, and apparently put it away somewhere." The Boots was working with his back to that end, but he had later heard him tap on a door somewhere down there and call out to some one that he was off downstairs to dinner. A moment later the borrower of the torch had passed him and taken the lift. He had not seen him again. That last time was about half-past seven.

"Had that torch any initials scratched on it?"

"It had something better," laughed the Boots. "I had lost the bottom off it, but I found a peroxide bottle's screw top what fitted just as well, and used it. Inside the cap is stamped the word *peroxide* very small. You can't see it from the outside, but it's there."

Pointer got the numbers of the twelve rooms, from one

of which the Boots was certain that X had come. There were only bedrooms and suites in that part.

"He might just have come from and gone back to a friend's room."

"Must have been a very silent bloke," said the Boots. "I had been working some five minutes on that switch, and no sound of talking to be heard." The Boots was not able to describe the clothes the borrower of the torch had worn. They had been quite unremarkable, he said.

The register showed that five of the twelve rooms on his list were double rooms—all, as it happened, occupied by couples who were still in the hotel. That left Pointer seven single rooms. Three of these were still occupied by the guests who had been in them on Saturday last. That left only four. The names of their occupiers on Saturday had been a Miss Jackson, a Mr. Blythe, a Mr. Inskipp, and a Mr. Holme-Kennedy. The room numbers of the last three ran consecutively. And, as it happened, the name of Blythe came next but one on the register to that of Inskipp. Blythe—Rackstraw— Inskipp—Norbury, all from Paris, preceded and followed by names from London, and some distance down came the name of Holme-Kennedy—again from Paris.

The home addresses of Blythe and Inskipp were very sketchy. Pointer had himself put through at once to the Worcester police. Holme-Kennedy's address sounded like a largish place. The police knew the name at once. Mr. Holme-Kennedy was an elderly gentleman much interested in ornithology. Very wealthy. Very much liked. Yes, he was back at Lampton Park since yesterday. According to the local papers, he had been over to Italy to see the San Michele Bird Sanctuary. The superintendent speaking had, by chance, seen him walking past just half an hour ago. Pointer hung up. Holme-Kennedy might be Y, the murderer, but he certainly was not X, the dead man.

The hotel detective came up at this juncture and offered his services.

Pointer was quite frank with him, though with him alone. It looked as though the man found murdered in a shelter on the cliffs might be a man by name Blythe or Inskipp who had had room 313 or 314 here in the hotel last Sunday evening. Had there been any suspicious characters about? The hotel is not one which accepts criminals within its doors, but in every place of that kind it is impossible to keep out wolves if the sheep's hides fit well. The detective, an ex-Scotland Yard man, thought that he could give the hotel a very clear bill of health all this last week, and, with that, his usefulness to Pointer was over. He might, however, yet hear of some talk or fact which would link up with the crime, and if so would at once let the chief inspector know.

That arranged, Pointer went on now to No. 313—Inskipp's room. It was empty at the moment, though it had been occupied each night since Mr. Inskipp had had it. If he had even had one night at the hotel, and if he really were the murdered man—Pointer had not much hope of coming on anything useful. On the other hand, he had before now found surprising evidence which had been lying unnoticed for longer than the couple of days which separated to-day, Wednesday, from last Sunday night.

One careful look about the room, and he knew that if anything was to be found here it would have to be in the drawers. They all seemed empty, but he took each lining paper out in turn, and in one of the small top drawers of the chest he found that what looked like lining paper was in reality a watercolour drawing, folded inside a piece of white paper which had been taken from one of the longer drawers. The sketch was signed J. Inskipp. On the back was pencilled: "*For Mireille.*" The drawing represented a couple of lemon trees growing beside a blue-painted door with a glimpse of maize fields to one side, and with a mimosa in the middle distance. It was an attractive piece of work, though entirely photographic. An artist would never have allowed that mimosa to stay where it was. It broke up the lines in a most unfortunate way. But the painter had managed to get into it some of his own sunny mood. It was gay—and it was curiously young. And the colours were charming in their unaffected purity. It had been done in the full summer time—August, one would guess from the darkness of the foliage and grass. As a picture it had no merit, but as an indication of where Inskipp had been, it might be most useful; though there were very many places where those lemons and that mimosa could have grown. South Africa certainly was one of them. And then Pointer stiffened. There, in a field of maize almost off the picture, was a scarecrow—complete with dangling sleeves, striped trousers and straw hat. Bar the latter, it might have been a painting of the garments in which Inskipp's body had been found. The very cut of the frock coat with its accentuated waist was the same.

Pointer slipped the sketch back into its wrapping again and put it away in his case. He rang for the Boots. But the man could not remember whether No. 313 had put out his shoes or not. Pointer knew that last Sunday had been extremely wet. It was most unlikely that any man would not have changed wet shoes for dry ones. He was told that they would have been placed, cleaned, outside the door by seven-thirty Monday morning. That meant, Pointer thought, a possible shock to the murderer. He might have caught sight of them in the morning, known that if they were allowed to stay on they might cause comment. . . . They were not hidden in the room anywhere. They would be dangerous to take outside the room. Pointer went to the hall window. It was topped with wooden gable painted white. Pointer got out and stood on the ledge.

Leaning far out in a curve, he saw a parcel wrapped in white paper lying on one of the wooden, sloping sides, and another, similar, white parcel on the other. They had been wedged against the wall.

Getting inside again, Pointer tried the distance. Any man of average height and arm-reach could have put them there. He picked them from their positions as carefully as though they had been peaches—and with gloves on. As he hoped, each parcel held a shoe. The shoes were of brown leather, and were marked with chalk on the soles: 313. He had with him all the measurements, and an outline of the feet of the dead man, on the off-chance that the presumed tramp might have left some clothes behind him somewhere.

He now stood the shoes on the outlines. They would have fitted perfectly, and when casts were taken of the feet, as would be done at once, they could be shown to have been the dead man's. Here was a definite link.

The shoes themselves told little. They were Bally shoes, bought somewhere abroad, by the number. They had not been mended, so there was no hope of getting at some new fact by that means, and there were no fingerprints on the wrapping paper. But they helped to establish that the dead man had had room 313 at the Lord Bishop—and was therefore called Inskipp. Pointer went carefully through the rooms of Blythe and Holme-Kennedy. He found that one of the brass knobs on the bedstead in Blythe's suite had only been dropped on to the upright, not screwed on. It was too large for it. Inquiry by the hotel detective showed that this was quite a recent defect. Further inquiries by him proved that the over-large knob in question had come from a room on the fourth floor, where one of the beds was minus this ornament. The bedroom in question had been empty over the week-end. Meanwhile Pointer turned his attention to the accounts, and then followed another of those close hunts for apparent trifles that must form part of all but the most exceptional police cases. There was no wine charged to Inskipp's account. But two bottles of Batard Montrachet, 1932, were put down to Blythe, who had yet only had one dinner and no lunch at the hotel. It was from the wine-waiter whom Pointer promptly interviewed next that he got his best and his most unexpected help.

The name of the wine stirred the man's very good

memory. It had been ordered by a party of four men, he said. Yes, one of them had been undoubtedly the dead man whose picture was shown him. He remembered the four men particularly because of the discussion they had had with him about wine in general. One had wanted Chateauneuf du Pape, and though the others had prevailed at the moment, he had had a bottle of it next day for lunch. One of the four—an older man—owned vineyards of his own, for the one who had wanted the Chateauneuf du Pape said, "This gentleman is a wine grower, so be careful what you set before us." They were all four English—or rather British. The waiter thought that in age they were around thirty, except the wine grower—from South Africa, probably, as he was so tanned—who appeared to be about forty to forty-five years old.

A wine grower! South Africa! Pointer thought of his idea that the rags in which the dead man had been found had come from a scarecrow which had stood out in some very hot, dry place. . . .

The wine-waiter thought that all four men had been on very good terms with each other.

A scrutiny of the bills made out showed that the name of the only man who had had a Chateauneuf du Pape with his lunch on Monday was Henry Rackstraw. So the man who had registered next to Inskipp had also come from Paris. Henry Rackstraw had left Monday afternoon. And Rackstraw had ordered a whole bottle of Chateauneuf. . . . Pointer asked the wine-waiter whether one of the four men of the Sunday evening dinner had not also lunched with Mr. Rackstraw the next day, and shared the bottle of Chateauneuf.

The wine-waiter was vexed with himself that he had not remembered it at once. The chief inspector was quite right. It was one of the same men as at the dinner the evening before—the older one—the wine-grower. The one who had ordered the Chateauneuf was tremendously talkative at lunch, he had noticed, and seemed in very high spirits, as though he had just pulled off something very good.

The table-waiter was able to add that the older man seemed deeply interested in some catalogues of farm ploughs, and that sort of thing, which he studied off and on during lunch. He had hardly left any room on the table for plates.

So far, so good. But was the man's name Holme-Kennedy or Norbury? Both came from Paris, but Norbury, unlike Holme-Kennedy, had no wine or beer entered to him for Sunday night or for Monday lunch. He seemed to fit the probabilities best. An effort to find his address in the telephone book was not helpful. Apparently all four men who came in a group from Paris put down the first one that came into their heads.

As for luggage, the hall porter's notes showed that the luggage of No. 313 had been dispatched later—Tuesday afternoon, apparently. He would find out just what had happened to it. . . .

The hotel detective followed Pointer into the room put at his disposal by the hotel.

"This bedstead knob, sir?" he began with interest. "The one we've traced and the one that's missing." He gave his detailed report and asked its significance.

"The man found in the shelter had his head crashed in, after he had been stunned with a sandbag. Done with something hard. Rounded end of a metal bar, it was thought. It rather looks as though it might have been done with the knob from No. 312." Pointer ran over the facts.

"The sand from the bag was emptied out on the floor of the shelter," he continued. "It was thought that the murderer did that to save carrying a sandbag home. But it looks now as though he had emptied it, dropped in the knob, given it a twist, and brought it down with all his force on the man's head. The injuries fit the notion. Incidentally, Smith, the housemaid, will find herself still a knob short in that suite. I borrowed one of the three

remaining originals and have it with me. You'd better
make her think that there's a collector here in the hotel
who has a mania for these things, but that fortunately
you have your eyes on him. Now, I want to find out
whether any price lists or catalogues of farm
implements—any things which might interest a farmer—
were taken out of room 477." This was the room of the
man who had signed himself Norbury.

The detective soon had the maid for that room
fetched. And they learnt that she had on Monday cleared
out a quite unusual amount of printed matter—
catalogues, price lists, advertisements from the room in
question. All to do with agricultural implements big and
small. Pointer would have dearly liked to have one of
those thrown-out folders or price lists, so as to get into
touch with the firms in question, but the hotel detective
hurried down to the cellar, only to learn that all Monday's
waste paper had been used up Tuesday morning in the
boilers.

Meanwhile Pointer sent word to the police station to
have plain-clothes men look along the sands for a brass
knob off a bedstead, and for trousers, coat, waistcoat,
shirt, socks and hat. He could not offer a reward for them,
but he fancied that the knob at any rate, and possibly the
clothes, would have been buried in the sand as near to
the shelter as possible, the murderer relying on the
garments found on the tramp to keep any search from
being made for the weapon that killed him. As for a
probable umbrella that he had pre-supposed from the
weather, and the position in life which he thought that
the man had occupied, Pointer fancied that it had been
opened up and merely turned adrift, to be blown where
the wind took it. On such a night as Sunday, this would
be attributed to a careless grasp rather than to intention.
Pointer stepped to the telephone again.

He was just about to ask for a trunk call to Mr.
Holme-Kennedy, when the manager himself came in. He
looked as though he had something important to say.

"Mr. Inskipp has just been asked for on the phone," he said, "it will be switched through to you in here," and with that he very tactfully vanished.

Pointer stood listening for the voice to come through with a stir of his pulses. What was he about to hear?

A voice spoke, a clear, woman's voice, pleasant in pitch. Not the voice of a very young woman, Pointer thought. He would expect her to be well dressed, quick in her movements, apt to stride when she walked, be good at games, and not very sympathetic to any one ill or in trouble. The kind of woman who smilingly suggests that by making an effort you might throw off that chill, or get out of that difficulty. Yet he would expect the voice to belong to a very loyal woman, however hard, and a generous woman too—though only in material things.

"This is Mrs. Thompson of Norburn Cottage speaking. So you're interested in tortoiseshell cats, Mr. Inskipp?"

Pointer was not often surprised. But he was now. Were the words a password? He must chance that. "Very much," he said promptly.

"So am I, and I've some beauties. But first of all, thank you for your letter. I've only just returned to the Cottage and got it. Now, if you'll make an appointment for any day this week, I will send for a couple of good ones I've just taken to a farm near by."

"I must explain that I'm only speaking for Mr. Inskipp," said Pointer then. "I'm sorry to say he has met with an accident and can't come to the telephone himself. Could you explain a little more?"

"I have had a letter from a Mr. Inskipp giving as an address the Lord Bishop at Dover. He asked for an immediate reply to his request to be allowed to come and see my tortoiseshell cats. I live in Cirencester, and was away till to-day noon, and as I hadn't been able to write back at once, I thought I would telephone him. You say he's met with an accident?"

"Yes, a very bad one. I'm one of the hotel managers," Pointer went on unblushingly, "and we can't find out who his people are. Or his home address. I hoped when you rang up that you might be an old friend."

"No, I don't know him at all," came in a tone which carried conviction.

"Would you be so very kind as to read me the letter aloud which he wrote you?" Pointer asked. "There might be some sentence—or word—which would help us."

"There isn't. But I'll read it aloud with pleasure. Just a minute!" and within a minute he heard, "Are you there? This is what he writes. The heading, a written one, is, *The Lord Bishop Hotel, Dover.* It's dated last Sunday, and is postmarked Dover, of the same date. He says:

" *'Madam,*
" *'I have just seen a notice about your tortoise-shell cats. May I come and see them, as I would like to buy one? I should be much obliged by an immediate reply to this, making as early an appointment as possible.*
Yours faithfully,
John Inskipp.

Pointer heard the crackle of the letter being laid down. "There!" the voice went on, "I'm afraid that's not much good, is it?"

"I'm afraid not, and it's addressed to you, where?"

"At my home, Norburn Cottage."

"May I come and have a look at the writing?" Pointer asked. "We can't be sure whether some papers found are in his writing or not. He signed his name in our books very illegibly. By chance, I shall be close to you late this evening. Will you hold the line just a moment?" and Pointer turned over an A B C. "I shall be dining in Cirencester and could drop in for a moment around seven-thirty. Would you excuse my coming in at that hour? I shall only keep you a moment; just a glance at the letter and its envelope. We really are badly stumped."

"Come, by all means," said the voice indifferently, "but

I can post you his letter, you know—-"

"As I shall be so close to you it doesn't seem worth while," said Pointer, and asked for directions as to how to find the cottage. That done, Mrs. Thompson hung up, leaving Pointer rather puzzled. Some inner voice, which he never disregarded, had told him to have a personal talk to this unknown woman. But he assured himself ruefully that he would have his journey for nothing. Inskipp might have wanted to buy a tortoiseshell cat for himself, or more likely as a gift. Surely his note could not be connected with his brutal murder. . . . The voice on the telephone was not the voice of a woman likely to be linked with any crime gang.

Voices over the telephone tell character with amazing exactitude. Nearly as much so as over the microphone.

But the speed with which Inskipp had wanted to get into touch with the lady of the cats—it might be that he wanted to make a very immediate gift. Pointer rang up the Cirencester police station and sent a four-word query along, two words of which were in code. The first word meant, "what can you tell me about"—the next two were "Mrs. Thompson"—and the last meant that the inquiry came from a C.I.D. chief inspector of New Scotland Yard.

The reply came very quickly.

"Mrs. Thompson is a widow lady, sir. Looks about fifty-five years old. Bought a workman's cottage about a year ago and an acre of land beside it. Goes in for cat-breeding and shows. Lives very quietly. One maid. Nothing known here against her. Address? Here it is, sir—Norburn Cottage, High Road, Cirencester. That's all, sir."

It did not sound interesting.

Pointer hung up, and then asked to be put through to Holme-Kennedy. In due course a very quiet, elderly, precise voice asked him who was speaking at his end. Pointer said that an accident had happened to a Mr. Inskipp, a man who had had a room at the Lord Bishop last Saturday night next to Mr. Holme-Kennedy's. Was he

perhaps an acquaintance of Mr. Holme-Kennedy's? They
wanted to get into touch with Inskipp's family, if he had
had any. He had had no address on him when found.

Mr. Holme-Kennedy seemed very shocked at the idea
of a sudden end to any one, and said that all he could say
about the man in the room in question was that he had
been a model neighbour. He had never seen him, much
less spoken to him. Mr. Holme-Kennedy was a very poor
sleeper. On the night in question he had not slept at all,
and he had heard his neighbour come in very late—
around three—doing his best not to disturb others, and
move about in his room with the same thoughtful care. A
most unusual trait nowadays. And he had had an
accident next day? How sad! Car accident?

Pointer was vague in his reply. He hung up, and
drafted an advertisement to be sent to all the London and
local papers stating that the unknown man found dead in
a shelter on the cliffs at Dover on Monday morning was
now believed to be a John Inskipp, who had landed in
Dover the afternoon before, coming from Paris. Would
any one who had any knowledge of, or about, him, kindly
communicate at once with New Scotland Yard, who
wanted to get into touch with his people.

He handed it to Grayson, and gave him a swift
account of his work—and its results.

"Well played!" said the superintendent warmly. "It's a
jump from a nameless tramp—who would have been
handed to one or other of those two frauds but for you—to
Inskipp, a man with three friends all coming from Paris
together, with whom he dined on Sunday evening. A man
who can sketch jolly well, who has been where lemons
and mimosas and—by jove, yes—scarecrows are. One of
whose friends is a wine grower—the friend probably who
furnished the scarecrow's garments—it's a splendid
jump!"

CHAPTER 12: A COTTAGE IS A MYSTERY

"Where are you off to now?" asked Superintendent Grayson, as Pointer laid down the hotel and boarding-house lists collected by his men for Sunday last.

"In one of the smaller hotels quite close, a Miss Florence Rackstraw is entered as having arrived last Sunday from Paris. Her home address is Capetown, S.A. It may be pure coincidence, the name is not uncommon, but I'll go there now, and ask for her."

He was told that Miss Florence Rackstraw had left this morning (Wednesday) by the nine twenty-three for Victoria. Pointer had called, he said, about a book, a small paper pamphlet which Miss Rackstraw had borrowed from a Mr. Inskipp who had stopped at the Lord Bishop. Miss Rackstraw had gone there first, hadn't she, and not been able to get a room?

The manageress said that all she knew of the lady in question was that she had taken a chill on Sunday night and kept to her bed till she left this morning, and that she had asked for the cheapest room in the house. The manageress, who was very busy, and not interested, once she learnt that neither Pointer nor the young man with him were looking for rooms, handed him over to an untidy housemaid, on his suggestion that Miss Rackstraw might have left the book behind her.

The maid took him to the top of the house and to a small room which had not yet been tidied.

"We're short-handed—as we always are," she half-whispered. "Here is her room. But she hasn't left anything. Nice lady she was—and looked so ill. And this morning when she crawled down the stairs and paid her bill! She looked bad enough when she came Sunday. She told me she went for a walk in the evening thinking it would help her head and that just did for her. Monday morning, I found her lying on her bed in all her wet things. It was the smell that made me look in here. Her felt hat had caught fire when she put it down to dry"—the maid pointed to the gas-fire,—"being felt and the band being leather, my goodness, you can think how it smelled! Burnt to a cinder. You can see where it stained the radiators. But the lady was past caring for hats or anything. I was frightened at the look of her, but she wouldn't have a doctor."

"I wonder if it is the Miss Rackstraw I wanted to see," said Pointer, as though half-thinking it was not. "What was she like?"

"Wears her hair looped over her ears, sir. Dark hair. Tall and nice looking. She looked round forty to me, but you can't tell when people feel so badly, can you—would that be the lady you wanted to see?"

"Sounds rather like her. She has a cousin who is a friend of mine. He was at the Lord Bishop. I wonder why she didn't try to send him a message?"

"As near as that! How funny! I asked her when I got her undressed, Monday morning, whether there wasn't any one in Dover I could get for her, and she said she was from South Africa and didn't know any one here, and didn't want to worry her friends in London. A cousin at the Lord Bishop!"

"That's what makes me think it can't be the same Miss Rackstraw. Didn't she leave anything behind her? No papers anywhere about?"

"Not one, sir. She left nothing behind."

"What luggage did she have? That might settle it. Had she two suitcases, one purple leather—one brown?"

"Only one suitcase, sir. Brown leather. Very good leather it was, and heavy!"

"Fitted with silver-stopped bottles? That's the one!"

"I didn't see inside it, sir."

Pointer tipped her, and asked again about the burnt

hat. Was she able to wear it going up to town?" he asked, turning away.

"Oh, my goodness, sir, it wasn't a hat at all! A proper cinder it was! She said she had put on any old thing because of the weather Sunday night. Lucky, wasn't it, that it wasn't her big travelling hat?"

Pointer learnt no more. He took a long look at the signature in the book, which was written rather slowly and rather shakily as though by some one who did not feel well. Then he left the little hotel and walked back to the police station. A hat

destroyed. . . . South Africa. . . .

At the police station he found that the offer of a reward had already produced an umbrella, and that the plain-clothes man had found a brass knob just where Pointer had expected to find it. The umbrella had been picked up early on Monday morning by a stationer of the place. It was on the cliffs, some distance away from the shelter, and pretty badly damaged. But it was recent damage, and might well have been the one used by Inskipp when he went out on Sunday night. If so, it told absolutely nothing, except that it was English—a Fox-frame, and the sort of umbrella that a man would buy who was not wealthy, but who wanted something reasonable and hard-wearing. The price, so Pointer learnt, would be around fifteen shillings. The cover was a stout "union."

The next thing was for the police to get out a notice saying that the umbrella had been found and giving its description. This one might yet turn out to have been lost by a visitor. But there was no such question about the brass knob. It was the mate to the one which Pointer had abstracted from the bedroom of the hotel. There were no fingerprints on it. If any had been left, which Pointer doubted, the wet sand would have seen to them. But it was badly dented on one side, with just such a dent as would be expected if the dead man had been killed by its means. It was the first official find so far, and as such was carefully labelled and locked away in the station safe.

Then Pointer had to rush to catch the aeroplane which he had ordered. He used the time till he reached the pretty Gloucestershire market-town of Cirencester in making notes which would be sent in to headquarters.

At Cirencester, a taxi was waiting for him, and Pointer reached the address given him over the telephone by Mrs. Thompson well on time. There was a lamp-post close to the gate. It lit up a narrow, gravelled path leading to a door with a rustic porch over it. It was seven-thirty when he rang the bell.

His ring went unanswered for some moments, though he could hear feet apparently running to and fro inside. The sound suggested that the lady of the house was absent, and that the servant was having a private caller of her own and was flustered by the ring.

He rang again. This time the door was opened, but in a furtive way, just wide enough to let a woman in a servant's uniform peer out at him, and peer with peculiar intentness. Beside her showed the pink muzzle of a bulldog.

"My name is Pointer. Mrs. Thompson is expecting me," said the chief inspector. The opening of the door did not widen.

"She's out, sir."

The door was closed. Pointer rang again. There was no reply, but he heard more of those light, scurrying footsteps which sounded so frightened, and so uncertain of what they were doing, where they were going. Then absolute silence.

Pointer hesitated. The servant's voice had not suggested guilty terror to his ear, and that is a note which once heard can never be mistaken. He had no reason to think that a crime had been committed on which he was intruding. But he was uneasy.

One murder easily brings a second murder in its train. He walked to the gate and was about to get back into his taxi and apparently drive off, only to stop when out of sight and sound, and return to Norburn Cottage on his own silent feet. But a little car came swiftly along, and pulled up. Out jumped a slender woman with a mop of silver curls. She peered at the taxi.

"Is it Mr. Pointer?" she asked in the same pleasant voice that he had heard before, over the telephone.

Pointer was beside her in a moment. Those furtive movements inside the cottage had made him glad to see her.

"If you'll go on to the house and ring, I shall be with you in a moment," she said cheerfully. "That's the best of a cottage. Everything is within arm's length—garage—gate—garden."

"Let me help you run her into the garage," he said, pleasantly.

"Well—thanks. The door there is a bit heavy to shove up," she said gratefully. It was but a step to the garage shed, where he switched on the light, helped her up with the shutter-door, and in with her little car.

"You want the letter of that poor Mr. Inskipp. By the way, I hope he's better?" she said, watching his swift, sure movements approvingly.

"No," said Pointer. "I'm sorry to say he's not. There's no hope of that."

"How sad! Well, you can have his letter in a moment. I left it out on the mantel for you—" she stepped towards the front door as she spoke. "But I could have sent it to you, you know, and saved you coming out. Like to have a look at my pussies while you're here?"

He had expected Mrs. Thompson to be a good business woman from her voice.

"With pleasure," he said instantly. "I was going to ask you to let me have one. A kitten, if possible. For a little niece of mine."

"Oh!" Mrs. Thompson stopped. "A child! I hope she'll be good to it! Children aren't always, though, of course, they mean well. I would much rather sell you one for your little niece's mother," she smiled as she spoke. She was a pretty woman still, and must have been a very pretty girl. And Pointer liked her care to sell her cats only to good homes. She evidently was more than just a business woman. She had her key in the door now, and turned it. The door did not open.

"What's the matter?" she asked, perplexed—and tried again.

At that, the door was opened by the same woman who had peered at Pointer through the crack. She now showed as a middle-aged woman whose face bore the marks of tears. Very recent ones.

She fairly pulled her mistress across the threshold, and tried to shut Pointer out in the same gesture.

"What on earth has happened, Miller? This way, Mr. Pointer—" Mrs. Thompson opened the door of a room next to her hand. "The letter is on the mantel. I won't be a moment. Now, Miller, what is it?" The door was closed between Pointer and the two women.

He was in a pretty little white-painted room with chintz covers, old and faded, over still older chairs, and chintz curtains closely drawn over the windows. On the mantel was no letter whatever. The shelf was still warm from a recent gas fire in the grate. The light had been on when Mrs. Thompson had opened the door for him to enter. He heard the two women now move down the passage into another room. But there was no sound of voices. Whatever had upset the servant so curiously was being told in a whisper. A moment later, and he heard footsteps go up the little stairs. Those of Mrs. Thompson, he thought, and then his own room door was opened by the maid.

"Mrs. Thompson says will you please excuse her, sir, she has had bad news, and doesn't feel able to see any one.

"Of course! I'm sorry to have come at such a moment. But—er—I came for a letter which she told me would be on the mantel here. Could you find it for me? It's

addressed to her by a man who's met with an accident."
Pointer was quite chatty, hoping to give her time to pull
herself together.

But Miller only looked like bursting into tears. "I'm
sure I don't know anything about any letter, sir. Oh, will
you please go! The mistress needs me. And—and—" she
was holding the front door open and motioning him out.

Pointer could not stay. There was real trouble here.
The woman's face was working, even as she tried to keep
her voice steady. He let her close the door behind him and
walked down the path, then turned and came back to the
little house. The letter which he had come to fetch was
gone. He thought that it had been taken, and, if so, its
loss was very probably connected with the mysterious
disturbance in the little house. He had not been able to
ask Mrs. Thompson to take special care of the note.

He knocked once more, this time with a postman's
knock. The door was opened on the instant, and Pointer
stepped inside before the maid could close it.

"Sorry," he said as he did so, "my gloves, I left them in
there—" He was back in the room in the same instant. As
Mrs. Thompson had said, everything at the cottage was
within an arm's reach. He had left his gloves behind him
on purpose. As he moved to the door, Mrs. Thompson
herself came down the stairs. There was no sign of the
dog.

"Miller, make some strong tea at once for us." She saw
Pointer and her whole face, a grey one, stiffened. She
drew herself up and stared at him coldly—and
suspiciously.

"I left my gloves in my hurried going," he said, in
answer to that look, " but I didn't find the letter you said
was on the mantel. I'm very sorry if I have called for it at
an inopportune moment—perhaps you will let your maid
bring it to me?"

"I made a mistake about the letter," said Mrs.
Thompson. "It's been lost. I don't know where it is. I will
post it on to you if I find it. But I'm afraid at the moment

it's impossible to look for it." She was desperately uneasy, terrified of something connected with the note which she had so easily promised to hand over.

Pointer picked up his gloves and left—this time really left. As he shut the garden gate behind him he wondered what had so absolutely changed Mrs. Thompson. She had now no intention of letting him have that letter. Yet when they had been in the garage, he was as sure that she really had left it out on the mantel for him, and had no slightest objection to his taking it away with him. Then who was in the house? Who had rushed up there to get the letter, or warn her not to hand it over—not to admit the man who came for it? One of the gang, as Pointer called the foursome of the Dover hotel? But if it had been one of them, it was curious that Mrs. Thompson had telephoned as she had done earlier this afternoon, and left her cottage with the note laid ready for him. If not one of the four— there was Miss Florence Rackstraw who had been out and got soaked, and then burnt a hat on Sunday night. She had left Dover this morning. Could she be in this? The order for "strong tea for us" suggested another woman.

He made a careful but, because of the bull-terrier, distant circuit of the cottage. There were no lights in any of the bedroom windows. But the kitchen, and the room back of the one into which he had been shown, were brightly lit. It looked to him as though some plan was on foot which precluded not only sleep, but going to bed. That looked as though some one there intended to leave the house secretly and before very long. For if there were illness, a bedroom would have been in use.

From the hedge where he sat down to watch, Pointer could see the garage. He kept his eyes and ears open as, wrapped in a mackintosh that he had brought with him, he thought over the possible meanings of the reactions which his coming to get Inskipp's letter had caused. He had stepped into some swirling tide of emotion, and had added to it. Therefore was linked with it.

What could account for the emotion of the maid and Mrs. Thompson's changed face? Both women had had a shock of a kind that had frightened them. The maid had shown it first. She was flustered. She had lost her head. As for Mrs. Thompson, she clearly must have learnt in those few minutes while he had waited in the empty room and been shown out, that she had been on the verge of making a dreadful blunder.

Pointer was puzzled. Very puzzled. Apart from any question of who had taken it, why should that letter of Inskipp's be of sufficient importance to be taken? It looked as though the question of his writing, unimportant at the moment, might become of capital importance later on. It was the only specimen of his handwriting so far found—except for the scribbled entry in the hotel register, and the two pencilled words on the back of the sketch. A sketch which had, Pointer believed, escaped the notice of whoever it was who had taken Inskipp's things away. But whether the letter had been taken to serve as a pattern for a forgery to come, which, given the peculiar circumstances of the finding of the body seemed very possible, or to prevent the police, or some one else, comparing a false with a genuine letter or piece of writing, it was too soon to tell.

Or was it that the visitor of the gas fire and the steps, was not to be linked, even for a moment, however remotely, with Inskipp, because of some share in his murder, as yet unsuspected?

It was about two o'clock in the morning, when Pointer saw a light go up in the hall of the cottage, stay on for a minute, and then be switched off. Then he heard the front door gently undone. A moment later a woman came down to the gate and tied it wide open with some string. She did not see Pointer, though she stood in the road a moment and looked carefully up and down it. She was so bundled up that her face could not be seen, but her gait was that of the maid.

At half-bast two a car came along, driving as though

not sure of the way. It turned into the gate and stopped! at the front door.

Pointer, his torch in his hand, ready to switch on, was by this time lying full length along the foot of the garden wall, and a very cold place he found it. Out of the car jumped a big, young man. The door was cautiously opened. He stood a moment on the sill before stepping over it and Pointer had a good view of his face.

The person who had opened the door was Mrs. Thompson. In about fifteen minutes the door opened again, out ran a slight woman whom Pointer had not seen before. Getting into the car, she was covered up with rugs by Mrs. Thompson, and by the young man who had driven up. The maid went on to the gate and stood outside it in the road, looking up and down it. Finally, Mrs. Thompson gave a last, lingering smooth to the rugs and stepped back reluctantly, speaking in a whisper to the young man. He murmured something in an encouraging tone, jumped into the driving seat, and was off in reply to a wave of the hand from the maid. Mrs. Thompson went down to the gate and stood with her arm through the maid's, watching the car drive away. She had done her work skilfully. At a glance, it looked as though the only occupant of the car was the young man driving it. The woman crouched on the floor inside was completely hidden under the rugs.

Pointer had no right to object. He did not follow the car, because the cottage might not have finished its activities yet. As he watched it, he turned over the little scene of just now. His final idea was that some one—a woman—had arrived unexpectedly, and had told Mrs. Thompson not to let the letter pass out of her hands, was apparently proving right.

What woman was connected with Inskipp so far? "Mireille," and the mysterious Florence Rackstraw. A young woman who bore a name linked with one of the four men who interested Pointer, who had gone for a walk late on Sunday evening, burnt a felt hat, and left the

Doverana this morning, or rather, Pointer glanced at his watch—yesterday morning, at an hour which would let her get to Mrs. Thompson's cottage before he, Pointer, got there, but after Mrs. Thompson had left. Mrs. Thompson over the telephone had spoken of being out all day.

As Pointer sat watching and waiting, he speculated on what could make this cottage the focus for Inskipp and for Florence Rackstraw. Had they planned to meet here, both under some pretext connected with cats? Why? What interest had the cottage for either or both of them?

Mrs. Thompson's manner to the woman whom she was helping to hide showed deep affection. The young man, a big, burly figure who had driven the young woman away, had seemed very friendly with Mrs. Thompson, but he did not seem to know the way to the cottage.

It was eleven o'clock before there were any signs of life in the house. Then the gate opened and a taxi drove in.

After a little wait, out came Mrs. Thompson, carrying a big basket from which came frenzied, indignant mewings to which the bull-terrier beside her listened with evident contempt. To Pointer's joy, the maid came out to get in beside her mistress, with another equally vocal basket. The dog jumped up beside the chauffeur and the taxi drove away. Pointer felt that he was in luck. He whipped round to the back, where, he found a choice of windows by which to enter. He owed that dog a grudge, he felt, as he undid a catch and stepped inside. But for him, Pointer would have done this much earlier.

There were only two rooms and the kitchen on the ground floor, and three little bedrooms above. The kitchen told nothing. The room behind the one where he had been last night, told nothing. He passed on into the room where he had been shown by Mrs. Thompson. As he glanced keenly around him he noticed something that had not been there last night. A small electric pocket torch was now lying on front of some books on a shelf. He picked it up and looked inside its cap—merely as a matter of routine. Inside was stamped the word peroxide. Pointer stood a full second with it in his hand. The dead Inskipp—the Dover torch—a young woman who had been in Dover that same night and left the next morning—had he found this earlier, the woman hidden under the rugs would not have been allowed to be driven off. He put it carefully away, and continued his swift but careful search. He found nothing more. Bar that torch the cottage showed an absolutely innocent character. And yet— Pointer acknowledged that it was only because of that torch, and of the connection with Inskipp's letter that he thought that the house was too bare of personal notes. There were no photographs whatever in any room. There were no letters from any old friends or relations that he could find. The cottage might have been a cattery office as far as things outside of business went, except for recent invitations.

True, death might have been busy in Mrs. Thompson's circle, and she might object to photographs, but she was very unusually friendless. What was her position? He placed her definitely on the plane of Major Pelham's womenkind. He was chiefly interested in her, because of trying to guess the reason which had made the visitor (whom for the moment, at any rate, he called Florence Rackstraw) go at once to that cottage and be received as she must have been and be helped as she certainly had been. Mrs. Thompson looked an upright woman, if ever there was one. She had bought cottage and land freehold unfortunately, which would mean that probably no references would have been asked for, though he would try for them.

Pointer had not been able to see the woman's face as she ran down the steps, wearing a big felt hat and a cloak of the highwayman type, but something in her run had given him an impression of youth. And there had been a very maternal touch in the way in which Mrs. Thompson had smoothed the rugs over her. Certainly only relationship, or great friendship, would account for the facts.

He stepped in at the police station, and there learnt that they had no knowledge whatever of the lady beyond what had been given him, but the sergeant too, he could see, agreed with his own ideas as to the class to which Mrs. Thompson belonged, in spite of her poverty.

From the station, Pointer telephoned to the various ports and aerodromes. If she had not already left the country, Florence Rackstraw was to be detained until he could question her about that electric torch. He learnt that a Miss Rackstraw had left early this morning in an Air-France liner for Marseilles. Her passport, he was told, had been issued in Durban, South Africa, three years ago. Durban. . . . Pointer thought of the tan on Inskipp's face, of the sketch of a farm where grew mimosas, and lemons and maize—of the remark about Norbury being a wine-grower—and cabled the Durban police for fullest particulars of a Henry and Florence Rackstraw, the latter of whom had obtained a passport in Durban three years ago, and for any possible connection between them and any one in Cirencester, especially a Mrs. Thompson.

As he hung up, Pointer felt that he indeed owed the bulldog a grudge. But for him, the chief inspector would have got into that cottage and found that most incriminating torch earlier. As it was—Marseilles is a good port from which to leave for South Africa; he might get on her track again there. Whether she had been alone, or accompanied by the big, burly young man who had driven her off from the cottage, he could not learn.

None of the names of the other users of passports this morning interested him, though he had them noted down. He left word at the station to have the taxi driver questioned as to where he had taken Mrs. Thompson and her maid, though Pointer did not think the answer would be of any importance. The women had not left the cottage for any length of time. A meat stew was simmering on the kitchen fire, a milk pudding was standing ready for the oven, some cat food was soaking.

As for the car that had driven Miss Rackstraw away last night, that would be traced by the Yard's special department for such work, and it was to the Yard that he returned from the Cirencester police station. His thoughts keeping time to the hum of the propeller.

CHAPTER 13: AN OLD CRIME THROWS ITS SHADOW ON THE NEW ONE

At his room in Scotland Yard Pointer found a note to say that Major Pelham was waiting for him. He went at once to the latter's room with a step that suggested the gait of a wolf dog, silent, swift, and springy. This was not the quiet, reserved detective officer of the Dover Mortuary. This was a man swift and sure and efficient—in other words, this was Pointer on his job.

The A.C. listened closely to the condensed, yet detailed, account of the events since Pointer had first been shown the body of the supposed tramp.

"The curious thing is," Pointer wound up, "that the passport-office can't trace any one of the name of Blythe as having arrived in Dover last Sunday. Rackstraw is there, so is Norbury, and next on the list to Inskipp. But no Blythe. As for Florence Rackstraw, she crossed by the same boat it seems, but her name comes some distance down, as though almost the last woman off the boat."

"That's odd!" said the major. "You think the man Blythe is using a false name?"

"It looks like it, sir. One evidently known to the other three men—instead of, or as well as his own."

"Four crooks?" Pelham asked, lighting a cigar.

A sudden vision rose before Pointer of the face of the dead Inskipp. There was nobility in that face—a quality not often seen alive, or dead.

"I see no reason—as yet—to think so," he said evasively. "As to the clothes found on the body, sir, Hendon reports that the dust collected and analysed shows that it consists of fig seeds as well as quantities of particles of the blossoms of lemons, oranges, olives and mimosas. Further, that there must have been many roses around, as well as some carnations, much lavender, thyme and juniper. The earth shown is chalky, with a good deal of rock— sandy rock. There's quite a paragraph of geological data as well which would fit many places."

"Durban among them?" asked Pelham promptly.

"I wonder, sir!"

"Think not?"

"Well, not one specifically South African flower—as we know them—is mentioned. Roses and carnations are all right, but what of the Veldt daisies and the many flowers which are found in masses in South Africa and nowhere else. I think their omission is odd. Incidentally, I had the recent lists of arrivals from South Africa looked through, and the report here says that not one of the names in which I'm interested can be traced. That means little, of course, the party may have made a longish stop in Europe—France or Italy. That's where I think of trying, sir, for that sketch was done on French paper, so our paper analyst tells me. Of course, any moment we may hear from some one who knows one or other of the parties concerned. But, first, I'm going to try to find out more about Mrs. Thompson's background, if that's possible. Meanwhile, I'll get Inspector Watts to look into the Mireille trail. There's the well-known film of that name, as well as the opera. It's just possible that the sketch may have been intended for something connected with either of them, or that, if meant as a gift for a lady, she may be connected with them."

Pointer was just leaving when the telephone rang again, this time from his own room.

His clerk thought that the chief inspector might like to know at once the contents of a cipher cable which had just been received from the Durban police and decoded. It ran:

"Frederick Rackstraw head master of private boys' school here. Married a Miss Knightly of Bournemouth, England. He died fifteen years ago.

Whole family very popular and highly respected.
He left three children, May, Henry and Florence.
Born thirty-seven, thirty-five, and thirty-two years
ago respectively. He left his widow an annuity of
three hundred a year, and directed that the school
was to be sold for the benefit of the children. It
fetched five thousand pounds. May married a
Rhodesian farmer. Has never been back since.
Henry got a scholarship to London University and
has never been home since. Florence became
librarian at town library here. Three years ago
mother and she joined son in Europe. Both had
highest of reputations locally. Last November
thirtieth, Mrs. Rackstraw sent some books from
Bulawayo to the library here as a gift, informing
them that Florence had just died in Europe as the
result of an accident while out climbing and that the
books had belonged to her. Letter has not been
kept by library authorities but authorship un-
questioned. Since then nothing has been heard of,
or from, any member of the family."

"What do you make of it. Pointer?" asked the major. "Beyond the obvious fact that, if the information is correct, some one has been passing herself off as a dead girl. But was it with, or without. the knowledge of Florence's brother and the three other men at the Lord Bishop?"

"On the whole, sir, it looks as though they might not be aware of it," Pointer said, "seeing that she seems to have avoided the hotel in question very carefully."

"Looks to me more than ever as though you had got hold of a gang of crooks," said Pelham.

As Pointer made way for the next man who wanted to see the assistant commissioner, his mind was very busy.

So Florence Rackstraw as a real person was out, or might be out, of the whole affair. . . . Unless her name had been chosen for some special reason, it suggested that the user of it could not obtain a passport herself. The fact that she could use it, threw some light as to her height, general age, and looks. It also suggested that she was aware of Florence Rackstraw's death. Beyond that, it only opened up some very interesting speculations as to why she could not use her own name, or get a passport of her own.

And yet, she had gone straight to Mrs. Thompson without, Pointer was certain, giving her any preliminary warning! The lack of doing this—added to the use of a false passport—suggested that she had not dared to send a message. Not from any fear of not being received. Which meant that such fear must be lest others should hear of her visit. This fitted in with the way in which she had left . . . hidden under rugs . . . driven off in the dark. And he saw too that if that were so, it might explain the taking of that letter to Inskipp, if it was all-important that no attention be attracted to the cottage. It all might, of course, merely be extreme precautions to avoid an arrest for debt; but it looked more as though the visitor had been a wanted or escaped criminal of some kind. And, if so . . . was it possible that that was the link between her and Inskipp . . . that he was on her track? That that was why he had been murdered?

Pointer changed his step and walked on to his room with eyes that only saw automatically.

Secrecy was at the heart of this murder. Inskipp's death had been very skilfully, because very simply, made to look like the result of a tramp's quarrel.

Inskipp's name—if his own—was to vanish with his body into an unknown pauper's grave. It had all but gone down into the grave of a Simpkins of a Harding, but that had not been part of the plan— he thought. The two women were, he believed, entirely outside the crime, though both were being watched.

Now, secrecy would have to be part of the crime if this unknown visitor could not even use her own name to go and come from England, her own country apparently, as she had struck the maid at the Doverana as undoubtedly English. Pointer felt as though his hand might be on the thread which would lead to the heart of the labyrinth. But he did not alter the plan he had made while sitting in the A.C's room just now. He went first of all to the secretary of the coming cat show at the Crystal Palace. Was a Mrs. Thompson an exhibitor? he asked.

The secretary said that she generally showed some cats, and that whenever she did so, she always carried off at least one prize, especially for tortoise-shells.

"That's what I heard," murmured Pointer, who looked much older and rather colonial. His card—Mr. Parnell—had a Durban home address pencilled on it. "She's one of us by the way, isn't she? Connected with South Africa, I was told, I mean by birth, or was it by her marriage?"

The secretary had no idea.

"Is Mrs. Thompson her own name?" asked Pointer heavily. "I've heard it whispered that it's just a trade name. If so, she might have bought the goodwill of some already established cattery. Which isn't what I want. I want—"

The secretary broke in on Mr. Parnell's wants to say that as far as he knew Mrs. Thompson was Mrs. Thompson, not that that mattered as far as he could see. "Anyway, she lives at Norburn Cottage, Cirencester. They might be able to answer your questions better there," he ended.

"Has she written on cats at all?" Pointer inquired imperturbably. "I've more confidence in people who write. And as I want the best possible blood for the cattery which my daughter is thinking of starting—"

"You couldn't have a better strain than Mrs. Thompson's," said the secretary, wondering how he was going to get rid of the bore. "Look! Here's a little par. on her in the last *Looker-On*"—he showed him a picture of Mrs. Thompson and the lines below. Pointer thanked the man, and, to his relief, left at that, to buy a *Looker-On* and tear out the page. From the date it would have been on sale in Paris or Menton at the time that Inskipp was travelling home, and so could easily have come under his notice and, if so, might explain the reference in the note sent to Mrs. Thompson supposing that Inskipp had wanted to get into touch with that lady for some reason or other—whether connected with cats, or with the strange visitor.

He drove to the office of the *Looker-On*, and there— still as a guileless Colonial—asked for the assistant editor. He had seen a picture purporting to be of a Mrs. Thompson, he said, "but why didn't the article on her say anything about Durban? Surely, in any paragraph dealing with Mrs. Thompson there ought to be some word about Durban, and her connection with Durban?"

He had been shown into the office of a very young under-secretary, who happened to be feeling bored with life. She looked at the photograph with marked distaste.

"One can't put everything in, and whatever one writes, people always complain that a lot ought to have gone in instead."

"But it's not a good likeness now, is it!" expostulated her visitor. "Can't you put another one in, and give more details of her life next week?"

"Oh, no, I can't put in another one, not even if she wins a prize at the coming show. Mrs.Thompson was ever so upset about that one appearing. Yet I took it myself, and I think it's very flattering. I had to interview all the exhibitioners at the last Cirencester show. I had thought she'd be so pleased with the advertisement. I really put it in because I wanted to help her."

"But why call her Mrs. Thompson?" Pointer asked fretfully. "Why not give her other name?" He was polishing his glasses, but he caught the look that just flitted across her transparent face. It gave him a thrill such as Miss Walker's glances rarely roused in her fellow mortals. He was right! He had correctly read that cottage empty of all links with the past. And here was one who might be able to throw some light on that emptiness—if she were handled carefully.

"She exhibits as Mrs. Thompson," she said evasively. "She is known as Mrs. Thompson. You've a right to call yourself anything you like, Mr.— " she glanced at the card—"Mr. Parnell, so long as it's not for purposes of doing something wrong." She little thought how apposite was the remark.

"But I think she makes a mistake," he said judicially, "I mean, from a business point of view. Much better use her own—her other—"

"Oh, I agree with you!" interrupted the girl warmly. "Especially as everybody would only be sorry for her, and want to help her in her plucky fight. I think husbands should be forced by law to insure, don't you? My father was a second division clerk in the War Office, and worked under Sir Seabright. That's really why I want to help Lady or rather Mrs. Thompson, as she calls herself—now. I think it's cruel! To find yourself left a widow with nothing but what you can sell your furniture for—and then on top of it to lose your daughter in that awful way. Most women would have gone out of their minds!"

"But *did* you think Mrs. Whin-Browning guilty?" Pointer asked, not a muscle of whose face told of the feelings within him. As he heard the name of Sir Seabright Thompson, the dead father of a Mrs. Whin-Browning who was wanted—if alive— for two murders.

"What else could one think?" The girl dropped her voice—her eyes wide—" She wouldn't have drowned herself—if she did—if she hadn't done it, would she? Or run away—if she did run away. I think Mrs. Thompson's a marvel, though, like you, I think it would be a better advertisement to use her title. After all, one's only the sorrier for her— one admires her grit the more."

"Does she know you know?" Pointer asked, really idly this time.

"Oh, no! It's only because of father I recognised her at once. He was taken in a presentation group with Sir Seabright and Lady Thompson some twenty years ago.

He had a copy of the photograph framed. It hangs in the dining-room at home still. And so, when I saw her—I recognised her at once, but I didn't know she knew Durban at all."

"Lady Thompson stayed there and very much liked she was there, too," improvised Pointer. . . . "Lucky you knew all about Mrs. Thompson. I wouldn't have spoken of her real name if I hadn't felt sure you knew all about who she is—"

"And *I* wouldn't have breathed a word, if I hadn't been sure you knew!" said the girl in all sincerity.

"Well—I suppose the thing is to do as she wants, and keep silent, eh?" So saying, Pointer picked up hat, gloves and umbrella, and apologised for the length of his visit. Then he stepped out into the street. Even he had had a jolt. This was far beyond anything that he had expected. This—the linking, even indirectly, of the famous Whin-Browning case with the murder in the Dover shelter on last Sunday night.

Nor was it indirectly, if the visitor was, as he now believed her to have been, Mrs. Thompson's daughter, Edna Whin-Browning answered every query that he had put to himself as he lay watching the cottage, and the later question as to why a false passport had been necessary, for though the Brighton superintendent had expressed his certainty that Mrs. Whin-Browning had been drowned while bathing—he had got out a warrant just the same, and if alive, if recognised, she could, and would be, arrested at sight. The electric torch linked her directly with the shelter where Inskipp had been murdered, or with Inskipp himself at Dover, just as her taking the letter suggested a previous connection with the murdered man. But where had that connection started? Had Inskipp got on the track of Mrs. Whin-Browning? Was he killed to prevent his giving information to the police? Or to stop blackmail?

The letter to Mrs. Thompson now suggested that Inskipp had not been certain who the latter was unless it was a genuine and most incredible coincidence that it had been written just at that time and sent to just that address. Mrs. Thompson had not known his name—but her daughter had! Her daughter who had taken the letter from the mantel-shelf, and left in the room the torch that Inskipp had borrowed from the Boots on the evening of his murder, and who in doing so had looped a very dreadful and a very strange loop.

CHAPTER 14: THE CHIEF INSPECTOR RUNS OVER THE POSSIBLE LINKS BETWEEN MRS. WHIN-BROWNING AND INSKIPP

Pointer went at once to the newspaper-room at Hendon, and there he obtained copies of all the portraits of the people linked even remotely with the tragedy which had some twelve months ago agitated England. There was no picture of young Mrs. Whin-Browning's parents, but they were absolutely out of even the widest picture of the double tragedy at Brighton.

As to the Whin-Brownings, there had been only her husband and his younger brother Hector and some scattered cousins, besides May Whin-Browning, the poisoned sister.

Pointer satisfied himself that there was no portrait of any Whin-Browning which could by any chance stand for Inskipp. But he asked for copies of all the newspaper prints.

As it happened, Inspector Watts had dropped in to the same room at Hendon to look through the newspapers for any mention of a performance of *Mireille* in England or any showing of the film lately.

Pointer explained what had brought him there. "Drop Mireille for the moment. I want you to fly down with me to Dover, and there take some of these portraits of the men associated with the Whin-Browning case to the Lord Bishop Hotel. Find out if any of them can be recognised as any of the three so-called friends of Inskipp who arrived at the same time with Inskipp and dined with him. Here is the list of numbers which will tell you who the portraits represent—should any be identified. I'll go on to the Doverana with these portraits of Mrs. Whin-

Browning."

They were driven to the police plane and were soon deposited outside Dover, where they separated, to meet later at the pier entrance.

Pointer walked to the Doverana and asked for a room. The assistant manageress who showed him around, had not seen him before, and he took the second one whose door she opened.

He took it for a day. It was on the same floor as Florence Rackstraw's room had been. He had been recommended to come there by her, he said unblushingly.

But to the chambermaid he held out the portraits to which Christopher had objected.

"Between ourselves, Miss Rackstraw has run away from her home. That's the truth of the matter. Now her people want to get her back again—without calling in the police, of course."

"Of course!" said the maid, "who would want *them* poking round!"

"Now, is this the lady who left here early yesterday morning? You know—Miss Rackstraw—the one who let her hat catch fire?"

The maid studied the portraits carefully. Finally she took one out and had another look at it.

"She didn't look like this when she came, nor when she went away, sir. But it's the very spit of her as she looked lying in bed. She looked quite different when she went out. It's the way of wearing her hair that does it. Besides, she looks as though she had light hair in these pictures, but it's quite dark, really."

"They're only snapshots probably," said Pointer.

"She looks just as ill here, though," said the maid, handing back the photograph, "and, my goodness, just as unhappy!"

The picture had been taken of Mrs. Whin-Browning just before the adjournment of the inquest on Saturday— just when she had begun to realise the awful fate that lay before her.

Pointer went off to "see about his things."

But a telephone message reached the manageress shortly afterwards, explaining that "Mr. Parnell" had had to change his plans and would not be able to take the room after all.

He turned from the instrument as Inspector Watts tapped on the door of the kiosk. "One of the three men at the hotel has been using a false name. Which one do you think it is?"

"Blythe," Pointer said.

Watts stared at his superior and his distant relation.

"We can't trace Blythe's passport—which looks as though he were using a false name," Pointer said.

The inspector made a sign of self-disgust at his stupidity. "And can you also tell me, sir, who Blythe is— since he isn't Blythe?"

"Hector Whin-Browning?" was the query which really did startle the other, who only looked a question too surprised to be put into words.

"I had an unfair advantage there," Pointer confessed. "I recognised his portrait when I saw it in the papers at Hendon as that of the young man who collected Mrs. Whin-Browning from her mother's cottage. Were the men at the hotel certain of him?"

"Absolutely. The head waiter, the wine waiter, and the hall porter all three will swear to him. Here are their signatures on the backs, together with their addresses. I explained that it was a case of trying to collect a gaming debt. Hector Whin-Browning! Amazing! I didn't know that Ambrose Whin-Browning had a brother—was he mixed up in the affair?"

"Ambrose only had one brother, this Hector, who is some years younger than he. As far as is known, Hector was away from England when the two deaths happened. 'Oriental cruise' is what is entered against his name in those papers that I looked through this morning."

Pointer spent the time on the flight back to the Yard in thinking over the facts as so far known, which seemed to be interlinked, if not interwoven, with the death of Inskipp in that shelter last Sunday night. He was dividing them up into coherent groups. It took accurate thinking to accomplish even that much, to see all the possibilities of each group, realise which of them negatived which, and what other possibilities there were that might negative any or all—partially or entirely. Once that is done with any mass of detail, the facts—and the theories arising out of them—become available. Until that much is accomplished, the mind merely turns them over and over, like a child with a pack of cards, or runs here and there like a dog at a fair in loops and circles.

Back at the Yard, Pointer had another interview with the A.C. who listened in profound silence to what the chief inspector had discovered. Then he held out a message from the Passport Office, which had been waiting for Pointer nearly half an hour. It stated that Hector Whin-Browning had arrived in Dover by last Sunday's boat, and had left by the Thallassa aeroplane for Paris this morning at quarter to eight. He had landed at Le Bourget at quarter past ten.

"Has he gone to meet her? Or did Rackstraw wait on the other side for the lady who bore his name? Look here, run over the facts again—to me."

Major Pelham pressed the button which meant that he was not to be interrupted.

"Putting the older crime on one side," Pointer said, "the facts surrounding Inskipp's death would seem to have been as follows:

"Inskipp arrived from France in Dover last Sunday evening in company with three men, Hector Whin-Browning, who signed the hotel register as Blythe, a man called Rackstraw whose dead sister's passport is used by Mrs. Whin-Browning—"

"Which may have been why Florence Rackstraw died—' by accident'!" threw in the A.C. under his breath.

"—and with a man called Norbury," continued Pointer. "We are told that a letter was handed to Inskipp

which had just arrived and was stamped *Air France*. We
know that he had written a note to Mrs. Thompson about
a tortoiseshell cat, posting it on Dover pier on his arrival.
As it was a wild crossing and was pouring at the time,
that fact suggests that he considered the note important,
though its contents seem trivial. We know that he and
the other three men dined together, and that Hector
Whin-Browning—as Blythe—signed for the wine. What
happened later on Sunday is still unknown. But—"
Pointer proceeded to sum up the facts of the puzzling
case. Then he passed on to what he knew of Inskipp's
three companions. Of Rackstraw there was nothing to tell
beyond hours of arrival and departure, and the fact that
he had paid Inskipp's bill. Of Blythe as Hector Whin-
Browning there was much to say. Finally he came to
Norbury.

"We are told that he was referred to as a wine-grower
or farmer. In other words, a man who could be connected
with scarecrows. Inskipp's sketch shows a scarecrow with
just such garments on it as were found on his dead body,
and the analysed dust of the garments confirms the idea
that they may actually have been taken off the identical
scarecrow which he painted in his sketch."

"Good God!" murmured Pelham.

"The fact of Inskipp having painted what looks like
part of a farm, suggests that he may have been stopping
there. And, if so, possibly the other two men stayed there
as well. The sketch shows lemon orchards and a maize
field, among other things. Where these two things grow,
grapes ought to do well too. That suggests that the farm
may have been Norbury's."

"If so, the farm could easily be the link, the outward
link at any rate, between the four men who came over
from France last Saturday afternoon, if not from farther
afield," said Major Pelham slowly.

"They were linked together in another and far more
peculiar way as well, sir," Pointer reminded him, "or
rather interwoven. Blythe is Hector Whin-Browning,

brother-in-law of Edna Whin-Browning, who is using the passport and name of a dead sister of one of the other men—Rackstraw."

"Don't say dead, say 'probably murdered too.' "

"That may be, sir," agreed Pointer, "but keeping to the murders we do know of, she must have had some secure hiding-place all these months. What about a farm—such a farm as Norbury's? And since Hector used the name of Blythe to the three other men, what more likely than that Mrs. Whin-Browning used it too? She would alter the relationship of course, probably to sister, for in that case Hector could register her without showing any but his own passport at the smaller, more careless hotels. That she had not passed as his wife seemed indicated by the absence of any communication which can be traced between them after her arrival, and by the evident willingness of Mrs. Thompson to call on his help, when her daughter needed help to get away. The odd thing is that none of the four men at the Lord Bishop would appear to have come to see her, though under her new name, it would have been quite safe, one would think. She had been very ill —especially all Sunday, the day after the murder of Inskipp. . . ."

"Was Inskipp about to mix himself up in that old tragedy? I suppose he'd found out, or was on the point of finding out, something absolutely fatal to her?" said Major Pelham.

"I thought that too at first, sir, but I don't see what he could find out which was more damaging than the facts ascertained by the superintendent and the coroner," said Pointer, looking intently at his shoe-tips. "Mrs. Whin-Browning was not like a securely placed woman about to be thrown into danger by some unexpected discovery. She is already in the depths. The worst is known."

"That's rather subtle."

"If the older tragedy is at the root of Inskipp's murder, it must have been quite simply that he had found out who she was, and was about to betray her, or had started blackmail. Yet—" Pointer stopped.

"Well?"

"He doesn't look in the least a hard or merciless character, sir. Not at all the blackmailer type. Then, too, she had got hold of that other woman's passport, and so could have disappeared, one would think. At any rate, she didn't slog Inskipp first with a sandbag and then with the hotel knob. That at least was definitely beyond her—or any woman's strength."

"The knob would suggest the man who called himself Blythe," said Pelham. "That putting another knob on in its place in his suite—"

"But the larger knob, sir, came from the floor above his, from a room which Norbury and Rackstraw would have had to pass on their way down the stairs or to the lift." Pointer thought that even the affair of the knob was not simple.

"It certainly does point, so far, to one of the three men in the hotel as Inskipp's murderer. And, of course, if Mrs. Whin-Browning was at the bottom of it—and if her brother-in-law was her fellow-criminal—he is clearly indicated as Inskipp's murderer. But it was a curious murder. I mean oddly planned," said Pointer, again in the tone of a man talking half to himself. "Carefully planned, and yet—and yet—a suggestion of the improvised —the hurried—abouт it—"

"She must have been in it to have burnt that hat and taken that electric torch," said Pelham in a questioning tone.

"There was a gale blowing that night from nine till past eleven," said Pointer. "If the torch had rolled into a corner, and the murderer had not seen it and emptied his sand over it, it might be—I don't for a moment say it was so, but it might be—that the gale blew the sand off it sufficiently for any one who later stepped into the shelter to have seen its shining end and picked it up to use it."

"But why should Mrs. Whin-Browning step into that particular shelter on that particular night?"

"It's possible, sir—not likely, but possible—that she knew nothing about the murder, even so. But that the same gale which blew the sand about blew the hat about, too, and blew it out of the shelter towards her as she walked on the cliff promenade to recover after a bout of seasickness. Now, the scarecrow in the sketch is wearing a very wide-brimmed felt hat. Suppose that Mrs. Whin-Browning recognised the hat? Stepped in to see where it had come from, saw the bright end of the torch shining in the corner where the sand was emptied—which, as it happens, is the only spot lit by one of the promenade lamps—picked up the torch and used it— to see Inskipp lying there murdered. I am supposing that she knew him as well as the scarecrow's hat from her stay at the farm," he added with a faint smile. "Her actions afterwards are consistent with innocence of his death. Given her position! She could not let the police know. But it might have been the shock of finding it which drove her to make for Cirencester and her mother. I feel sure that she had not given them any warning that she was in England. Evidently Mrs. Thompson had no idea of any link between Inskipp and her daughter, even if it existed. It's possible, of course, as I first thought, that Mrs. Whin-Browning took the letter merely to prevent any inquiries about any dead person drawing attention to the cottage to which she had rushed for at least temporary shelter. But Mrs. Thompson—to call her as she prefers to be called—hasn't sent the letter on to the Yard yet, I see. But now that her daughter has left—and without any one knowing of her visit, as she would think—she could do it safely, and, I think would have done it unless there were another closer and more permanent link which she now— not before— knows all about. I rather think the link is the farm, which is still to be the daughter's refuge."

"Wherever it may be."

"It's where there are lemon groves—orange trees—maize—figs in bloom—thyme—lavender blossoms—roses and carnations," said Pointer.

"Sounds entrancing." Pelham looked at the cold drizzle outside. "And, I still think, sounds like South Africa. Cape Town has some marvellous spots around it. But why on earth that woman left it— What necessity drove her?" Pelham's cigar had actually gone out unnoticed.

"Money couldn't account for it, one would think," said Pointer, eyeing his shoe-tips still more closely. "In the first place, Hector Whin-Browning is a rich man, and, apart from him, she could get nothing by a personal appeal to bank or solicitor which she couldn't get far more safely by writing. Unless it was just some sudden impulse or home sickness which the opportunity to get hold of another woman's passport rendered possible—" Pointer did not finish his sentence for a moment, but sat gazing attentively at his shoe-tips.

"They made great play at the inquest about her being a woman of sudden impulses. But you were saying?"

"Unless an impulse, I can only imagine one pair of motives," Pointer finished slowly. "If she is innocent, and hoped, or had reason to think, that she could get at some fact to prove this, it would be well worth her while to run the terrible risk. And if she is guilty, and believed that she could fasten the crime on to some one else—that, again, would be worth it. Either way she would be proved innocent legally, and could touch her husband's considerable fortune, and once more take her place in a normal way in a normal world."

"Which do you think of the two is the more likely one?" asked Pelham.

"I don't see how she could hope to bring the crime home to any living person," Pointer said slowly. "Of course, sir, I know nothing about it, for I didn't attend the inquest."

Pointer fell into a reverie as he sat at the table. The other two waited.

"I don't see any woman in her position safely abroad, returning to an island in order to prevent some one giving

her away. She would have killed him abroad with much
more safety for herself. Our little island and the passport
difficulties are some of the things foreigners and
Americans remind us of when we boast of the number of
murderers we catch."

"But what if she didn't know till he got here that he
intended giving her away?"

Pointer only shook his head. "Whoever murdered
Inskipp thought until they opened their papers this
morning that they had succeeded in hiding his identity.
Yet Mrs. Whin-Browning, once she had seen him dead, as
we think that torch must mean, wants to get away. It
suggests—it makes one wonder"—he frowned at the
floor—" whether Inskipp was—not a danger, not an
enemy—but an associate—a partner. She would have
needed one— if she intended stirring up that old case."

"But there's her brother-in-law! Her devoted brother-
in-law!"

"I only saw them together the once—and under very
peculiar circumstances—but I got an impression that she
was afraid of him—or at least unwilling to go with him,"
Pointer said slowly.

"I suppose Hector really was out of England at the
time of the two poisoning cases?" asked Major Pelham.

According to the papers, he was supposed to be," said
Pointer. "But—well—some one helped her to escape. She
couldn't have done it alone. And he certainly helped her
away from the cottage. Yet she's hardly likely to have an
army of helpers. It rather suggests that Hector wasn't far
from Brighton when she went bathing on Saturday
afternoon—which suggests that he was there when at
least the sister-in-law was poisoned."

"By Jove!" muttered Pelham meaningly. "Upon my
word, I can see why you think she may have wanted to
come to England! Lurid possibilities, eh? And you think
this Inskipp?"

"Not 'think,' sir, 'wonder'—'speculate on the possibility
that—' " Pointer corrected with a smile.

"I don't know if it's any point," said Pelham, "but Superintendent Walker of Brighton told me, when he dropped in here about the stolen ingots, and the Whin-Browning case came up in conversation, that he believes that the sister happened to come across so definite a proof of Mrs. Whin-Browning's guilt that she had to be silenced. Which is what may have happened to Inskipp. Though your suggestion, Pointer, that he was here to help her is very alluring."

"Well, sir, we may find out the truth when we locate that farm," said Pointer equably. "That's the next thing to do."

"You've been reading up the case though you didn't attend the inquest. I take it you, too, think she's guilty," Pelham asked.

"Unless she lied about those trays, certainly. But if she changed trays with her sister-in-law, I see a possibility of her innocence."

"You mean you think the man's sister did it?"

"She stood to gain a sufficiency by his death, sir. She was entirely dependent on him. But for her own death, she would have been as likely a suspect as the wife."

But for her own death—" echoed Pelham; "by poison meant for her sister-in-law?"

"She would have had all her brother's fortune if Mrs. Whin-Browning died, sir," Pointer reminded the other. "As the facts seemed to be, no one brought that out clearly, but it is so."

"And you think you can prove it?"

Major Pelham's look suggested that he thought the possibility to be very remote.

Pointer did not tell him that he had commissioned an ex-Scotland Yard inspector, a man called Earnshaw, to look up the case. Starting with Ada Greenlee, who, Pointer fancied from what she had not said at the inquest, might have seen her mistress touch the breakfast trays which were left outside the doors of widow and sister-in-law. There were two small pieces of evidence given by the cook which tended, in his mind, to suggest Mary Whin-Browning as herself the criminal.

The telephone rang. Several messages had arrived over the telephone for Pointer. He returned to his own office, and there looked at the latest information. Mrs. Harding was definitely eliminated from any possibility of having been on the cliffs last Sunday night. So was Mrs. Simpkins the charwoman. Mrs. Thompson's taxi had driven her and her maid, and her cats and dog, to a nearby cat show. The cats were left in their new quarters, and the two women and dog had returned a couple of hours later to the cottage, where they still were at the moment of telephoning.

CHAPTER 15: LEMONS GROW IN MENTON

News had by now begun to come in over the telephone about Inskipp. The first was from Mrs. Thompson. Mrs. Thompson had just seen the paper, she said, and though she did not know anything about Mr. Inskipp personally, she recounted the facts about the letter that he had written to her. She had unfortunately mislaid the letter when a manager from the Lord Bishop Hotel at Dover had called for it, but it had turned up since, and if the Yard would like it she would at once send it on by registered post. On Pointer's vigorous nod, the constable at the telephone thanked Mrs. Thompson, begged her to do so, and after a moment hung up.

"Sensible woman, Mrs. Thompson. She realised that the so-called manager of the Dover hotel would get into touch with the police, and she intended to be first," said Pointer. "Also, now that her daughter is safely out of England, the absolutely non-committal letter can be shown. She could truthfully say that she had never met Inskipp and did not know him. The letter will be useful as affording a specimen of Inskipp's writing."

Then came two mistaken people who thought that an Inskipp whom they had known years ago was the dead man, but the description and the age negatived that. Then came a Stock Exchange man, a Mr. Barrett, who described a former partner of his, who was undoubtedly the Inskipp lying dead in the Dover mortuary. He was asked to go down to Dover and see if he could identify him. He agreed at once. He had not heard from Inskipp since he left the city, which was about seven years ago, after mopping up quite a nice little pile in Marochis.

Had Mr. Inskipp any artistic tastes? Music, Pointer

knew, was a strong point on the Exchange, but Inskipp did not belong to any of its recognised choirs or theatrical companies. Did he sketch? Pointer wanted to know. The man at the other end could not say. He looked the sort who might, he added guardedly. A few more inquiries, and Inskipp was given a very good character. He was the kindest of chaps, said the speaker. Generous, too. Always anxious not to do the other chap in the eye.

Pointer fancied, from something in the other's tone, that that lovable characteristic had been rather a handicap on the Stock Exchange.

Pointer asked Mr. Barrett if, supposing he identified Inskipp, he would be kind enough to call in at his rooms at the Yard, and was told that few things would interest the speaker more.

Other telephone calls came in. They were either obviously no good, or they only bore out what Pointer had learnt from Mr. Barrett. By evening Mr. Barrett had definitely identified the dead body as that of John Inskipp, but Pointer nevertheless went to bed feeling that the Inskipp street was turning into a cul-de-sac. Durban on Miss Rackstraw's passport . . . wine-growing . . . Norbury a wine grower . . . lemon groves, mimosa and maize. . . . But, apart from the lack of any of the typical South African field flowers, there was one other little point against the farm being in South Africa.

Rackstraw had only stayed two days in England. He had arrived on Sunday afternoon, and gone back to Calais on Monday. That short stay, supposing him to have also come from the farm where stood the scarecrow, seemed very unusual, if

one assumed that the farm was in South Africa.

None of the three men linked with Inskipp came forward. Yet Blythe, for one, must have heard of the inquiry through his connection with Mrs. Thompson. Rackstraw might not have seen the notice in the papers— but what of Norbury? Pointer had had another notice sent to the papers asking the three men known to have been with Mr. Inskipp at the Dover hotel to get into touch with the Yard, and giving their names. The next morning passed, however, without any news from them nor of them.

"Blythe we can understand," said Major Pelham, "if his whereabouts would point to Mrs. Whin-Browning's hiding-place. But the other two? Looks as though all three were mixed up in something shady."

Pointer agreed—with reservations—that it did. The trouble was that so many people nowadays only glanced at the leader, the chief political events, and the stock markets in their papers, and then gladly dropped the rest of its mass of verbiage.

Pointer wondered whether any of the three could give him any light on Mireille. The name did not suggest South Africa. He had once read a translation of Frederic Mistral's epic poem while convalescing from an injured leg in Marseilles. He had seen the film of the name because of having read that poem. He knew that it was an entirely Provencal name. . . . And he knew that mimosas and maize grow well in Provence. Inskipp was by way of being fond of sketching. There are artists' haunts in Provence which are very attractive.

He thought of Cassis . . . where more easels than trees in the summertime outline its old port, and Aigues-Mortes, that enchanting dream of a town near Nimes. . . . Other names came crowding to his tongue. It is a lovely region, thyme and juniper and lavender scented. *Mireio*— she was of the very essence of the hills behind Hyeres. What about the lemon groves? Pointer was not sure about lemons. . . . He looked the fruit up in his encyclopaedias. There was only one place where, in Southern France, lemons ripened in sufficient numbers to be a paying proposition, he read, and that was at Menton. Pointer made a note of the name. A young man on a visit to the assistant commissioner passed him in a corridor, a young man who went everywhere to play tennis.

"Mr. Richards, do you know Menton?" Pointer asked

him swiftly.

"And Voronoff's apes? I do. Why?"

"What's it like?"

"Sort of place Queen Victoria liked. Punch had a cartoon some years ago with lines under it which just fit in the case:

*'For Tooting Beck and Wimbledon, and
Streatham Hill and Cannes
Aren't nearly so respectable as Menton-
Garavan.'*

"Menton-Garavan is the east bay. Menton, *tout court,* is the west. The old town holds the centre, and keeps the two other bits from cutting each other's throats in the effort to prove that each suffers more from the Mistral than it does. The tennis courts are quite good. They're in the east part."

"Any farms around?"

"Flower farms. The earth is said to be marvellously fertile. It isn't. But the sun is. Roses and carnations grow like cabbages. But no vegetables."

"Any good vineyards?"

Richards shook his head. "Not good ones. But plenty of places where the sour local wine grows, though I except Castellar, which can be quite drinkable."

Richards would have passed on, but Pointer had one more question:

"Many lemon groves to be found there?"

"Lemons—" Richards made a sign of holding off an avalanche. "Menton gets a swelled head every time you talk of lemons. They're not bad, the Menton lemons, though they can't touch Sicilian ones. Don't let them know that it was I who told you that, will you?" he added in mock fright. "They'll stone me off the courts next time I play there. I doubt if even 'Mr. G.' could get off with such a sentiment."

"But are there farms which specialise in lemons?"

"Look here." Richards shook his head. "Evidently a lemon has committed a crime, or the answer to one of our criminal hunts had been a lemon, and you're on your toes to get it arrested. Every hillside around Menton has at least one lemon grove on it, I should say. Lemons, mandarins—as they call tangerines, being ignorant and foolish—and olives simply swarm on all the hillsides. Add mimosa bursting at you from every comer, with roses such as we don't dream of in England, thirty feet up the trees, and you have a fair picture of what the traveller out there has to put up with." And this time Richards was gone.

Menton. . . . That scarecrow had hung and swung in hot sun and plenty of wind, whether Mistral or Bise. . . . A man might rush to Dover from Menton and return the next day, provided there were great need of hurry, much more easily than he would from South Africa. . . . Menton lemons are small . . . so were those on the trees in the sketch. . . .

There is no aerodrome at Menton, but if you have a pull, even in winter you can leave London at quarter to nine, and be in Cannes at quarter to four; and from Cannes it was only a question of an hour and a half by train, or an hour by motor-car along the Grande Corniche. Some eight hours in all would do it. . . .

Pointer had himself put through to Menton. The popular British Vice-Consul was out, unfortunately, and he could find out nothing about any one of the name of Norbury, either as a vineyard owner or as a farmer in the neighbourhood,

At Nice is a Consul-General. Pointer had met some of the members of the consulate there while on the Eames-Erskine case, whose end came in that sunny town. He was put through at once, and learnt that there, too, the Consul was away at the moment. So was the first secretary, but one of the assistant secretaries was speaking. Pointer wanted to know whether the name of Norbury was known there. It was not. He ran through the

other names. Inskipp? No. Blythe? No. Rackstraw?" No—
oh—sorry! Wait a moment. There was an accident to
some one of that name. . . . Wait, hold the line a moment,
will you?" Within that variable measure of time Pointer
was told that a young English woman named Florence
Rackstraw had been killed by a fall from a mountain path
only this last September, "and, oh I say—awfully sorry—I
see here in the account that it happened at a farm called
La Chevre d'Or, not far from Menton, which belongs,
apparently, to some one of the name of Norbury. You
asked about Norbury, didn't you? Sorry! Mrs. Norbury
apparently came in and officially identified the body and
so on, and oh— look here—I see that the other witness
with her was a John Inskipp whose address is also given
as *La Chevre d'Or*. Sorry! That what you want to know?"

In considerably more detail it was, and Pointer soon
got all the recorded facts out of the hasty young man,
including the one that a man called Blythe, also stopping
at the farm, had been out alone with Miss Rackstraw
when she had had her fall. The nearest police to the
Domaine de la Chevre d'Or had sent in their report,
having been at once called in by the owner, Norbury. The
report ran that after carefully looking over the ground,
and taking all the evidence, they had made quite sure
that there had been no foul play. As for Norbury, the
secretary had a vague idea that Inskipp had come in his
stead, as he had the 'flu, or something of that kind, or
was too busy to come down to Nice. Or it might have been
Blythe. Yes, Miss Rackstraw had some relations out there
at the time. Her mother and her brother. "Oh, sorry! I see
the mother had gone back to South Africa not long before
the accident."

"And the brother?" asked Pointer.

"He had gone, too. Oh, sorry! This is a note to the
effect that he was exploring the Red Caves at the time of
the accident, and no one had been able to get into touch
with him. His name was Philip. Oh, sorry! No, it is
Henry. Henry Rackstraw."

"Had Miss Rackstraw's passport not been handed in?" Pointer asked.

"No, there is a note here to say it couldn't be found. Probably dropped in the ravine somewhere: it's thought she had it with her as she was going to the Red Rocks."

Pointer kept him at it until he was satisfied that there really was nothing more to learn. Then he was put through to the police of Castellar near to the farm of the Golden Goat. He explained that he was the solicitor to Madame Rackstraw, and that there was some tittle-tattle . . . enfin, might he ask just what had happened to Mademoiselle Rackstraw? He heard the same story in French as the Consul's secretary had given him, with added details of the baboon and the baboon's keeper.

"Wasn't there a Mademoiselle Blythe among the guests of Monsieur Norbury?" Pointer asked.

Yes, the police officer thought that there was, but she was in Nice at the time, he believed. Anyhow, she did not come into the story at all. As to the farm, he gave it the highest character. Norbury had bought it some five years ago, and had been prompt in paying all taxes, and so on. . . . He employed only French labour, which was another good mark in the police eyes, and paid good wages to them. He gave Pointer the exact address of the. farm. Monsieur Norbury was there now? Oh, yes, he had returned after making arrangements for the sale of his produce in London. When? He had returned home on Thursday. No, he rarely left his farm. Once a year with his wife he would go down to Marseilles to replace broken tools and buy the seeds and necessaries for the winter sowings.

What did the farm produce? Lemons chiefly, but also oranges, mandarins, olives, with some cereals— corn, maize—and a small terraced vineyard. What of the guests at the farm? Were they still as when the accident had happened? No, the man thought not. There seemed fewer. But he could not speak with any certainty. Certainly he had met one of them only this morning. Monsieur

Rackstraw. He often came in for a permit to pass into Italy about the *Rochers rouges* just across the border. The Domaine itself was very close to the borderline, which twisted and turned like a serpent.

Yes, Monsieur Rackstraw had told him that he had just returned from a swift rush back to England in Monsieur Norbury's company. He was about to start on a magnificent film of the region which, so he had told the policeman, would bring travellers from all over the world up there in the hills. Yes, he was a film writer as well as a *savant*, he and his friend Monsieur—Monsieur—*enfin*, these English names!

"Was it Inskipp?"

"*Parfaitment*! It had just that extraordinary sound . . . who was also a film writer and had also a great interest in local legends."

"Where was Monsieur Inskipp?"

He had asked Monsieur Rackstraw about his friend, and had been told that he had returned to his home in England and wasn't coming out again for some time—possibly not at all. Pointer heard also of Mrs. Norbury, and of the respect in which the quiet, very *comme il faut* lady was held. No, she had not left the farm at all since going to Marseilles last December.

"Was there any one in the neighbourhood of the name of *Mireille* or *Mireou*?"

"Only the little baby of the schoolmaster."

"Did they take any English papers at the farm?" came the final question.

The constable speaking had no idea. As to the Blythes, he did not know if she and her brother were still there or not. That ended the talk.

It had been a wonderful haul, all springing from the sketch left in that drawer of a Dover hotel. The murderer imagined that he had been so clever, but he had not thought, or not had time, to lift out the papers lining the drawers, and so find what looked like a white lining, but which was in reality a most important piece of evidence.

What interested Pointer most was that he now understood how Edna Whin-Browning could have got hold of the passport of Florence Rackstraw without—necessarily—Rackstraw's knowledge or connivance. Apparently the brother had been absent at the time of the accident and for some hours later and Miss Blythe might have found it easy to take.

The apparently total lack of communication between the two "Rackstraws" at Dover was also accounted for. As for the death of Florence— Pointer had no great opinion of French detectives. There was a time when it looked as though the murder of Englishwomen in France were going to become a regular sport and one, moreover, in which there was no close season. Was that death what it seemed—a real accident? Or had Inskipp's murder to do with some unexpected discovery on his part of foul play concerned with it—not with the older crimes? Time alone could show, but it added yet another possible motive to be sifted and followed up.

He left instructions with Inspector Watts as to what to do should Inskipp's suitcase turn up. A suitcase sent, Pointer thought, to some distant place in England, and containing at the present moment, he believed, the watch and various oddments, such as cuff-links and fountain-pen, which the murderer would not want to leave on the sands in case there was a hitch in the acceptance of the body as that of a tramp. There would probably also be Inskipp's passport with the photograph of him as a living man. Carter Paterson were already busy searching through their books.

Pointer was asked to go to the assistant commissioner's room again when he had finished his report.

"I want you to pick up my nephew, Christopher Pelham," said the major, "and take him on with you to the farm. He might be very useful. He's quite an ordinarily intelligent lad, and speaks good French. He's at Cannes. He'll meet you at the aerodrome. Use him as you would any constable. He'll like the experience. He's rather thinking of going to Hendon in the autumn. Tell him all the facts of the case that you care to. He won't leak."

CHAPTER 16: MR. PARNALL GOES TO THE FARM OF THE GOLDEN GOAT

To Cannes, the nearest air station to Menton, Pointer flew by *Air France* next day. He found a pleasant, fresh-faced young man waiting for him. Christopher Pelham looked as though he might be of real use, Pointer thought. During the drive, an hour's along the Grande Corniche, he gave him all the details of the case. Pelham's silent interest was of good augur, so were his few but intelligent questions. At Menton, Pelham, acting on instructions, went to the Casino, to find a taxi whose driver knew Castellar. Once at Castellar he would get him to drive him round, past the Domaine among other places, where Pelham was to stop for a drink, and— struck with the peace, or the beauty, or the warmth of the place—take a room. Pointer was walking up. When he should finally arrive they would meet as strangers. Pointer believed that Miss Blythe would be already at the farm, or would arrive very shortly, and that Blythe would follow soon. He would not want to stay far from his sister-in-law if there were any love affair between them, or even if the love were only on his side, for she needed some one with her. As for her, even though she now had a passport which she could show, money must be always a serious problem. And there were very few places where she could stay without being asked questions which she would find it difficult to parry.

It was a charming walk, but at last Pointer came to the gate with its gilded name. He pushed the gate open and walked on to a rambling two-storied farmhouse. He made for the back. There he stood. He had seen that blue door before—in a sketch which was locked in a safe at Scotland Yard, though a photograph of it was in his pocket. And from it he knew those lemon trees on either side, and that field of maize. But not the scarecrow, for this one was a fat gentleman with a blue working blouse tied around its shapeless middle over what looked like pyjama legs, so stuffed with straw that they nearly split. Yet the hat—as he glanced at it—was like the one in the sketch—a tall-crowned black felt with a great flappping brim.

Pointer rapped on the back door. A very pretty girl opened it.

"I want to see a gentleman who is staying here—a Monsieur Inskipp."

She led him round to the front of the house. A swift glance up showed him a pair of green shutters closed, save for one hinged middle part, which was hooked up. In the opening, a pale face, shadowy and almost hidden, was looking down at him.

"I will call Madame. The patron is in the orchards. But Monsieur Inskipp has gone back to England. He left over a week ago. You are a friend?"

"I am," Pointer said, smiling. "I expected to find that he had returned already. If not, he's coming back here almost at once. I'll have a drink, please—orangeade. And then perhaps I can have a talk with Madame—her name?"

"Norbury," said Sabe, and went on into the house.

A minute later Mrs. Norbury came out.

Pointer presented himself as a solicitor friend of Inskipp's who was on a holiday, but who had to see Inskipp about some shares that the latter owned in a company which was being taken over by another company. Pointer was discreetly vague as to details.

He had by chance, he said, run into Inskipp just as he—Parnall—was leaving for abroad, and Inskipp had told him that it would only be a question of a couple of days before he, too, would be returning to the Farm of the Golden Goat, and had suggested his going there if he wanted to have a really enjoyable time.

Mrs. Norbury thanked him for repeating the compliment, but warned him that life here was very simple, and the food extremely plain.

"I smell roast kid stuffed with thyme," said Pointer to that, "and a better dish can't be found anywhere!"

He suddenly smiled, and let her see him at it. Following his glance, she saw he was looking at the scarecrow.

"Stout fellow!" he said approvingly.

She laughed assent.

"Your friend Mr. Inskipp and a Mr. Rackstraw, another of our guests, made him. We had a lot of straw lying about from some china which had just been sent up, and they used it to stuff him. Apparently they thought scarecrows should look as fat

as snowmen."

The figure had a round head of cotton stretched over loops of twigs, with button eyes under black brows, a huge black moustache over a red mouth and a tuft of goatskin for a beard. Bar its big hat, it looked like a very puffed-out clown.

"He's a most effective watcher," Mrs. Norbury said. "Of course, elsewhere scarecrows are rarely seen nowadays. But we're conservative here. By the way, his name is Horatius. Percy, who used to stand here, changed places with him—and lost all his clothes that very night, I'm sorry to say. Indeed, he isn't really Percy any longer."

"An ancient tragedy?" Pointer asked lightly, following her into the house.

"The very night before my husband left for England, we think. My husband had only moved Percy on the Thursday morning, for Mr. Rackstraw always thought that Horatius should stand nearer the house; he fills the eye better, he says." And she laughed. Then she looked back. "That hat's all that's now left of poor Percy," she said pathetically. "When another guest—a Mr. Blythe—packed, he donated such a magnificent grey felt to our cast-offs on the very last day he was here that I gave

Percy's old black one to Horatius, and let Percy have the grey to make up to him for being moved so far from us all. With the result that that was lost, too. I hope our herdsman and general factotum wasn't for anything in its going. He thought it at the time far too 'noble '—his word—for a scarecrow."

So the hat of the sketch had not been with the rest of the scarecrow's clothes. And Blythe had thrown one away just before leaving, which had been placed on it instead. And Edna Blythe had burnt a felt hat in her gas-fire the night of Inskipp's murder. . . .

"But didn't the owner, or the donator, have his name in it? I always put mine—not merely my initials, which might fit other names, too."

"Oh, yes, he had his name on the hat-band. But a hat-band can always be changed."

By this time they were standing in a big but bare bedroom. He looked about him. He feared that it would be too sunny. "Where was Inskipp's room? He has, of course, kept it on. He spoke of it as so delightful and shady."

"He didn't keep it," said Mrs. Norbury. "We don't expect him back for some time—not for months, perhaps."

"But didn't he leave his trunk here?" asked Parnall in a perplexed tone.

"Oh, yes, but another friend of his is occupying the room—a Mr. Rackstraw."

"Well, will you put me as near to it as possible," said Parnall, "so that when Inskipp blows in we shall be near each other."

He was given a smaller room next door to the one temporarily being used by Rackstraw. A little talk, and Pointer skilfully found out that Rackstraw, on his return the other day, had asked for Inskipp's room, and that Inskipp's trunk was being used by him as a table for papers.

Then dinner was served. At any other time Pointer would have found the low-arched, white-washed, red-tiled room very delightful, but he had now no mind for things

that did not concern his quest. As he came on in he saw—
and recognised from her portraits—a young, very pale
woman, who was standing by the fireplace. She looked
tired, and there were dark shadows around her eyes.

He was introduced by Mrs. Norbury to Miss Blythe.
Edna stared at him with dilated eyes for a second as her
hostess added that Mr. Parnall was a friend of Mr.
Inskipp's, who was, it seemed, coming back almost at
once.

Her eyes spoke of illness, mental or physical—
probably both, thought Pointer.

"*A la bonheur!*" said Laroche, coming on in. "So
Inskipp is returning. We miss him."

This was a new member of the party at the farm to
Pointer, who liked the look of the Frenchman from the
point of view of learning about his fellow- guests. But
otherwise the indolent, cynical, clever face told nothing of
its owner's character, and character might yet turn out to
be the best thread to follow in this maze. For men, in the
last analysis, murder from choice—not, as they try to
believe, from necessity.

Christopher Pelham came in and was introduced.
Norbury followed. He welcomed Pointer cordially,
especially, he added, as a friend of Inskipp's.

"His forerunner," Pointer said, taking the chair
assigned to him beside Mrs. Norbury. He mentioned
again how he had run into Inskipp, and how the latter
had spoken of returning to the farm almost at once.

Norbury looked surprised. Edna, opposite Pointer, did
not move, she did not seem to breathe for a moment, but
with her eyes on the tablecloth, looked nearly as white as
it. Mrs. Norbury, as though that would add weight to
Pointer's words, mentioned that Mr. Parnall was a
solicitor.

"But Inskipp told me that he didn't know any
solicitors," said Norbury bluntly. Pointer wondered of
what they had been speaking when Inskipp had said
that.

"Inskipp and I haven't seen anything of each other for at least five years," Pointer explained easily. "But now I need his signature. It's a question of one company buying out another company in which he owns some shares. My firm has to do entirely with company law. I rather wonder what's detaining him."

Edna rose with an apology and left the room. She had hardly touched her food.

Mrs. Norbury looked after her with a wrinkled brow. "She shouldn't have come by plane," she said then, "if it upsets you, it does so frightfully."

"Fortunately she expects her brother back to-morrow or the next day," said Norbury, "and he may be able to get her to see a doctor down in Menton, where there are some good ones." Then he turned and asked Parnall about Inskipp's return in the near future—a piece of information which surprised him, as Inskipp, when he last saw him in Dover, had dined with him and a couple of other men who had been at the farm. He had spoken as though he would be away for quite an indefinite time.

"It was at Dover that I ran into him—on Saturday afternoon," Pointer explained. "I crossed by the night boat. He had only just arrived. Bad crossing, I believe?"

"Vile!" said Norbury feelingly. "Ah, well, I may have misunderstood him at dinner—or he may have changed his mind suddenly."

Pointer showed surprise at the farm having gone in a body to Dover, as it were, and all of them except Inskipp, apparently, for so brief a stay.

Norbury explained that the four of them had each been meaning to go to England for some little time, and had eventually decided to return together. But Inskipp then, at any rate, had thought that he was going to be away some months, and Blythe would not be returning so soon but for his sister being so obviously under the weather. "The two seem to be quite alone in the world," said Mrs. Norbury. Laroche spoke of the scenario from which Inskipp had hoped for such great things. Pointer did not pretend to any knowledge about it, and listened with interest to the account now given him of the joint labours of Inskipp and Rackstraw.

Had Norbury been told something about Inskipp's plans, which made it very unlikely that the latter would change them suddenly? Something in his tone suggested some such knowledge. Otherwise no one, except Miss Blythe, seemed to have any idea that all was not well. If Norbury had left England on the Tuesday—as he must have done, if not earlier—then it was quite possible that he had not even seen an English newspaper. Besides, nowadays with wireless, many people hardly ever really read a paper.

"Dreadful affair that about Miss Rackstraw's death, wasn't it?" Pointer now said. "It seemed to have upset Inskipp quite tremendously. At least I gathered as much when he told me about it."

"Ah," said Mrs. Norbury with a gentle and pitying smile, "had it? He is so reserved that one can't tell with him. . . ."

"Think he was in love with her?" hazarded Pointer on that.

"I'm afraid so," said his hostess.

Laroche burst in vigorously.

"*Vous n'y etes pas, chere Madame!* No! No! Inskipp was not at all in love with that young lady. She was the fisherman, he the fish. But he did not do more than nibble at her line just at first. Oh, I assure you I am right."

"Well, then, let us say that they were very close friends," suggested Pointer.

"As distant as he could make it at the end," insisted Laroche, who liked to label things correctly. "Of the dead no harm should be spoken, but she was a dangerous, a very dangerous type. Malignant and clever. The kind to do real harm when her pride was hurt—as it was. Her grotesque pride. Had she lived—there would have been trouble."

"I think you don't allow for the total lack of malignancy in us English," said Norbury. "Besides —she is dead, and I think my wife is right, and so is Mr. Parnall here, that Inskipp was much more deeply hit by her death than one would have guessed at a glance."

"Ah, but I don't guess and I don't glance!" was the retort from Laroche, with a flash of white teeth and a glint of narrowed eyes.

But Norbury stuck to his guns. "I am convinced that in this case you underestimate the tenacity and the strength of Inskipp's feeling. He said something in the train, too, which bears us out. Something about never altering once he loved."

"*Mon Dieu!*" said Laroche, opened-eyed. "He was not such an imbecile, surely!"

"I don't think he was an imbecile at all." Norbury spoke with warmth. "But I think he was a man who had had a hard blow and who, for the time being, thought the effects of it would never fade. There are people whose affection goes deep." And he looked at his wife.

Laroche shot them one of his mocking smiles, but he let the subject drop. Pointer now had a chance to ask him what he had meant by his speech about Inskipp and the Golden Goat.

Laroche explained at great length. He had an attentive listener. But he told Pointer no new facts—only he shed some interesting lights on the character of the dead man, the dreamer—the follower of Fata Morgana— taking illusion for reality.

Rackstraw came back from some expedition, rucksack on back, and was introduced. Mrs. Norbury chanced to send a dish up to Miss Blythe a moment later.

"Is she ill?" asked Rackstraw.

"She looks frightfully ill. I think it's possibly some sort of low fever that she caught in those valleys."

"If she walked about in Florence's hat, no wonder she caught a fever," said Rackstraw, half under his breath. "It's as thick as a bearskin."

"Florence's hat?" asked Mrs. Norbury, evidently all at sea.

Rackstraw nodded. "Quaint but true—like some of the customs of the Albigenses that Laroche here won't admit. Florence's hat disappeared when she died. She had promised it to the Honey-woman, who asked me for it later. It was nowhere to be found, nor Florence's cloak, either. I thought Sabe must have helped herself to them, though neither seemed much in her line."

"Any more than helping herself to the property of the guests here, I hope!" said Mrs. Norbury with spirit.

"Oh, quite! Nothing insinuated against the service, Mrs. Norbury. The two valuables in question have reappeared with Miss Blythe's return to the farm. They're back in the cupboard on the landing where they used to hang. Which proves, I think, that she took them with her—for a fancy dress, possibly, but took them, none the less."

Mrs. Norbury shot him a very indignant look. "I don't think that joke's in good taste, Mr. Rackstraw. Miss Blythe is a lady. A lady doesn't help herself to other people's clothes. The idea is preposterous!"

Pointer, when he first saw her, had thought that Mrs. Norbury looked the kind to speak very plainly when she didn't like things. In her very carriage too, straight-backed and unbending, there was something uncompromising. What Mrs. Norbury thought should be rebuked she would proceed to do in no smothered tones. What she thought should not be tolerated, she would proceed to remove, and nothing could stop her. So at least the very accurate judgment of the Scotland Yard man decided. He noticed that, though she looked confidently towards her husband for support, Norbury said nothing. As for Rackstraw, judging by his general appearance, the day had seen some hard and dusty work on his part, and he had evidently quenched his thirst somewhat too deeply.

Laroche now made a reference to the Red Rocks, and

the talk drifted to them.

Blythe came down shortly after, and the two new guests were introduced to him.

"You don't look as though your holiday had done you much good," said Laroche frankly

Blythe nodded and made no reply. But he took a seat at table, so that his face was in shadow, as Pointer made some reference to Inskipp, and asked when he had seen him.

"Saturday before last." Pointer told him what he had the others, and went on to speak of Inskipp's apparent certainty, at that time, that he was returning very shortly indeed to the farm.

Norbury and Rackstraw repeated their own certainty that he would not be back for months.

"Yes, he wrote me, too, that he would be away for months," said Blythe, as Rackstraw looked at him.

"Well, all I can say is that it's very odd—very odd indeed." Pointer let his face seem troubled. "He as good as gave me an appointment here—since I was starting on a holiday to these parts. He certainly would have written me if he had changed his plans so radically. I told him about the papers I'm carrying with me, which must be signed some time before the end of this month.

"I *can't* get it straight! None of you saw him at breakfast. Pity!" as the three said that they had not, "for I must write to my firm at once if he's really not coming soon. Look here, when did he pay his bill? Perhaps he's still in Dover. He mentioned that he must go to the money changers first thing on Monday morning, as he had only French money on him."

"He asked me to settle that," said Rackstraw, "and send his things on after him to the Cumberland Hotel. And he might have included a cheque for it—but didn't."

And then Pointer let him swing the talk to the money and tokens used by the ancients along these shores.

Pointer caught Norbury's eyes resting speculatively on him more than once during dinner. As for Pelham, he was only the enthusiastic traveller delighted with the weather and the scenery, and the novelty of his surroundings. It chanced that they both drifted out together for a stroll after dinner.

Mrs. Norbury got up and made her way to the garden, where her two new boarders seemed absorbed in the skies above them.

"If you want to see a local celebrity," she said, "come this way and meet our bailiff—and shepherd —and astrologer all in one."

They followed her into the kitchen. The pretty girl who had first spoken to Pointer was standing by a stove with a very sullen look on her face, while over her towered her father, brown-faced, smelling of the thyme and juniper boughs on which he always slept. He was talking warningly to her in the Menton patois, most of which Pointer had no difficulty in following, for it was but a mixture of French and Italian, but some of which escaped him altogether, as for instance her reply: "*Soch di', non es ve, paire men,*" spoken tearfully as they came in, and she fairly ran from the room. It was an awkward moment, till Norbury coming in with instructions as to some wattle repairing which he wanted done in the morning, changed the atmosphere. But Mrs. Norbury did not leave well alone.

"What were you saying to Sabe that she says isn't true?" she asked sharply. "You haven't any call to talk so crossly to her, Du Metri. She's a good girl."

"She had better be!" said Du Metri with a flush on his swarthy cheeks. "But who gave her her new dress? The one for the festa? Eh? She won't say, and I don't know."

"She bought it herself, probably," said Mrs. Norbury.

"And the new shoes to go with it?" persisted Du Metri in a low growl. "What is the use of being able to read the stars as I can, when I can't find out that? I know what the animals are up to, I know what the swifts will do when they come back in May, but I don't know what my daughter is up to—no, I don't! Not for this whole year past."

"She's up to no harm," repeated Mrs. Norbury. "I look after her quite as well as you could, Du Metri. But we shan't be able to eat her cooking if you worry her so." Du Metri after a second turned silently away, but Pointer followed him, asking the

name by which Du Metri knew this and that star. Then he said casually, " retty names the Provencals have. Take Mireille, now—is it a usual one around here for a girl?"

"Around here rarely, though *Mireille mes amours* used to be said, in my grandfather's time, to any pretty little girl. Monsieur Inskipp asked me the same question once. He thought *'Mireille mes amours'* a quaint love-name."

Pointer was staring up at the stars.

"I wonder what the sky is doing at home to-night," he said finally. "It was a wild night on the Thursday, the night before Monsieur Norbury and his guests left for England. We had a tremendous storm, yet they tell me it was very clear here."

To his amusement Du Metri confirmed this idle statement. "The best of the mid-January orange crop was picked that day, and if necessary we could have finished by moonlight, the moon was so bright."

"You picked at night?" Pointer asked, as though he had not understood the other.

"No, no! We finished late, but not so late. All was over by ten, when I see to the locking of the folds. It was a wonderful night."

"Do you mind telling me why you were interested in the skies here last Thursday night?" Pelham asked as Pointer and he drifted back to the little nook where they had been standing when Mrs. Norbury found them. "I caught your eye and heard what he said. But why the interest in the skies out here?"

"I wanted to find out if possible whether whoever stripped the scarecrow, which stood in the maize field when Inskipp painted it, could have done so easily late at night—as far as light went. According to the man in there, he could have."

"And according to the dog?" asked Christopher.

Pointer laughed. "Just so!" He said no more; but up in his bedroom he walked the floor with a very grave face. Whatever he thought, was it safe to leave Miss Blythe and her so-called brother free? A message to Brighton, and the French police would arrest her for murder, and Blythe for aiding her.

Major Pelham had left Pointer an absolutely free hand in the matter.

Her face was very distinctly before his eyes. So worn—so young. It was not in the least a poisoner's face, for it was not subtle, and it was not cruel. And if she were not the poisoner, what a hell on earth her life must have been since the inquest started. If she were not the poisoner. . . . If— not—

There came a knock on his door. Pelham entered.

"I say, can you lend me a box of matches?" he asked conversationally before he closed the door on himself. Then coming close he whispered: "Does that woman strike you as innocent? She doesn't me!"

As Pointer closed the window without replying, he went on earnestly: "That white face of hers gives me the creeps somehow!"

"Yes, but are your creeps or her white face evidence?" asked Pointer dryly.

Christopher gave a chuckle. "My creeps are a subconscious warning," he said.

"Don't let it make you show your feelings consciously." Pointer was very grave. "Not a look—not a tone of your voice must suggest that you have any other knowledge of the Blythes than that of meeting them here as a complete stranger."

"You yourself are sure of her guilt, aren't you?" Pelham asked swiftly.

"If she was telling the truth at the inquest—yes. But if she was frightened, and told a lie about not having moved the two breakfast trays outside her and her sister-in-law's door the morning when the other died—there's a chance, just a chance, that she's innocent." Pointer explained his theory briefly.

"Yes, but how to find out? What about giving her a shot of sodium evipan and then chatting to her?" suggested Christopher.

"Your uncle might think we were getting too modern for the Yard," Pointer objected with a grin. "But there are more prosaic ways. For instance, I started a private detective looking into some questions for me before we left London. He's a very clever chap—an ex-inspector of the C.I.D. who had to retire owing to an injury he received in the course of his work. I sketched the lines I want his inquiries to take, and, if he can get into touch with the parlourmaid—Ada Greenlee was her name—he may learn something useful. The coroner obviously cut her short in something she wanted to say. He thought it irrelevant—but I fancy it may be vital. As a matter of fact, Earnshaw, the man I'm having look into things, told me that the parlourmaid—this Ada Greenlee—took a situation in Dover. If so, it's possible that she was connected with whatever took Inskipp out that wild night of last Sunday."

"A note could have been slipped under his door," suggested Pelham, "by this Whin-Browning woman, who then—" He stopped. Laroche was coming up the stairs, and, after a second, Pelham slipped across the passage to his own spartan apartment.

CHAPTER 17: POINTER IS INTERESTED IN A PHOTOGRAPH AND TWO FRAMES

Later in the night Pointer drafted a telephoned cable and with Pelham slipped down to the dining-room. He found to his joy that the Menton telephone and cable service was open all night, and he buzzed through his message very quickly to "Fraser of Lincoln's Inn Fields."

"*F comme France. R comme Rouen. A comme Angleterre,*" he chanted. The telephone was in a quiet corner. Pelham watched by the stairs, but Pointer was not overheard, though he sent the message itself in code. Next morning, when he would tell Norbury of it, he would say that he had cabled to his firm of Fraser and Fraser, Lincoln's Inn Fields. In reality, his cable was a set of instructions to one of his men to go at once to the Cumberland Hotel, get Inskipp's luggage, which had been sent on there by Rackstraw —supposing it had been sent and was still there— and let him know the contents by coded cable. If the passport was there, he was to send it him at once by registered air-mail. Beyond this, with its photograph, Pointer did not expect anything interesting, though he would have been glad to go over the luggage himself. But it did not seem important enough to justify the expense of flying back to England for it. Inskipp was killed before ten on Sunday night. The luggage was not sent off till some time on Monday at the earliest. The murderer would have had plenty of hours to see that there was nothing incriminating in it.

The message sent, Pointer and Christopher were free to go to bed.

Next morning the chief inspector was up early— waked by the swifts at their morning hunting, by the rattle of pails, by the clank of farm implements, by the

myriad sounds of even a small farm. Looking out, he saw
Blythe in the garden. The young man's face showed grey
and pinched in spite of its fullness. His eyes were heavy.
His lips compressed. Turning, he faced the house, and
gave Pointer's room that long, considering stare which
means that the eye was but the servant of the mind
which had outstripped it.

Pointer slipped on a raincoat, hung a towel around his
neck and went out, too.

Blythe gave him an unfriendly stare. "There's no place
to bathe up here—except the drinking-water tank. And I
have an idea that Mrs. Norbury doesn't really like us to
do that."

Pointer looked disappointed. He stood chatting to the
very unresponsive young man about the journey to and
from England. As he expected to be returning in a
fortnight, he explained that all information as to the best
trains would be useful. He wanted privately to know just
what had caused the delay of a day in the itinerary of the
three men on the way from the farm to Dover, now that
he knew when the four had left the Golden Goat. But that
was not his chief interest. He could learn that from either
of the two others. What Pointer was after was not a
detail, but another possible trail.

If the Whin-Browning double tragedy of a year ago
was the real cause of Inskipp's murder, as seemed
probable, then beside him might stand a treble
murderer—cunning and ruthless. But on that question
Pointer's mind was as open as the field which he was
facing. So for the moment only his surface attention
listened to what the other was saying in a curt,
unresponsive tone. But at one word Pointer's whole mind
was alert. Inskipp, it appeared, had got out at Marseilles
in order to go on to Clermont-Ferrand, and had come on
to Paris by an express from there, reaching the capital
quite late on Saturday night. Skilful questioning on
Pointer's part drew out the fact that no one was prepared
for this sudden solo flight.

Pointer ate a quick breakfast, but he had time to get Blythe's information confirmed. He must follow this up, and see if it did not lead to a Mireille somewhere.

The post was just being delivered. There was a bundle of newspapers for Albert Parnall, Esq. Among them would be some of last week asking for Inskipp's companions in Dover to come forward. Pointer had intended to undo these now at table, hand them around, and wait for the reactions, but learning of Inskipp's stop on the way to Dover had changed that. For, since arriving at the farm, Pointer had been asking himself what sudden change in Inskipp's plans had only made his murder necessary when Dover was reached, seeing that the farm, so close to the border of Italy, would have presented far safer opportunities to get rid of him to any one who knew how the frontier ran. For a frontier murder is the hardest and the slowest to get cleared up, since each side maintains that it is the duty of the sister nation to start the inquiry—among her own nationals. But for the clothing found on Inskipp's dead body having come from one of the two scarecrows—from Percy—Pointer would have decided to assume, at any rate at first, that the murder was unconnected with the people staying at the farm, and that therefore its causes must be hunted for in Inskipp's life before he came to the Golden Goat.

As it was, it looked to him so far as though the choice of Dover for the murder had been imposed by some inexorable time-pressure, rather than deliberate preference, since the obvious advantages and simplicity of a local end had not been taken advantage of.

That meant that something new, unexpected, unforeseen had happened on, just before, or just after, the arrival in England which had made every hour dangerous to the murderer. Pointer thought that only one brain had been engaged in this crime. The sudden jaunt to Clermont-Ferrand suggested that Inskipp might there have learned of some fact which he had to be prevented from following up.

And yet . . . no apparent effort seemed to have been made on his life; on the boat train from Paris, which had been very empty as it always is at this time of the year, nor on the boat itself, though the rough crossing would certainly have given a determined murderer more than one chance. Still, Clermont-Ferrand seemed to stand for something unexpected, something suddenly altered, in Innskipp's programme, and Pointer intended to find out as much as possible of what took the dead man there. That the murderer had gone to England prepared to commit the crime seemed evident from the clothes which had been stripped off the scarecrow. And though Pointer thought that that might prove to have been caution rather than a definitely drawn-up plan, they suggested to his very acute brain that something underhand was possibly going on which the murderer knew might force his hand at any moment. And that suggested the corollary that Inskipp was worth more to the murderer alive than dead, and that his death was only looked on as a possible contingency—as the lesser of two evils.

At breakfast Pelham professed a great interest in the neighbourhood. Pointer had asked him to get the men away from the house if he could, and for as long as he could.

There was a certain hermit's cave not far away of which Christopher had read in his guide-book, and about which he asked many questions.

As Norbury was going to a farm on business which was fairly near it, he offered to show it to Pelham. Pointer professed a great desire to come, too. Laroche was interested, so was Rackstraw; in the end even Blythe was captured by the prospect of a long walk, a sharp climb, and a wonderful view from the hermit's "window."

At the last moment Pointer announced that he had blistered his heel yesterday in walking up to the farm, and had, to his apparent disappointment, to give up the picnic, but the others went off, their luncheons swinging on their sticks, or tucked into their haversacks. Even

Edna Blythe went as far as Castellar with them.

Pointer hobbled about the garden watching, without seeming to do so, until Sabe clattered away with pail and mop from the Blythes' rooms to his own part of the house. Then he made his way to the wing she had just left. It consisted of two bedrooms, a sitting-room and a couple of empty rooms, which could be used as cupboards and box-rooms. The furnishings were simple. Edna Blythe had not cared to have any luxuries sent her from Menton or Nice, he saw. Her belongings, too, were almost pathetically few. Not a scrap of anything was in the room linking her with her past, except a few photographs of English country scenes. Taken away, Pointer saw, from her mother's cottage in Cirencester. He had noticed one snapshot of some dogs playing with a kitten standing on her mother's desk when he had been shown in by Lady Thompson herself. Edna had considered them evidently as quite "safe." Locked in her simple suitcase he found Florence Rackstraw's passport. It had been recently used into and out of England. There was nothing else of any interest.

And in Blythe's belongings, nothing whatever of any interest bar his pass-book leaves, a passport in his own name, and letters from his solicitor to him, as Blythe, c/o T. Cook & Sons at Nice. The Nice branch had sent these latter on to their Menton branch, and there, apparently, Blythe had called for them. There was no reference whatever to anything but financial matters in them. Blythe showed as a man of considerable means, drawing on only a fraction of his income, and keeping an unusually large sum of money at Cooks in Menton.

As soon as he had put everything back as he had found it, Pointer went down into the garden and walked the little earth paths deep in thought. Under ordinary circumstances he would have notified the superintendent at Brighton at once that he had found the woman for whose arrest a warrant still ran, but the circumstances were not ordinary. Pointer doubted if Edna would have a chance of her life if she were arrested by Walker, or handed over to him. Or if a chance, it would be but of penal servitude. Her flight would tell enormously against her, and the public prosecutor, he happened to know, believed firmly in her guilt, and was a man who thought it high time to show that if sex did not count in committing a crime, neither should it count in its punishment.

Pointer decided to hold his hand for the moment. Even if guilty, he could not see that there was any other person at the farm who ran any danger by allowing Mrs. Whin-Browning a little longer freedom. It was a tremendous risk to take, but Pointer

decided to run it.

Catching sight of Sabe's pretty face looking dreamily out of the window of Pelham's room, he went up to his own, locked his door, opened with one of his own master keys the door between his room and that now used by Rackstraw, after locking that farther room's door into the passage. Then he set to work on Inskipp's trunk. It opened easily enough to his practised fingers, and the contents kept him busy for some little time. There were no private papers whatever among them, but at the very bottom was a set of five cabinet photographs of Inskipp himself taken in Menton.

There was an unexpected find, and a most welcome one. So far, Pointer had only the police photographs of Inskipp's dead face to show, and he saw by these how different Inskipp had looked in life. There was here none of that serene tranquil calm which had so struck him. On the contrary, it was a dissatisfied face, yet a very attractive one, in spite of the fact that Inskipp had no claims to good looks. He turned to the backs, and there, in the middle of the batch which were fastened with a paper band, was one with some writing on it.

He read in Inskipp's neat, clear writing:

"It's much too flattering, as you will find when we meet, so don't say then that I didn't prepare you, *Mireille, mon amour*." The last words were scratched through, and

"*Mireille mes amours*" was written above. The correction was probably the reason why this photograph had not been sent.

Pointer abstracted it, and passed on to the study of some newspapers which were tied together with tape. There he found the accounts of the Whin-Browning affair which had appeared at the time. How had they come here into Inskipp's possession, supposing him to have been the one who had put them in the trunk? At any rate, they meant, if laid there by Inskipp, that he had learnt who the Blythes were, and so confirmed Pointer's idea that Inskipp might have offered his help—his very much wanted help—to the cornered woman. Had any one else seen the papers? If they were Inskipp's, how had they got into his possession? Had he come to the farm, knowing whom he would find there? But, in that case, why the long delay before undertaking, as Pointer thought he possibly had, to look into the case on Edna's behalf It seemed on the face of it more likely that he had come on these papers a short time before he left for England. They had been roughly handled, whether by him or another. Could he have found them somewhere on the farm? That meant the possibility of others having read them, of others also knowing the facts about the Blythes. Pointer did not think for a moment that no personal papers had been left behind by Inskipp in his trunk any more than in his suitcase. Whoever had taken these away might easily have undone the bundle of newspapers and glanced over them, seen the portraits—and recognised at least Hector Whin-Browning.

Pointer replaced the papers and locked the trunk again.

He passed on to Rackstraw's own belongings, and soon found himself confronted with a thick wad of sheets neatly fastened together and headed *Haroun the Christian*. They were in Inskipp's writing, and, as he turned them over, out dropped a Clermont-Ferrand tram ticket dated the 16th January of the current year. Pointer ventured to replace it with a scrap of paper. Apparently Rackstraw was using or incorporating the pages wholesale in some work on which he was engaged.

Next, he found tucked in a pocket of Rackstraw's suitcase a page cut from a film magazine, which announced a three-thousand pounds prize for the best film scenario dealing with Transmigration of souls, showing the same set of at least three characters in prehistoric, mediaeval and in modern times.

Any scenario dealing with religion or religious topics would receive—if successful in winning the prize—an additional two thousand pounds. There were various clauses about what would happen to those which were good enough to use, but not good enough for the prize, but a pencil mark around the prize conditions showed that Rackstraw was after that alone. The entrance date was only some three months off. The scenarios were for a talking film, and apparently for a long one. It was quite clear what was going on here.

Rackstraw was using *Haroun the Christian* for the middle portion. But there might be some clause in his agreement with Inskipp which permitted this. Pointer had never seen an agreement between two writers. He found the letter which Rackstraw had shown Norbury at breakfast the morning after Inskipp had been killed. It was hastily written, all but a scrawl. The kind of thing on which hand-writing experts hate to pass judgment, as well they might, since they rarely agree about them. Certainly, if any one had wanted to stave off inquiries about Inskipp, nothing better could have been drafted, or if Inskipp had himself wanted to be free of troublesome inquiries. But it seemed very unusually comprehensive in letting Rackstraw do what he liked with what was, after all, the work of many months, what must have carried with it accordingly very high hopes. Certainly by it, the scenario was tossed to Rackstraw to do with as he liked. Convenient but hardly likely, Pointer thought. Unless Inskipp had learnt of something so vastly more important that the scenario was, as it were, wiped off the slate, at least for the time being. But this letter was not merely for the time being. Any time after its receipt, Rackstraw might have sold the scenario for a sixpence, and Inskipp could not have complained. Most convenient for Rackstraw—with this prize in the offing. But was it likely that Inskipp would have troubled to write something of no advantage but to Rackstraw? Even if he had had no time at the moment, would he not rather have put everything off till sometime when he should be free?

On the whole, that letter looked very incriminating, though nothing in the characters suggested Rackstraw's writing. Not a letter nor punctuation stop was as he made them.

But one thing was certain. Rackstraw had had the opportunity—to put it at the lowest, of reading those newspapers which referred to the Whin-Browning affair. Once again, Pointer left everything as he had found it, and went for a turn in the sunshine. As he walked, his mind turned over what he had found. Quite apart from the possibility that Rackstraw knew who the Blythes really were, the use that he was making of the dead man's papers strongly pointed to a knowledge of the writer's death. It also, in itself, given some natures, furnished a sufficient motive for that death. Pointer's mind went on to the words on the back of Inskipp's photograph. Strange words. Evidently Mireille was some one whom Inskipp loved—and yet had apparently not met. This last, if so, set her aside from any possibility of being the cause of a murder from jealousy. "*Mireille, mes amours*". . . the caressing words were strangely pathetic. But, so far, no help in the hunt. He must go to Clermont-Ferrand once he knew what he wanted to do there.

The fact that Inskipp had stopped over there—unless for some antiquarian interest—suggested that he had an appointment with some one who lived in the town, since he could have arranged a much more convenient meeting place directly on the Marseilles-Paris line. Or, if not an appointment, then that he intended to pay a short visit to some one who lived there. If Mireille were the answer, Pointer would have expected Inskipp to have stayed longer than just over a train or two. As for blackmail of the Whin-Brownings on the dead man's part—Pointer cut that possibility out for the present, unless it obtruded itself. Everything to him suggested the contrary.

In the late afternoon Pointer got the reply to his overnight cable. Inskipp's suitcase had been handed over to the Yard against their receipt. Its contents were given one by one in cipher in the cable. There was a passport— now of no importance since Pointer had found the photographs. There was a watch —which Pointer thought had been dropped in after being taken from Inskipp's body. The main spring was broken. The hands pointed to three o'clock. The murderer had probably had the sense to alter them to a perfectly safe hour. He had made few mistakes so far. The careless hiding of boots—the oversight about the brass bed-knob at the Dover hotel, were not more than slight blunders.

There was no cheque-book, nor any papers or letters whatever inside the suitcase. But stuffed down at one end was a grey felt hat—with Inskipp's name inside. The murderer collecting Inskipp's things from around his room had probably put it there, Pointer thought, the considerate murderer who had so roused his neighbour's gratitude! So no cheque-book had been left in the suitcase. That was indeed a very striking omission. Was something recorded in its counterfoils? Was the murder connected with money? But there was something found by the searcher in the suitcase which was odder than the absence of the cheque-book. It was either an omission or a presence according as one looked at it. On top of all, said the cable's order of coding the contents, were two silver photograph frames—empty, which by their size had contained cabinet photographs. They were identical in every respect, made of handworked silver, representing wreaths of olive branches. They had the French hallmark on them, and had been made within the last five years. Pointer at once asked for one of the frames to be registered to him by air-post.

If the taking away of the cheque-book and all money records looked as though money might be mixed up in the crime, as it so frequently is, then the fact that the silver frames were empty looked as though jealousy could not be ruled out, unless here was a trail of the Whin-Browning affair. But, if merely for any purpose connected with that tragedy, Pointer could not see why the frames should have been so handsome, and the photographs of what appeared to have been cabinet size.

"*Mireille mes amours*" rose to the mind as one thought of those frames. Mireille, the girl—or woman—to whom Pointer fancied that Inskipp had sent his own photograph, pointed the sketch. The girl—or woman—whom he, apparently, had never met. That had at once suggested a stage love. The film of Mireille, founded on Mistral's poem of the girl who loves a man whom her parents will not let her marry, might account for everything.

Pointer sent a short note to a certain French detective asking him to look into Laroche's whereabouts on the Sunday night of Inskipp's murder, and also requesting him to find out all he could of whoever had played the part of the heroine in the recent films of *Mireille*, and who had lately sung the part in Gounod's opera. If possible, Pointer wanted photographs and details of where the two had lately been played in France, sent to him. By "lately," he meant within the last year, for he did not think it likely that, had it been earlier than that, Inskipp would not have managed to meet his inamorata. Film stars and operatic stars are quite accessible to men with whom they correspond, though if Mireille had left Europe, that might explain the fact that though he had seen her she had not seen Inskipp—to notice him. The words on the portrait of the dead man suggested that odd state of affairs. It was possible, of course, that Inskipp had fallen in love with a star's mere picture, but the phrases used made that seem unlikely. Unless he had, as lonely men and women sometimes do, been carrying on an imaginary correspondence. Inskipp's face in his portrait suggested a nature to which that would not be at all impossible. But the sketch found in the drawer in Dover with For Mireille scribbled on the back opposed this notion. Surely that would be carrying a dream love-affair very far? Provisionally, Pointer thought that his first idea might prove right that it had been a film or operatic Mireille with whom Inskipp had fallen in love, and whom he had managed to captivate by his letters.

Though that idea too, presented difficulties. Such a person would not be lonely—isolated—willing to accept a stranger as a friend—and, apparently as a lover, merely from reading their letters. There was some real mystery here . . . was it a part of the mystery of his murder? Was it from jealousy that Inskipp had been exterminated? The difficulty was to associate the taking of the cheque-book, and presumably his money too, with the taking away of the photographs in the silver frames. They seemed to point in two opposite directions. He decided to spring his mine now, and follow up Clermont-Ferrand when this was done.

CHAPTER 18: THE GUESTS LEARN THAT SOME OF THEM HAVE GOT INTO PRINT

Pointer had his package of newspapers lying ready in his room.

With Inskipp known to be dead—murdered—people who had any information about him—and were innocent—would talk far more freely than if he were alive. That fact turned idle gossip into possibly useful information. But before that, he wanted to get a chance for a general chat on Inskipp separately with Rackstraw, and with Laroche, when they should return.

They came in around noon, hot, dirty, and very pleased with the scramble. At lunch, Pointer mentioned that he was going down to Menton shortly, and might spend some days there, roaming along the coast.

"He means Monte-Carl'!" said Rackstraw to that. "Better leave your return fare with Norbury, Parnall, just in case the luck's against you."

Pointer laughed and said that possibly he might riot get much farther than the Rock, and they talked of the casino there and of what you could win—and lose.

"So you don't expect Inskipp back directly?" Norbury asked.

On the contrary, Pointer said, he would wait till he had arrived before leaving, and so saying, he ran up the stairs for his bundle of papers. He was ripping off the wrapping as he came in, saying that most of them would be too old to be interesting, but that he had had the *Express* sent on to him for every day that he had been away, as a solicitor must "keep abreast."

He shook out the top one, and ran through it quickly. Then the next. Suddenly he gave an exclamation. Grasping the paper which he was reading, he rose as though under some violent emotion, the paper shaking in his hand.

"What's wrong?" asked Laroche, turning curiously. He had put Parnall down as a man of iron nerve and self-control. This yelp of distress surprised the Frenchman.

"Inskipp!" said Pointer in a strangled voice. "Inskipp! Good God, he's dead! and the police suspect foul play. A body, found in a Dover shelter and thought to be a tramp's has been identified as Inskipp's. Inskipp's!" His voice rose in a very telling crescendo of horror.

"Here! May we look?" said Norbury, getting hold of the paper.

Pointer seemed in too much of a trance to reply, and the men each helped themselves.

"Why, in this one, *we're* asked to communicate with the police, too," said Rackstraw suddenly.

"No, no!" said Norbury. "Just a general request that any one who knew Inskipp should come forward. Oh, I see— " as Rackstraw thrust the paper that he had secured under his nose. "Yours is later. Yes, you're right. We are named as having accompanied Inskipp to the Lord Bishop Hotel, and asked to get into touch with Scotland Yard as soon as possible."

"May I see?" said Blythe in a level voice. He was the only one who had not grabbed some paper from the pile.

"Well," said Norbury, "at any rate, now that we do know about it we must send a letter at once to Scotland Yard. I should think you, Parnall, will be their best hope of useful information, you are a friend of his. We're not."

"I haven't seen him for years!" protested Pointer. "Good heavens! What an incredible affair! Inskipp of all men!" Then he went on to: "What can lie behind his murder? Evidently the police have no doubt that it was murder."

"Men don't usually knock themselves on the head,"

said Rackstraw to that. "I wonder how much money he had on him? Obviously, that was why he was killed. Mistake to carry money on you. I suppose some heftly tramp pitched him a pitiful tale, and Inskipp out with his pocket book, drew forth a wad of notes, giving him one— and that was enough. I notice they don't speak of finding any money on him."

"They didn't find anything on him," said Norbury, reading on, "Amazing! It doesn't sound like Inskipp at all, surely there's been a mistake! But no, this is his portrait all right. But what was he up to? Nothing on the body but striped trousers, a frock coat and white canvas shoes. Nothing else! No shirt nor waistcoat. No underwear. In mid January! What became of his clothes? On the journey—and at the hotel that evening, he was dressed in—let me see, what was he wearing?" Norbury took a pencil.

Rackstraw and Blythe helped with the compilation.

"Where did he change?" demanded Norbury. "Why did he go to that shelter? When? The paper speaks of between nine and ten as the time when he was killed. Incredible! Seems fantastic—utterly!"

"I must let Miss Blythe know," said Blythe suddenly. Mrs. Norbury came in, and was told—and shown—the news. She, too, could hardly credit it at first. But as she read on, she suddenly gave a little cry.

"Striped trousers and a black frock coat. Both very worn. In holes—Arthur, it's Percy! The clothes that were taken from Percy!"

"Percy," echoed Laroche blankly, "Percy who?"

"The scarecrow!" she said excitedly.

Norbury shook his head slowly. "Impossible, Ellen. Those things weren't taken until after we had all left."

"Their loss wasn't noticed till after you left," agreed Mrs. Norbury. "Du-Metri had no cause to pass there on Friday, but he says that on the Saturday after you left he noticed only the bare cross-sticks of the scarecrow standing in the field."

"But," said Laroche, hardly able to keep his face straight, "forgive my smiling, I oughtn't to, I know—but the idea of Inskipp in my old frock-coat—and with your hat, Blythe—"

Rackstraw laughed outright—Blythe went very pale. Mrs. Norbury looked shocked. They were talking of a death—of Inskipp's murder! said her stony glare. Laroche murmured an apology, and tried to rearrange his face. Blythe slipped out and up the stairs.

"They are those clothes," said Mrs. Norbury obstinately, reading the description again.

"We'll put the possibility before the Dover police. But frankly, I can't see why Inskipp should have wanted to take them as a disguise"—the moment he had said the words, Norbury stopped as though silenced by some sudden thought.

Pointer looked doubtful, but before he could speak, the two Blythes came back into the room. Edna wasted no time on exclamations of surprise or horror. She asked for the papers describing the clothes found on the scarecrow, and read them through swiftly.

"No hat was found with the man," Mrs. Norbury pointed out. "I think some one must have stolen it, for I gave Percy's old one to Horatius and put your hat on, Mr. Blythe, your large-brimmed felt hat."

"I know. I only sacrificed it at the last moment, because my sister here loathed it so on me—or me so in it—"Blythe was looking excited.

Edna raised her face from her reading and asked to see the other papers giving the earlier accounts of the finding of the body. Pointer collected them for her. Then he replied to Norbury, who had meanwhile slipped out of the room and just returned.

"I rather think that I, as a solicitor, ought to be the one to more or less take charge of things at this end. I am sending a cable to that effect to Scotland Yard. Care to see it?" He held it out to Norbury who only grunted as he read it. It ran:

"I, Anthony Parnall, junior partner in the firm of Fraser and Fraser, 200 Lincoln's Inn Fields, am at the moment at the above address where John Inskipp has been living before going to Dover. I had a slight acquaintance with him some years ago and talked with him on the Saturday night in question. Firm will explain my presence here. Shall I take charge of depositions? It was to be sent reply paid.

Norbury asked him to hand it in at the little post office in Castellar himself if he could drive a French Ford on a French road—which Pointer truthfully assured him he could—he who had once, when trying to locate Joan Ingilby, driven a taxi from a Marseilles aerodrome.

"Meanwhile, no one should leave the farm for any length of time—or on any account," he said, as he rose to do as suggested. "I must be able to assure the authorities of that, or—"

"Or what?" asked Blythe curtly.

"They would call in the French police at once," said Pointer slowly, as though he had to think out what would be the steps most likely to be taken.

"I shall work at the Caves as always," said Rackstraw.

Blythe gave him a glance, and would have spoken, but Norbury said at once, "Look here, Rackstraw, don't make difficulties. You have plenty of notes on which you can work, I'll be bound. The Rocks are in Italy—"

"My permit is a daily one," was the reply, "I'd like to see who will stop me from getting on with my work!" and with that he won his point.

About half an hour after Pointer had left, Miss Blythe pushed the papers into a heap. She had been reading them feverishly, as had the others.

Blythe went over to her. "This is no place for you," he said in an affectionate tone, "you know all there is to know now, and you need a rest—from talking and re-talking."

She made no protest as he held the door open for her, but walked so slowly—wearily—heavily—out of the room

into the garden, that Mrs. Norbury rose. She paused a
moment at the door.

"I think we had better only tell the servants—and the
people at Castellar that Mr. Inskipp is dead."

"Killed in a motor accident," supplemented Norbury.
"Ah, there's Parnall back."

"Sent your telegram off?" Rackstraw asked, while
Blythe turned his back, and went on up to his room.

Pointer nodded. "I ought to get the answer within
three hours. Perhaps less." He knew that it would be a
good deal less, for his reply being from the Yard would
have priority.

Norbury walked with his heavy farmer's tread to a
door into the yard. Pointer followed him, for he had an
idea that Norbury was debating some question in his own
mind. Probably, thought Pointer, something which he
wanted to tell him—was it about the Blythes? Or was it
something which would link Inskipp to Mireille? He was
too experienced—and too wise—to try to hurry Norbury.
His type is self-starting.

Instead, Pointer got a lift in a camion hurrying down
from the farm with empties. At Menton, he cashed his
cheque at the English Bank. He had made arrangements
before leaving town which enabled Anthony Parnall to
cash cheques up to a hundred pounds at sight. He then
asked for a word with the manager, but the latter was
away, on the bank's business in Turin. His return would
depend on events there. The bank was empty of
customers. It would close in five minutes. Pointer lit a
cigar with the air of a man inclined for a chat. He
explained that he hoped to get some information about a
client of his as well as an old friend, a man called Inskipp
who had died very suddenly while home in England.

The cashier to whom he was speaking gave a
sympathetic exclamation and took his eye off the clock.
He knew Mr. Inskipp quite well—as a customer of the
bank. Why, he had only been in a couple of weeks ago.
And before he left, Parnall knew all that there was to be

known, for, to the dead man's solicitor, the cashier spoke
frankly. Pointer learnt that Inskipp had asked the
manager about a solicitor at Clermont-Ferrand . . . he
heard about the cheque for a thousand pounds changed
after a week into thousand-franc notes. The manager had
the numbers. . . .

That apparently exhausted the information to be
extracted from the bank, and Pointer thanked him, asked
that the numbers of the bank-notes taken by Inskipp be
considered very confidential, and left the bank by a side
door. Turning the corner past the British consulate, he
made for the photographer whose name was on Inskipp's
photograph. The man was no help. Inskipp had merely
come in for his portrait, taking six cabinet-sized ones, and
had not talked to the photographer at all. Pointer tried
artists' materials, and shops where silver frames could be
bought, with no better result. Inskipp had evidently
taken his purchases with him. He tried hotel after hotel,
asking whether Inskipp had ever called on friends there,
still with no result. The casino likewise knew him not.
Then he tried the two libraries that supply English
readers—at neither place was Inskipp known. Nor at the
bridge clubs.

Driving back to the station he thought over the case
afresh. Why had Inskipp asked for a cheque for a
thousand pounds in the first place, and then been
anxious, or appeared to be anxious, to exchange it for
notes? And this had been done in mid-November, and,
two months later, mid-January, had come the crime in
which a scarecrow's clothes figured so strangely.

The truth in a murder inquiry comes into view like a
distant landscape. At first only a far-off, faint blur shows
that there is anything to be seen. Then, little by little,
first one thing then another can be divided into their
respective kinds—a tree comes up as a tree—a mountain
shows as a mountain— water glitters. Next, the tree
proves to be an oak. The mountain takes on an outline
different from other mountains. The water must therefore

be a certain lake which lies near that mountain, and has a certain oak growing close to it. By that time, fields become recognisable, roads show their trend, and, last of all, people have faces—not mere discs, and, finally, by their features, they too are known.

Pointer was only as yet able to tell one object from another, that the tree was a tree—not, as it had seemed yesterday, a rock. He might guess who the murderer was, but that was only a guess as yet.

Back at the farm, Pointer found that a long-distance call from Paris had been taken down for him. It sounded like a message from his sister, but it told him that Laroche had been constantly seen in Menton in the company of a well-known writer, and had with him attended several local literary gatherings during all the days that interested Pointer.

As for the others who had been at Dover, Pointer learnt at dinner how impossible it would be to prove where any of them had been that evening or night in Dover. After finishing their coffee in the lounge, none of the little party of four had apparently seen each other again that night.

Pointer left the others talking, and slipped upstairs, but he was fetched almost immediately. The cable from the Yard had come. It seemed to have drawn the Blythes to the room as though it were a magnet and they were steel filings. Pointer merely glanced at the slip of grey-green paper before handing it to Norbury with the suggestion that he should read it aloud. He himself had drafted it before leaving town. It ran:

"Your offer accepted. Do not think it necessary as yet to apply to local authorities and hope not to have to do so if you take charge of inquiry at farm. Collect all possible evidence including signed statements from the three who were in Dover. Request them to remain in touch with you." It was signed New Scotland Yard, C.I.D. Branch.

"Very discreet," said Norbury, and seemed about to add something but, if so, changed his mind and handed the cable instead to Miss Blythe whose hand was half-outstretched towards it. She stared at it a moment before passing it on to Mrs. Norbury and then went on out into the fresh air, wrapping herself up in her thick cloak as though shivering.

"Now, there's another thing we can do," said Pointer cheerfully when the cable had gone the circuit. "Didn't you tell me, Mrs. Norbury, that Inskipp, poor fellow, left a trunk with you here? It ought to be corded up and sent untouched to Scotland Yard, or the Dover police."

"I'll see to it at once," Norbury promised. "Relieves me of all responsibility—if any one claims anything is missing."

Exactly!" Blythe's voice, too, registered hearty approval as he hurried after his sister.

"I'll help,' Rackstraw volunteered. Pointer left him and Norbury getting cords together and went on out to a corner of the orchard for which he had seen Edna Blythe making. And there, with the moon turning the violets to silver, he saw her looking up into Blythe's face with her own as white as the clump of wood-anemones beside her. Blythe's attitude suggested that he was comforting her— or was it reassuring her?

Pointer walked on and waited. Something in the woman's face made him think that the talk would not be a long one.

CHAPTER 19: MIREILLE

When Miss Blythe was finally left alone, Pointer limped into sight, and murmuring about blisters on heels taking an unconscionable time to heal, asked if he might rest a moment on the fence beside her. She nodded almost absent-mindedly, and let the ash of one of her constant cigarettes drop on to the eye of a sleeping narcissus.

Pointer watched Edna Blythe's absorbed face without seeming to do so. She was a profound egoist, he thought. Possibly her fate had made her so. For unhappiness can be a vitriol, and in that case it is the sweeter, softer qualities which are eaten away first.

"I very much want a word with you about poor Inskipp," Pointer said at length. "Have you any idea whom he could have meant when he mentioned the name of Mireille to me in Dover? Is there any one of that name known to you around here?"

"Mireille?" she repeated. "Mireille? That is the name of the lovely creature he was going to marry! I've quite forgotten about her. He told me before he left for England and asked me to keep the fact a secret, as there was some temporary obstacle to their marriage. He showed me her photograph. I never saw so beautiful a creature!" she added warmly.

Pointer had her describe the portrait shown her as closely as possible. "Did any one else see it, do you know?" he asked.

"I had him show it to Richard. She really is incredibly lovely, Mr. Parnall, and yet one felt that the photograph hadn't been retouched to hide anything. The lines of her were enchanting."

So Blythe saw the picture too. "Was it in a frame?"

"Yes, in a silver one, which Mr. Inskipp said he had bought for it down in Menton. It was modern, but a charming thing. A wreath of hammered olive leaves. He had a pair of her photographs, he said, and the frames were a pair, too. I remember his saying that he had hunted Menton through before he found them in the old town."

"Something he said made me rather wonder whether this Miss Mireille wasn't an actress or some one in a film company," suggested Pointer in a very casual tone.

"She didn't look like either," was the reply.

"Oh, no! She suggested a country parsonage much more than any theatre or cinema."

"Yet he was writing a scenario—"

Edna repeated that the face shown her might have stood for a portrait of unawakened girlhood.

A little silence fell between them. So her brother-in-law had seen this photograph. . . . And both frames were now empty. . . . "To how many more at the farm had Inskipp shown it?" he asked.

"To no one," Edna said very decisively. "I don't think he would have shown it to me but for fearing that I might think"—she hesitated as though she had spoken too quickly—"that he was talking rather a lot to me the last week," she added brightly. "I had an idea that he wanted no mistake to be made about his intentions," she added with a real, though short, laugh—and a very charming laugh, too. Pointer listened to its quality. Character is revealed in a laugh better than in hours of talk. This one that he had just heard was well bred and very sweet, with a faintly ironical undertone all the same. "And he made me promise not to tell any one about her," went on Edna.

"But what about your brother seeing the portrait too?"

Again came the look on her face as though she had been too outspoken. If he read it aright, she recovered herself very quickly—too quickly, some might think.

"That   was   to   be   sure   that   he,   too,   didn't misunderstand," she said again, with a meaning smile, "and think he was going to get me off his hands so easily." There was a note in her voice that struck the keen ear beside her as of real bitterness and real mockery.

She got up, and he fell into step beside her.

"Still, I can't quite give up my idea that—though she may not have looked it, she might have been connected with the stage in some form," Pointer persisted. "Now, your brother, for instance, when you showed him the portrait of this Miss Mireille, didn't he speak or look as though he had seen the face before?"

Pointer was turning to help her over a rough bit of the path. Her face showed surprise. "I don't think so," she began slowly. Then she frowned a little as though in an effort at concentration. "Yet, now you suggest the idea, there was something that might be explained that way— he didn't study the portrait as closely as I should have expected—I remember, since that you speak of it, thinking at the time that he must have seen it before, standing out in Mr. Inskipp's room—the frame could stand, if one did something to two corners otherwise it was quite flat and thin—though very strong. Dear me, Mr. Parnall, you're quite a detective!"

"Did Mr. Inskipp speak French well, or would the young lady have had to talk English to him when they met?"

"She was half-English, he told me. But now about his murder, Mr. Parnall," and her face changed at the words, and seemed to grow years older. "How in the world did he come to be wearing what really does sound like the clothes off the scarecrow that used to stand near the kitchen door? Mr. Inskipp in those rags—!"

No one at the farm had yet, as far as Pointer knew, suggested that it was not Inskipp who had put those clothes on himself—that he had not been alive when he wore them.

"But without the hat," he reminded her. "That's very odd. In a disguise a hat is the most important thing, one

would think. Yet no hat was found near Inskipp. One of
the papers says that the police think the omission most
important and are basing a very important theory on its
not being found."

She snapped off a branch of early orange blossom.
"How ridiculous!" she said, sniffing at its sweetness in the
short twilight. "Why, he was probably wearing the hat,
and something happened to it."

"I wonder if he had any money in the band," Pointer
suggested.

She tossed the sprig away. Pointer retrieved it. He
could not bear to see a flower broken and flung aside. No
human hand can put together those miracles, and it is
not for man to destroy one wantonly.

"Why should he have?" she asked shortly. "I feel sure
the hat blew away before, or after, he was killed. Quite
unimportant either way."

"But its loss suggests important possibilities to the
police," Pointer said to that. "Even to an outsider it does.
The murderer may have worn it so as to look like Inskipp
at some subsequent interview. What you've told me about
his engagement suggests jealousy."

"If I'd remembered it before, surely it wouldn't have
made any difference—"

She stopped, her face ashen. Silent by force of
circumstances, rather than nature, Edna, like most
people in that case, said too much once she started.

"But we can cable the news of his engagement at
once," said her companion calmly. "After all Miss Blythe,
a delay of an hour or so doesn't affect such things, I
fancy," and Edna turned her face away and hurried on.
She had nearly betrayed herself she told herself in terror.
Had this Parnall not been engrossed in his own thoughts
he would have guessed the truth—that she had known
that Inskipp was murdered, before the papers brought
the news. Known it days ago.

Edna finished the rest of the walk at a breakneck
pace. So much so that Pointer, mindful of his supposed

Scarecrow 193

blister, dropped behind and let her rush on in thankful solitude. He had plenty to occupy his mind.

So Mireille was Inskipp's fiancée, and was very young, and very lovely, and Blythe might have seen the portrait of her before—though whether standing in Inskipp's room, or in a portrait at all was another matter. His mind pigeon-holed Mireille the Beautiful for the moment, and returned to speculations as to what could have taken Inskipp to Clermont-Ferrand early on the Saturday morning.

Pointer had looked up the trains and knew that, two hours after the others were on their way from Marseilles to Paris, a train left Marseilles for the Rubber Capital, as it is often called, owing to the huge Michelin tyre works there—arriving in Clermont around half-past seven. To reach Paris as he had that same night, he must have taken a latest the half-past two afternoon train from the town. The morning hours suggested a business engagement. But what business? Banks? Or an investment? Or a doctor? It must have been something very urgent. . . . He had a bank at Menton. . . . that thousand pounds . . . was it business of an investment type? . . . The question overheard by the cashier about a solicitor suggested this. Also, a solicitor seemed a very possible man to try at that early hour. Had it been on or for some business of the lovely, mysterious Mireille's that Clermont had been chosen—that cheque changed for notes?

He reached the farm and went upstairs to where Sabe could be seen flitting about in the passage.

"You've heard, I know, that Monsieur Inskipp has died in England. Yes, run down by a car. Now, I'm acting as his friend or as his brother would, if he had one."

Sabe nodded. She understood perfectly, she said.

"But he may have a real brother somewhere. Or a mother? Now the only way to find out is to remember what kind of letters he used to get. Did he receive many?"

"Constantly, monsieur. Every ten days or so. Never

two weeks between them. From Clermont-Ferrand. From the lady in Rennes they used to come weekly. Every Saturday. Without fail."

"The lady in Rennes? She might be able to help us. Who was she?"

"*Sais pas, monsieur.* But the writing was beautiful. Perhaps she was English. The paper was English."

"How do you know that the paper was English?"

"Well, I suppose it is, as Mademoiselle Florence had some like it. It was found when she had the accident. It is not like paper sold here in the shops. Madame uses it now."

"I wonder if I can see a piece?"

She darted away like a dragon-fly, and was back in a minute. In her hand a used envelope of a peculiarly repellant shade of blue. But the envelope was the square, English shape—unlined.

"That was always the paper she wrote on. But the envelopes were thick! So thick! She sent many many pages. I will put this back on madame's desk." She darted off and back again.

"Are you sure it is the same paper? Not merely rather like it?" Pointer asked.

"Positive, monsieur. It is too ugly to be mistaken about, eh?"

"And you think a lady sent them to Monsieur Inskipp?"

Sabe's eyes danced.

"Monsieur, I saw him kissing the paper once! His door was ajar. And if you had seen his eyes when the postman handed him one. As if all the stars, and the moon, as well as the sun, were shining at once! And when they stopped he was inconsolable. A face as though he had not slept at nights. But he got over it! And soon he forgot all about his lady in Rennes and it was all Clermont-Ferrand. And fine silver-grey paper. But no more beautiful writing. No, the writing was like that of a child. And then it was typed. Always typed. And never another letter from Rennes

after the first one reached him from Clermont-Ferrand. I
think the other lady got married—or engaged—and the
affair had to end."

"And you think the letters from Clermont-Ferrand
were written by a lady too? Why?"

"Allez, monsieur! As if one could not tell by his face—
his shining eyes—the snatch of his hands to take it. The
reading of it when alone. Oh, he looked again just as
before—until at the last when he was worried. He told me
he had lost a lot of money. I asked him if it had been
stolen, and he said, yes, it had been. Is it not terrible!
People who steal should be guillotined. Except, of course,
food. Stealing food is not stealing, it is human nature. My
father won't let me say it, but I do say it!"

"Now about the letters from Rennes—did you ever see
any of them lying about? Were they in English?"

Sabe had only seen the envelopes of the letters in
question.

"Could you write down how they were addressed?"

Sabe at once wrote in her careful writing:

Monsieur Inskipp,
Domaine de la Chevre d'Or,
Pres Castellar,
A. M.

"And how were those from Clermont-Ferrand
addressed?"

"Precisely the same."

"The lines, too, arranged just the same?"

"Just the same."

"Did any one else get any letters from either of these
towns?"

"From Rennes? Mademoiselle Florence, the
mademoiselle who was killed, got one once a month. Also,
she knew this lady of Monsieur Inskipp's."

"How do you know that?"

"Oh, he used—in the beginning—to pull out his letter

and talk to her about it. And she would ask him about it. One could tell they were discussing the lady he loved. Monsieur Inskipp would blush—like a *jeune fille*, and mademoiselle would laugh, and laugh, when she left him! Oh, she thought him very funny, one could hear that!"

"Did you ever hear any girl's name mentioned?"

"Mireille," said Sabe instantly; "but do not tell madame I know so much. She thinks it indiscreet in a *pension*. There were two names they talked of when the letters came. *Mireille* and Madame de Pra. That is a name easy for me to remember, for Madame de Pra was the name of the woman who used to sell honey here when our hives went sick. Mademoiselle Florence used to talk a great deal to her. Our Madame de Pra lost her eyesight later, and had to go to stay over in San Louis with her son. She was so clever at getting honey, monsieur, she—"

"One moment, Sabe, you're sure they weren't talking of your Madame de Pra?"

"But no! She is always called the honey-woman. Only Mademoiselle Florence and we of the place, of course, knew her real name. Even madame does not know it. Mademoiselle Florence was very curious. She was always asking questions."

"Had this Madame de Pra any one called Mireille in her family?"

Sabe' laughed outright. "I should hope not, monsieur. She and her son are both hunchbacks. And Mireille only goes with beauty, we think. No, Madame de Pra has no relatives but her son."

"And when the letters from Rennes stopped, did Mademoiselle Rackstraw and Mr. Inskipp continue to talk of Mireille and Madame de Pra?"

"She had her fatal accident just then," said Sabe, thinking back with the ease of the peasant, whose whole theatre and library are the foreigners in their midst, and whose memory, trained to mark dates by the time of the year—the harvest of this—the sowing of that—is very lasting, and often very accurate.

She evidently did not connect the two facts except by time.

"And was it long after it, that the letters from Clermont-Ferrand first started?"

"About a fortnight. Gentlemen have short memories. My father is always telling me so—and he is a wise man. But what grief for the second lady, monsieur! She must know that he is dead because she has not written lately."

"Not necessarily. He would have told her that he was leaving here, and have given her an address in England to which to write."

Pointer did not believe this, but it would satisfy Sabers sympathy.

"Who else received letters from there?" he asked.

"The patron—at least he receives circulars—advertisements of things for the farm. Otherwise? Monsieur Laroche has a relation there—an aunt, he told me, who is going to die and leave him all her money. He hears from her now and then—no one else ever has letters from Clermont-Ferrand. Coming, madame—*J'arrive! J'arrive!*" and Sabe, with a polite little bow of excuse, flew down the stairs to Mrs. Norbury who was calling her.

Pelham stepped in. Pointer in a few succinct words told him of the latest developments. Christopher shook his head.

"I'm hopelessly out of my depth—but, look here, I fancied that hat having been altered on the scarecrow means something to Miss Blythe. But how could it have had any significance to her? You think it had? Don't tell me what. Let me at least reason that much out. The rest is beyond me," and he vanished on to the landing.

CHAPTER 20: MIREILLE'S IDENTITY BECOMES A PUZZLE

Miss Blythe had a late supper served in her room. But the others were in the dining-room, and Pointer mentioned to Blythe the portrait seen by his "sister " in the silver frame.

"Had you seen it before? In Inskipp's room?" he asked Blythe.

"Seen it before—yes," said Blythe shortly, "but in Rackstraw's room, not Inskipp's."

Every one looked at Rackstraw, who only stared at the speaker. Pointer repeated Edna's description of Mireille.

Rackstraw looked surprised and something else as well. "That's the portrait of a girl who died just before her film was to be shot. *The Cradle Song.* I was in Barcelona at the time. The portraits were taken to see how she would photograph. The director was a friend of mine—is still—and I took the portraits off with me one day when he wasn't looking!"

"But," said Mrs. Norbury, who had been greatly interested in the news about Mireille, "How could Mr. Inskipp show the portrait of a dead girl as his fiancée? It can't be the same girl!"

"Had the girl, in the portrait Inskipp showed you, golden hair, fastened back with a ribbon? Was she standing in a garden of lilies, bending over them? Old convent garden?" Rackstraw asked.

Blythe assented.

"That's Aagard Petersen! She was run over on her way to the film studio in Barcelona and killed instantly. Her mother was Spanish, but her father had been a Norwegian—hence her name and her colouring. She had the loveliest face and figure I ever saw. I missed the two portraits some time ago, but I thought they had got mixed with my mother's or my sister's papers, and that they would turn up again some time. Also, it was a face you tired of. No 'go' in it. No devil."

"It takes both to hold one in a portrait," agreed Laroche, " I think it does in real life too."

"But, Mr. Rackstraw!" expostulated Mrs. Norbury, who cared nothing for impersonal argument. "How *could* these portraits of yours be those of a girl whom Mr. Inskipp called Mireille?"

"Easily," said Rackstraw, " Inskipp was just the sort of chap to fall in love with them, and construct an imaginary love affair with his ideal woman—whom he called 'Mireille ' because just then he was full of things Provencal. He seems to have told Miss Blythe that there was an obstacle preventing his marriage to her—there was! Its name was death." His tone was mocking, his grin contemptuous. And yet, to Pointer, he had some other secret explanation of the name, or the choice of the photograph, or both, and one that amused him.

"But he made no effort to learn from you who she was?" Mrs. Norbury's tone was unbelieving.

"My mother or my sister might have told him. They knew all about the story of the poor little thing." Again something in Rackstraw's tone caught the keen ear of the chief inspector.

Looking at Blythe, Pointer saw the signs of suppressed anger in his face. Blythe evidently believed that Inskipp had used the portrait to lull him—Blythe— into a false sense of security. But Pointer thought of that sketch which had first brought him here, and of the words on the back of the portrait of Inskipp himself, which he believed that the dead man had sent to some one—somewhere.

"There's some mistake," replied Mrs. Norbury doggedly. Once she got an idea into her head she refused to allow it to be easily dislodged. "I feel sure there is.

You're talking of some one else, Mr. Rackstraw."

"Have you another portrait of this Petersen girl?" asked Blythe suddenly, "that would settle the matter?"

Rackstraw thought that he knew where he could put his hands on one. He went to his room. After a few minutes he returned with a bundle of old photographs. Taking out one of them, he passed it to Blythe.

Pointer remembered having been struck with the lovely face when he went through Rackstraw's things.

Blythe nodded. "That's the girl he showed me. Though his picture was far prettier. But that's she without any question. I'll show it to my sister if I may, and see what she says." He left the room.

"It seems impossible," murmured Mrs. Norbury, "to show a dead girl's picture. . . . It seems so—so unhealthy! And Mr. Inskipp always struck me as so—" There came a light run down the stairs, followed by the heavy tread of Blythe. Edna had the picture in her hand.

"Do you mean to say, Mr. Rackstraw, that this girl isn't alive? That Mr. Inskipp was only romancing when he spoke of her to me? I can't believe it! I simply can't! I wonder if he knew that she was dead? He spoke of her in such a tone, and his face lit up so when he spoke of her— it seems quite incredible! But this is the girl he called Mireille. No question of that!"

Laroche turned to her with tales of imaginative and solitary people, women as well as men, having had a dream-love to whom they gave real names, and of whom they spoke as of the living until at last they believed their own romancing.

Edna would not have it. "He didn't talk of her like that," she persisted. "He didn't look as though she were just a dream. Most certainly he thought she was alive! I'm positive of that."

"If you ask me," said Norbury—no one had, but he often prefaced his remarks with that opening, "I should say that those photographs which you, Rackstraw, say Inskipp pinched, were very like his girl, his Mireille.

Which would mean that he had no portrait of her, and took the ones of this other, this dead Petersen girl, as the next best thing to what he hadn't got and so to himself, and to you, Miss Blythe, let them pass for his girl's portraits."

"That's a very sensible explanation," said Mrs. Norbury approvingly. "In fact, I think you've got it, Frank."

Edna agreed with her, and so did Blythe and Rackstraw. Only Laroche would have none of it.

"No, no! the other is too much in keeping with Inskipp, who was the dreamer—the mystic—par excellence. It would be absolutely in keeping with him to have taken the portraits of a girl about whom he knew nothing, for whose real life he cared nothing, and out of them to make for himself the object of a secret worship. To me, the only explanation is that Mireille—like the Golden Goat—stood to him for the ideal—the never-to-be-realised— the symbol of unattainable desires."

He spoke with certainty, but Mrs. Norbury would not let this theory pass. She much preferred her husband's.

"I agree," Laroche said finally, "there wasn't much of exaltation left in Inskipp before he went back to England—when he got into financial difficulties, I mean. He went round with a very long face at the end—that much I do concede."

"What financial difficulty was Inskipp in?" Pointer asked. He heard again about the loss of interest—and possibly of capital—from his shipping investment. "Yet after it, he let you, Mr. Rackstraw, deal with his scenarios of Haroun as you liked," said Pointer in a very puzzled voice.

"Oh, by that time he had got his hands on something good," said Rackstraw very decidedly, "or thought he had. I noticed before he left the farm for home that he had lost all real interest in his writing. He was for ever reading over old newspapers up in his room. Going in for journalism, perhaps."

Edna's spoon rattled. She laid it down hastily. She had accepted some stewed fruit. A moment more, and she slipped from the room.

Pointer, when supper was over, went into the garden and out along the lane for a quiet smoke. His theory was proving itself. Inskipp had used a thousand pounds for some object, not long before he was in low financial waters. And apart from the money taken in thousand-franc notes, there was the odd, the very odd story of the portrait said by the dead man to be that of his fiancée, "Mireille," yet claimed by Rackstraw as the picture of a dead Norwegian girl.

Something about Rackstraw's manner—or voice—was peculiar. His story might be sheer invention, and he and Inskipp have both been in love with Mireille de Pra, for whom, over whom, they had quarrelled. But Pointer did not think so, though he decided to get the name of the Spanish producer out of him as soon as possible, unless Rackstraw were to claim that he, too, like Aagard Petersen, were dead. His story could apparently be investigated. And would be.

He saw a spark coming towards him. The watch-dog was silent, which meant that it must be Norbury, smoking a cigar, for after dark no one but his master could move in the garden without the dog giving due notice of the fact.

Norbury asked a few questions about Menton and the bank, but Pointer felt he had come out to say something which either was, or which he believed to be, important. Finally, after an interval of silence, Norbury leant forward confidentially.

"I had better tell you something—in strict confidence, mind—the Blythes aren't brother and sister. She's his sister-in-law. The widow of his dead brother. And neither of their names is Blythe. And I happen to know what they are. So did Inskipp. And I only hope that there wasn't a connection between his knowledge—and his death."

And with that, Norbury told Pointer exactly how

Inskipp had first learnt of the real identity of the so-called brother and sister staying at the farm under the name of Blythe.

Pointer showed himself as hugely interested, but pointed out that Norbury had placed himself in a very difficult position. Very. He strongly advised him on no account to mention the facts to any one else whatever.

"I'm a farmer—not an orator," Norbury replied curtly. "You needn't advise me to keep my mouth shut. As to giving that poor woman away—I couldn't. She's absolutely innocent of the charges against her. But whether Inskipp stirred up some hornet's nest when he took on the job—that's what I'm inclined to think."

"And was that when he spoke to you about knowing no solicitor to turn to in England?"

Norbury said that it was, and on that they parted.

Pointer went for a turn by himself in the cool, fresh air.

That thousand pounds . . . and Sabe's account of the letters which came first for Inskipp from Rennes—and then, after Florence Rackstraw's death—from Clermont-Ferrand, fitted together and fitted his idea that something underhand might have been going on with Inskipp as its hub.

Taken in conjunction with the discussion as to the identity of the photographs, Pointer believed that a very heartless game had been played with Inskipp, a game which had been continued as a crime. Begun, he thought, by Florence Rackstraw, as some sort of revenge—or retaliation, but continued by some one who saw in the love-letters purporting to come from the beautiful Mireille a chance to get some money out of the romantic dreamer. The idea would probably have been to claim that her marriage—or some terms of her husband's will if she were a widow—was a bar to her remarriage. Some such tale would enable the person behind the cruel joke—presumably Florence Rackstraw—to account for the difficulty in Inskipp meeting his lovely correspondent.

Pointer thought it more than probable that she had been represented as married to some jealous brute of a husband, from whom in common humanity she should be set free.

And here the thousand pounds might fit. Divorces cost money. . . . Divorces, too, have to be obtained through solicitors. Had Clermont-Ferrand a Court of Assizes? His knowledge of the place was nil. But he would try first to find out if the best solicitor there knew the name of Inskipp. That letter from France which had been handed to Inskipp on the day of his arrival—and murder—in England. Did it belong here? Blythe had spoken of the horrified look on Inskipp's face as he read it. Was it the alarm clock which had set the hour for the actual murder? Though that death had been decided on before that. For one thing was certain, if the thousand pounds had been obtained in any such way as he was supposing, then at the time that it was obtained whoever had got it must have known that the end might have to be the death of the deceived giver. The time might be uncertain—but supposing the money to have been sent in reply to a request of "Mireille's," there must come a moment when Inskipp would penetrate the deceit, a day when he would realise that he had been duped, and prosecute the person to whom his thousand pounds had really gone.

Was that apparently unexpected visit to Clermont-Ferrand due to some suspicion of Inskipp's? There were three men with him, had one of them let drop some word which had aroused that suspicion?

Had Inskipp followed up that word and asked for some piece of information to be sent to him at Dover which would clear the matter up? If so, was the letter handed to him at the Lord Bishop the reply to his query? Was that interview to which he had gone on the cliffs an interview arranged by the sender of that letter? An interview connected with Mireille and his thousand pounds?

As for the Blythes themselves being connected with the money, he could see no reason for Blythe needing to get a thousand pounds by any such means as he was presupposing, and Miss Blythe, by her conduct in England, by her return to the farm, did not suggest a person who had obtained a thousand pounds only three months ago.

At this stage in his reasoning, a hail reached him. It was Pelham's clear voice calling his name. Pointer called back, and a moment later the two met.

"Registered letter from England for you, Parnall. Come by air."

In France, no one but the addressee can sign a receipt for a registered letter, and Pointer accordingly hurried back to the farm, leaving Pelham to wait for his return. That young man did not have to wait long. He, too, spent the time in cogitation, and when Pointer reappeared, he greeted him in a cautiously low voice with the murmured remark that he still couldn't see what the changed hat on the scarecrow meant to Miss Blythe and would like to be enlightened.

"Well," said Pointer to that, "it suggests strongly that she was not in the scarecrow murder—either as accomplice or accessory. For if so, one would expect her to have been familiar with the idea of leaving him dressed as a tramp in garments taken off the scarecrow—to which Mrs. Norbury had just added Blythe's hat. What happened strongly bears out the idea that she came on the hat unexpectedly—just before she saw Inskipp's dead body, or just after it—recognised it at once, and connected Blythe with the murder. And so, partly for his sake, possibly for her own as well, since he was her only helper—she decided to get rid of the hat—by the means that we know of. But now about this registered letter, suppose you sit down over there while I read it. In case any one comes along we're not together. If no one comes I'll let you know what's in it."

Pelham walked away to the place indicated, and

Pointer, sitting down, switched on his torch and read the typed pages. It was from Earnshaw, and the contents were startling. He had obtained an interview with Ada Greenlee almost immediately after Pointer's departure, and another with the cook of the Whin-Brownings who was in Dublin at the moment, and then a third with the upper house-maid now in town. All three of them had seen Mrs. Whin-Browning change her tray for that of her sister-in-law, and the net results pointed conclusively to the fact that Mary Whin-Browning had poisoned her brother and meant to poison her sister-in-law, Edna. As instructed, Earnshaw had at once laid all the papers before the public prosecutor and—also as instructed—had an interview with Mr. Martin Blair of the *Morning Wire*. Pointer knew that Blair could be counted on to go all out to help the under dog, and his paper had taken up the case again on its front page under this new light. Blair's work and that of the Home Office had now proved that it was the alteration of the two breakfast trays by Edna— trays which at the inquest she had denied having so much as seen, that had saved her life, and ended that of the real poisoner. The warrant against her was being withdrawn, and she was free to return to England—if alive.

So Edna Whin-Browning was innocent. Pointer was very moved as he thought of what her life had been since the second death. He could imagine few more terrible— except that, being innocent, she could hope for the ultimate prevailing of the truth. Walking over to Pelham, he let him read the papers.

"Innocent!" whispered Pelham, "what an amazing affair. Poor woman, it's been a bit steep for her, eh?"

"A bit," Pointer agreed laconically.

"When are you going to tell her?"

"If she's still up, at once, on our return. I think her brother is still wrestling with the cording of that box. Naturally he's overjoyed to have it sent away unopened lest it contain—as it does—the old newspapers with pictures of himself and his sister-in-law. Papers which first told Norbury, and then Inskipp, who the two were— and very possibly told others as well. Rackstraw for one."

"Then if the Blythes had no motive to stop Inskipp's inquiries, they're out of it!" Pelham stopped himself. "Mrs. Whin-Browning is—yes. But I don't see that Blythe is necessarily free from suspicion of having murdered Inskipp."

For as to Hector Whin-Browning, it had been said at the short inquest and accepted for truth that he was away on a world cruise at the time of both deaths. But acting on Pointer's suggestions, Earnshaw had learnt that he had been in Paris at the time, and then in a villa near Boulogne, which would have let him come over to England on the day on which his sister-in-law had disappeared so completely in some small yacht.

"—He might have been jealous of Inskipp and Mrs.— er—Miss Blythe?" finished Christopher.

Pointer did not reply, only gave him a smile, and strode off back to the farm. His feet were winged. There are few more delightful sensations in the world than to be the bearer of good tidings.

CHAPTER 21: A PRISONER IS SET FREE

Pointer saw a figure lying out in a deck chair on the Blythes' balcony. He rapped smartly on the door of the sitting-room.

Her voice called to him to come in, and Pointer stepped through the room on to the balcony. For a moment she stared at him in surprise, and, he was sure, terror.

"What is it?" she asked wildly.

"Good news," said Pointer in a quiet voice. "Very good news indeed. But may we talk here in the sitting-room? What I have to say is confidential."

Her eyes searched his face. In silence she led the way into the room behind them. In silence she let him close the glass doors and the windows.

Then he turned. "I've just had a letter, which I think you will like to see." He held the pages out to her that he had just read.

Her face was very pale as she took them, and sat down. At the first mention of her real name she gave a low cry—a very pitiful cry, Pointer thought it—it reminded him of a rabbit when it is snared.

"Read on!" he said urgently and encouragingly.

She did so. Then, jumping to her feet, she snatched a glass of water from the table near her, drank a deep draught, and reread the papers. Then she turned to him, her face transfigured.

"Who are you? What does it mean? Is it true, oh, is it true?"

"You can take every word in it as absolutely certain and proven," he said gravely.

"My sister-in-law? Impossible!"

"The breakfast trays," Pointer said now.

"I thought—my solicitor thought—it would be fatal to speak of it."

"Because he thought you guilty," Pointer said to himself.

"I did change the trays, yes," she confessed. "They were just alike, only the wicker border of the one at my door was broken in one place. You couldn't see it if you didn't know it, but my sleeve had once caught on it and been torn . . . so I gave it to her . . . and took the one outside her door for myself."

"That's what I thought possible," he said reflectively.

"Mr. Parnall, as I said before, you really ought to have gone in for detective work. Scotland Yard would be the place for you! You think—it really is proved?" She was quite overcome for the moment.

"You will be able in a very short time to return to England for good. Mr. Blair is a power in the newspaper world—so is his paper."

"But this man—Earnshaw—how did he come to write to you about me?"

"Obviously Inskipp had got him started," Pointer said easily. "And knowing, evidently, that I am looking up Inskipp's murder—he has written to me. But now, in return, will you tell me several things I want to know. First of all, how did Inskipp learn who you were?"

For a while Edna could only talk of herself—her past danger—her present relief. Then she grew calmer and told him what Norbury had already told him and what he had divined for himself. She told him of the payment, unknown to her brother-in-law, of the two hundred and fifty pounds which he had spoken of, registered to himself somewhere in town.

There was a little pause and once again she was back at her own wonderful delivery from the very depths of despair. He let her run on for a while, then he said suddenly:

"Miss Blythe, Inskipp has helped you—through Earnshaw—"

"He has saved me!" she corrected, her voice quivering, tears on her cheeks.

"Then help the search to find out who murdered him," he said urgently. "For instance, I think you know more about that Sunday night that he was killed in Dover than you have told. Be frank, Miss Blythe. It can't hurt innocent people."

"But how can *I* know anything about Dover?" Her face was waxen again.

He said nothing, only waited. But his eyes spoke for him. She gave them a long look.

"I don't know how you guessed it. I think you must be a wizard, not a solicitor—but you're right —at least in that I, too, was there—in Dover. I was so homesick, Mr. Parnall. I loathe all this beauty around me, I want to be back in my own country— not condemned to exile for ever!" Her face worked and she covered it with two very thin hands for a moment before she went on quietly, "So when they all went home—I couldn't bear it, and I went too. They didn't know about it. Mrs. Norbury, like them, thinks I went for a few days into the valleys all around us. But I left on the next day—the Saturday—and owing to the chance of their having stopped over a night in Paris we crossed by the same boat. I went second class and third on the trains!"

"But how could you have got past the passport officials?" he asked as though suddenly puzzled.

"I managed it," she said with a flush on her cheeks. She did not want to confess to that horrid theft of the passport, though she did not regret it for a minute. And though it had brought her the terrible experience of the hat and Inskipp's dead face looking up from the floor of the shelter, it had also let her go to her mother's house and have a talk with her which had entirely relieved the mother's dread about her daughter's fate, for Edna had not dared to write the facts.

"Oh, Mr. Parnall," she said now, following back on those thoughts, "when can I let my mother know?"

"She'll read about it to-morrow morning when she opens her paper," he said, smiling at her. "You can exchange cables of mutual congratulation. And now, excuse the question, but how do you manage for money?"

At the frosty look in her face, he said quickly, "Forgive what seems an impertinence, but as a solicitor, it often happens that we can arrange loans—furnish supplies."

At that she looked at him very gratefully.

"I wanted my mother to try and induce her solicitor to help me—advance me something of my husband's money—which will come to me as soon as his death is cleared up. So far, he has refused. He—he didn't think I could be cleared," she said sadly. "But of course now— everything is changed! Everything. I can manage all right for the moment. Oh, Mr. Parnall, you can't know what this news means to me!"

"I'm asking for a return," he warned her. "Remember, I'm trying my hardest to find out what happened in Dover that night. So, will you tell me everything that happened to you after you left here?"

After a second's hesitation, she told him even, at the end, how she had taken Florence Rackstraw's passport, when she—Edna—ran away to Nice the day of Florence's death, and how, later on, she had taken the peculiar hat and cloak which Florence wore. How she had gone on to the cliffs for fresh air on the night of her arrival in Dover, and how she had by chance, stepping into the nearest shelter, trodden on a small electric torch, switched it on, and seen Inskipp's dead face not a yard away.

She said nothing about the hat, nor did Pointer. She told how she had stumbled back to the boarding-house, and then, when well enough to go, had made up her mind that she must get to her mother. How, when she had arrived at her mother's cottage, and been received by the old servant who had known her as a girl, she had found her mother absent and sat down to wait for her return. Edna, in telling it now, quite flung herself into this part. Pointer understood how, once the curtains were drawn, the lights lit, for the first time since she had seen Inskipp dead, poor Edna had had a feeling of being safe and among friends. Then she had noticed a letter on the mantel, and the maid, faithful Lily Bridges, had explained that that was a letter about which a gentleman was coming to inquire from the Lord Bishop Hotel at Dover where a Mr. Inskipp had met with an accident. Edna had immediately realised that that letter might put the hounds on the scent. She had carefully not given her mother's address to Inskipp, but evidently he had found it out for himself. Edna had snatched it off the mantel, and just then the front door-bell had rung.

"It was a manager from the hotel, a dreadful man!" Edna leant forward earnestly, "who wouldn't take no for an answer. Poor Lily was at her wits' end to get rid of him. Finally she thought she had done it, and then what does my dear mother do but bring him in with her? She met him at the gate and knowing nothing about any reason to be careful with him—she didn't know Inskipp's name, or that I had ever met him—she told him to come along in and she would let him have the letter. I still don't understand why they wanted it at the hotel—as a specimen of his writing, I believe. But at any rate—there we were! Luckily I had snatched up the letter when I ran upstairs on his first ring, so I was able to tell my mother not to have anything to do with any inquiries about him—it seemed a shabby thing to do—for I liked Mr. Inskipp—I liked him immensely—but I was in a dreadful position, Mr. Parnall." Edna for a moment was back in sad memories. Then she roused herself. "My mother thought I was mad to have come back and in dreadful danger of being discovered now that something had happened to Mr. Inskipp, and she was certain that only my brother-in-law, Hector, could help me back again. I didn't want him. Oh, I didn't want his help!" Edna's voice rose for the moment. "But my mother had telephoned to him before telling me what she had done, and together they smuggled me out of the house. They actually seemed to think there might be some one watching it. So absurd! But you know how, when one is frightened, one starts at every shadow." She stopped and suddenly smiled a real smile. "I don't think you know much about fear," she said then, "but *I* do. I do!" Her face grew sombre again. "So I came back here. There was nowhere else to go apparently. But now—now!" She suddenly looked to him for advice. "What do I have to do now?"

"Wait," said Pointer, "Wait in confidence. The warrant against you is cancelled and I think this inquiry into Inskipp's death won't take long to clear up."

"I haven't been able to make sense of that note he wrote my mother, nor has my brother-in-law. Mr. Inskipp rather disliked cats, so he told me. Hector says that Mr. Inskipp mentioned my mother in the train, but had then apparently no idea where she lived. Yet that letter to her, which so frightened me when I saw it on the mantel, had been posted in Dover, as she told the manager of the hotel over the telephone, when she had no idea that there was any connection between me and Mr. Inskipp."

It looks to me," said Pointer, "as though Inskipp had come on some notice of Lady Thompson's cats in some magazine or paper—"

"The *Looker-on!*" Edna said instantly. "That's possible. My mother was wild over an article about her cats in a number which had just come out, as she had dropped her title in order to be disconnected from my awful affair—it was a shocking blow to have her photograph published in it. It doesn't seem to have done any harm though. And now—now it won't matter!" Her eyes shone.

He rose. "One thing more. Did Blythe approve of Inskipp taking the job of clearing you?" he asked bluntly.

She shook her head.

"Why not?"

She fingered the chair arm in silence for a moment then she said in a low voice, "It meant that I should be free—like other people—able to get clear away—and he didn't want that."

"Why not?"

"He's fond of me," she said after a little hesitation. "He—he wants to marry me, and—and I had been indiscreet enough to let him see that I would get away if I could. That but for my helplessness I wouldn't stay a day—an hour. And he resented that. He thought that in common decency, gratitude, I should want to make up to him for all he had given up for me. And I don't!" she added with sudden fire. "Not a bit! You might as well ask a bird to be grateful to the man who keeps it in a cage. I only want one thing—one thing which most people have without asking for it—without having to scheme and suffer for it—freedom! I made the dreadful mistake of letting Hector see that—just as before, in Brighton, I made the dreadful mistake of letting the coroner know it, who thought that I had murdered my husband to get free. If I had been a murderess, I should indeed have been tempted to murder Hector these many months

She paused, quivering. Pointer brought the subject back to Inskipp.

"You really know nothing about his affairs—his people—his family?"

She did not. "Yet I have something to show you—something which has oppressed me frightfully," she went on. "But it was impossible until now to hand it over. Not that it had any connection with poor Mr. Inskipp's murder—" she stopped and rising, looked at him suddenly. "I wonder if you have any idea what is coming," she said.

"I hope it's some letter he wrote to you before setting out for his last walk," he said gravely. He had a hope that since it might have been to meet some one linked with the Whin-Browning affair, past!"

Inskipp might have sent a line to one of the Blythes. And that, if one or both of them was innocent, they might yet find it.

Edna's eyes were wide. "What a good guess! It is a note which only makes things more perplexing. But you shall read it for yourself in a minute. I always carry it on me with my money."

She went into her bedroom, but in a moment was out again, a folded envelope in her hand. Taking it, Pointer saw that it had been posted in Dover on the night of Inskipp's murder. It was addressed to:

Miss Blythe,
Domaine de la Chevre d'Or,
Pres Castellar,
Alpes Maritimes,
France.

Inside he drew out a sheet of paper. He read:

"Dear Miss Blythe,
"I have just reached Dover after a foul crossing.
Your letter to Ada has brought me a note from her
and an appointment for this very evening which I
am looking forward to immensely. Her promptness
seems a good omen. I shall write more fully
to-morrow morning.
"Sincerely yours,
"J. Inskipp."

"Your note to Ada?" Pointer queried.

Edna made a gesture of bewilderment.

"*I* didn't write to her. I knew she was somewhere in Dover, but not where. I can't think what Mr. Inskipp means. Nor who wrote him. How could Mr. Inskipp have got a letter from her so quickly?"

She stopped. Pointer was glancing at the door. He had heard steps outside.

"Blythe!" he said, under his breath. "Shall I tell him? Or—"

He made another gesture suggesting a silent departure. She stopped him. Her small head was high.

"I'll tell him," she murmured, as the door opened.

Blythe came on in. He looked very bulky in the little room. Stopping short, he glanced in surprise and wariness at the chief inspector.

Edna jumped up from her chair. "News, Hector! News! It was Mary—*Mary* who poisoned Ambrose and meant to poison me! Read this! Don't ask questions—read it!"

Hector Whin-Browning did so. His face grew very pale. He read the letter three times through before he looked up.

"*Mary?*" he said in what looked like real horror. "It doesn't seem possible—"

"But it is—it *is*! It's true! Oh!" Her hands clasped together, Edna pressed them against her heart. "And at last I'm free! At last I'm free again like other women— free to go and come when and where I like—"

Hector's head had dropped a little. He gazed at her from under his thick eyebrows. A struggle showed on his face. "How do you come to be in this?" he asked Pointer.

Pointer gave him the same vague explanation that he had to Edna. Hector was not listening closely. He only nodded and said, "Very likely, very likely!" in an absent-minded way. Then he went over to Edna and took both her hands. "How shall I congratulate you? I've begun to fear lately that only a miracle could set you free. And now it's come." His voice was husky.

She let him hold her hands but she gave him a very steady, searching look.

"I know," he answered it, "I know, Edna." Real regret seemed to sound in his voice and look from his eyes. "I haven't played the game. I know you don't love me. And now you never will. I thought I could force it. Well—"he gave her hands a squeeze and then stepped back, "all I can say is that I'm most devoutly thankful for this news. I'd begun to fear that it was impossible—especially since Inskipp was killed."

She stared at him as though not able to believe her ears. Then she held out her hand with a quite different gesture. "I owe Mr. Inskipp a lot, yes, but don't you suppose I shall always remember that but for your help—twice over—I shouldn't be in any position to profit by this news about Mary. Twice you helped me at the risk of your own freedom—you gave me a refuge here at the farm—oh, Hector, I can never thank you enough—shall always think of you with the most intense gratitude—"

"And forget?" he asked almost humbly.

She gave his arm a friendly squeeze and he went on into his own room. Then she turned to the chief inspector.

"My brother-in-law is too modest as to what he's done for me," she said, as though in explanation of what must have puzzled him in their talk.

Pointer again repeated his own good wishes, and added that he was leaving the farm early to-morrow morning for a trip along the coast and perhaps into the charming towns behind them. As he said good-night, Edna looked as though she could have hugged his tall, straight figure, but she contented herself with shaking his hand with the smile of one living in a fairy story. But when he reached the door her face grew grave again.

"Don't be misled about Mireille!" She spoke urgently. "Mireille lives, Mr. Parnall, and Mr. Inskipp loved her! Had you seen or heard him, you would feel as sure as I do that she wasn't a myth or a dream, but really was what he called her once when he showed me what can only have been her portrait—no matter what confusion has crept in. He spoke of her then as his 'heart's desire.' And I think she was. Just that!"

Pointer's fine grey eyes rested a moment on her.

"There's a proverb I heard once at Les Martigues—I don't know if you know the town? It's not far from here. It runs, 'Beware of the she-wolf and the heart's desire,'" he said darkly, as he closed the door behind him.

CHAPTER 22: AT CLERMONT-FERRAND THE END COMES IN SIGHT

On his arrival by air-taxi at Clermont-Ferrand, Pointer took a car, and was first driven to the police station where he handed in his identity papers, received a most warm welcome, and then asked for a list of the names of solicitors living in the place. He explained that there was reason to think that a murdered Englishman, who apparently spent an hour or so in the town about a fortnight ago, might have consulted one. The man's name had been Inskipp.

It meant nothing to the commissaire. Neither did the name of Mireille, or of Madame de Pra. As for first-class solicitors—there was only one good one in Clermont-Ferrand, but he, parbleu, was an honour to any town. This was Maitre Francois.

Pointer was told that his speciality was the divorce court, and that the district *Cour des Assises* was here.

The commissaire rang up Me. Francois. The lawyer was in the courts, but his head clerk said that he would be out in an hour, and, at Pointer's suggestion, an appointment was booked for an English gentleman who would bring a card from the commissaire.

And the commissaire and Scotland Yard man chatted of international crooks to their mutual interest.

At the time set, Pointer found himself before the door of a big house looking into the Place de Jaude. He was shown through a spacious office into a large, comfortable room where a very fat man rose to meet him. Apart from the reputation of Maitre Francois, Pointer would not have been misled by the stoutness of the figure, or the smallness of the eyes facing him, so swift were the man's movements, so neat his half-turn as he seated himself.

The body is closely linked to the mind, and Pointer knew that here was a man of unusually quick mentality—very sure, very certain of himself—and with unbounded energy.

His own card lay on the corner of the writing-table. The Frenchman looked inquiringly from it to Pointer. His face expressed a polite astonishment—a certain interested waiting. There was no sign of his having any clue, however remote, as to the object of the visit.

"*Monsieur l'avocat,*" Pointer began in his admirable French, "I have come to you about a letter which we at the Yard think has been written by you to a certain Mr. Inskipp at the Lord Bishop Hotel, Dover, a letter which reached him on Sunday, the fifteenth of January. He was murdered that night, and we want to collect all the scattered threads of his life."

The fat man drummed on the table. "Murdered," he said reflectively—"*Tiens!* And the motive?"

"We have no idea what it was, but there are several odd things connected with Mr. Inskipp. We have learnt, for instance, that he was interested in a lady called Mireille—and that her surname may have been de Pra. We know that he got off at Marseilles on his train journey back to England from Menton, and that he stopped some hours here in Clermont-Ferrand on Saturday morning, January 14th, before rejoining his friends on Saturday night in Paris. We fancied that he might have come to see you—or some other solicitor. But that is pure guess-work."

"What would the date have been? January the 14th? I wasn't here then. I was at Avignon in the courts. And no one of that name called here at my office." He was silent, looking rather sleepy. But Pointer had a certainty that his mind was debating something. He kept silence.

After a moment Maitre Francois spoke. "I may have something to tell you—I may have nothing—but I would like to be sure that my name does not pass beyond these walls."

"I may use the information—if it exists," said Pointer without a smile—"but not mention the source where I got it? Is that the point?"

Maitre Francois' large head with its fan-shaped black beard, bowed gravely.

"*Convenu!*" said Pointer to that.

"You see," Francois said, speaking in a brisker tone, "the matter concerns another solicitor who would appear to have been making use of my name. And that—if it got spread about, would do me infinite harm. Who would care to write of their private affairs to a solicitor who might be quite another man altogether? That is why I did not go to the police about the matter, but have had private inquiries made on my own account. My connection with Monsieur Inskipp is limited to one letter with an enclosure which I sent to him by air-mail at the Lord Bishop Hotel in Dover, posting it here on Friday the thirteenth. Here is a copy of the letter and of its enclosure."

He opened a drawer, and took out two sheets of paper from a folder. "They explain themselves," he added, handing them to Pointer, whose face was impassive as he handed them back and agreed that they did, but he was overjoyed. At last he had struck oil. It remained to find out how much.

"Now, there is no other solicitor of my name in the town," continued the lawyer, "which was why this letter being merely addressed to *Maitre Francois, Clermont-Ferrand, P. de Dome,* was handed here. But my clerk has found out that there is an avoue, a Monsieur Oreille, who was struck off the rolls some years ago, whose first name is Francois. He lives, and has his office in a little street, the rue Jaude, which is at the other end of the town, and apparently he does some shady business still—chiefly money-lending, I fancy, at illegal rates of interest. There is a bare possibility that this other Monsieur—not Maitre—Francois was the man for whom your Mr. Inskipp meant his letter. But if so "he paused—"

obviously there was a postman bribed, and kept bribed, to deliver without comment to that address any letters that came."

"You think Mr. Inskipp was under the impression that he was addressing the well-known Maitre Francois?" finished Pointer.

The Frenchman nodded. "It has that air—" he said. "But to continue, Francois Oreille shut up his office— such as it was—on Monday the sixteenth, it appears," said Francois with a meaning look—his eyes were small but very expressive. "And in the confidence which binds us mutually, monsieur— my clerk learnt that he had received a telegram early on Monday morning from Dover consisting of the word—*Finished*—in English."

The two looked at each other for a long moment.

Pointer asked for copies of the copies that were in the lawyer's possession, and then told him of the Mireille affair—as he saw it.

Maitre Francois was enchanted. This was a tangle after his own heart. Here were events stirring on the plane of the mind—the only plane where he cared to live.

"Usually a murder"—he wrinkled up his lips in disgust—" bah! Sordid and stupid generally. But this tale of the photograph—that was a woman's trick, monsieur— in the first place! *De Pra* is quite a common Provencal family name. *Mireille*, of course, is not common—but not uncommon. The society of *Filibriges et Filibrigesses* keep it alive. They are what one might call the Mistral Society of France. And now what?"

Pointer was off to see the place where he believed that the other, spurious Francois might have been visited by Inskipp on the last day before his murder. And Pointer believed that here lay the real motive for Inskipp's murder, though the letter from the real Maitre Francois had been the actual cause. Its arrival—even without knowing its contents—would have told the criminal that the time must be counted in hours during which Inskipp could be continued to be hoodwinked. Inskipp, so Pointer thought, and so the criminal would think, would have returned as soon as possible to France and to an interview with the genuine Maitre Francois. Yes, Pointer thought, he had the motive now. But how was he to bring the crime home to the man whom he believed to have done it?

"I would like to see the office of this pseudo Maitre Francois," he said now.

"Nothing to see—literally," said the avocat, facing him, "the office furniture was sold by auction the day after that' Finished ' cable reached Oreille."

"Is the office to let? Could I get an order to look over it?" Pointer persisted.

"My head clerk can manage it, doubtless," said Francois carelessly. "He tells me that Oreille's son works in a film studio, and that a film of some sort was to have been taken—'shot'—is the term, I believe—there, but the cable stopped that apparently. It would have been worthy of the best Hollywood traditions, that office-scene! Lambert—my head clerk—learnt that the furniture intended for the occasion was the same as that used for the filming of some scenes from the life of one of our multi-millionaires—one of 'the twenty' as we call them nowadays."

He pressed the bell. His head clerk, Lambert, a big, stout, fair-haired Norman, took Pointer to Francois Oreille's late office. He obtained the key, and let Pointer in to the two rooms. The back room was but a cupboard, but the front room was of noble proportions, with a beautiful ceiling, freshly tinted.

"That must have been the work of Yvon, the son," explained Lambert. "He used to be an interior decorator's assistant before he took to working for the *Films d'Auvergne* Company. And the guilded woodwork— parbleu, it must have been done for that film that they intended to take here."

The gilding meant to Pointer that the woodwork was not to be tacky next morning. It is the quickest drying

medium known to the ordinary decorator. He asked
Lambert to find out for him on what date the film
furniture had been taken away. Lambert went a little
way down the mean street, and came back to say that it
had been the night of Friday, December 15th, when the
furniture had been moved in, and therefore the day of the
sixteenth when the last of it had been moved out again.

Pointer had opened the locked letter-box during the
clerk's short absence, and secured the contents which
were one letter addressed to Maitre Francois, and four
bills for M. Oreille. They were all postmarked from the
Tuesday to the Friday after Inskipp's murder. Pointer
guessed that after that date word had been sent to the
post office to forward Oreille's letters to a given address,
but that these had been delivered before the fact was
known that the office had been given up. In due course,
when the office should be let, the box would have been
emptied. He was anxious to be off now, for the letter
postmarked Calais was in Inskipp's writing. It had been
addressed merely to Clermont, and was pencilled with
writing which showed that it had gone first to Clermont
in the Oise department, north of Paris that was to say,
and then to Clermont-en-Argonne not far from Verdun,
and then to Clermont-l'Heroult down in the south, before
some brilliant postman scribbled on the envelope to try
Clermont-Ferrand, Puy de Dome. Its travels alone had
prevented it arriving before Oreille had decamped, for it
had been posted on the Sunday. As for the *film manque*,
the film which had never been taken, Pointer did not
think that that was the reason for the moving in and out
of the lordly furniture, which just covered the morning of
Inskipp's visit. Inskipp was to have any suspicions lulled
by the magnificence of the interior. The furniture, having
been often used, would not look new, and therefore be the
more impressive. The gilding had been skilfully done—a
pale, dull gold. The ceiling had been tinted to suggest
mellowness. That Inskipp had accepted things as
presented to him seemed indicated by his having left

Clermont-Ferrand so immediately for Paris and England. But Pointer would soon know.

He thanked Lambert, paid him for the time spent with him, sent many polite messages of thanks to the solicitor, and drove away.

On the way he opened Inskipp's letter. Inside was another letter addressed to Madame de Pra, with no address below. Around the enclosure was a piece of paper with the formula, *Faire suivre, s.v.p.*

Opening this enclosed letter, Pointer read:

"Between Paris and Calais,
"Sunday morning, 17th January.
"MIREILLE MES AMOURS,
"This isn't a letter, merely a word to you before
going on the boat which is to take me back to
England, away from France where my darling lives.
But only for a short time, sweetheart. Soon your
duty visits will be over and we can meet at last.
And now for my news. I had an interview with your
Maitre Francois in Clermont yesterday. He's rather
a rough diamond, isn't he. But a diamond all the
same. I had got nervous over the many delays about
your affairs. But he quite reassured me about the
divorce. Indeed he said that the news which we may
expect to get about it any day now is so good, that
he did not want to spoil the surprise for us. I don't
regret my visit, as my mind is now quite at rest, for
he was able to tell me too that the transference of
the loan is being immediately put through. That
means a lot to our future, darling. I can't put down
here in the swaying train half of what is in my heart,
as I think of you—my heart's desire. You know
what I wrote in my last. Every word of that long
letter holds good. Every word, most beautiful—
most dear. Farewell for the time being. To think
that there's a likelihood of our meeting soon—of
my at last seeing that lovely face, not merely its

portrait.
"With the fondest love of your own
"John."

"P.S.—I have a little water-colour sketch made
by me at the farm, to me it will always be the
wonderful place where I first saw and fell in love
with the portrait of the most beautiful girl in the
world. I didn't need poor Florence Rackstraw's
assurance that you were the sweetest too. I'm
going to have the sketch framed in town by a man
who does really good work. It'll be far too good for
the gift, but not nearly good enough for you to receive.
"J. I."

Pointer copied the note carefully, and sent it by
registered post to join the other copies of the case in the
Papers Department of the Yard before he got into the
plane and flew towards Cannes. At first, his thoughts
were busy with the letter. His mind traced the course of
the Mireille affair. Florence Rackstraw had started it,
with photographs taken from her brother's collection,
photographs of a dead girl to whom she had given two
Provencal names, the one all poetry—the other that of the
old woman who sold honey at the farm. There was malice
in that choice The loan spoken of in the letter as being
transferred was the thousand pounds. Pointer saw just
what had happened . . . and his mind swept on to the rest
of what had happened—that, too, he understood. And
now—the end was very near—and he ought to be able to
have the murderer arrested very shortly. But at Nice he
found that owing to the unexpected absence of the
prefect, the warrant requested must be taken out at
Menton. After the arrest—or rather detention—would
come the formal procedure of extradition, and the
handing over of the criminal to be taken back to England
there to stand his trial.

On to Menton, therefore, Pointer went in a car, and

found himself in a little town temporarily gone mad, for this was the afternoon of the third day of the lemon festival. The police station is a part of the *hotel de ville*, outside the door of which a pair of particularly engaging lemon trees hang their pendant balls of sunshine sky.

Pointer had no eye for their charm as he strode past, only to find that there was no question of his business being even considered to-day, for all the heads of departments were out at the unveiling of a monument by a cabinet minister.

Pointer handed in a letter against a receipt and asked that, as soon as the commissaire returned to the office, it be handed to him, as the matter was extremely urgent.

That done, Pointer went to the post-office telephone and rang up the farm. There was no reply. The telephone branch to Castellar was momentarily out of order, he was told, but they hoped to have it repaired within the hour.

He stood awhile outside the handsome post office building, deep in thought. A passing woman ogled him, and flung a handful of plaster confetti into his face. He did not look up. A band of young people went singing down the winding street a famous old song of good King Renews.

"O Magali, me fas de ben
Mais, tre ve veire
Ve lis estello. 0 Magali
Coume au pali."
He heard nothing.

It was late afternoon. The hour when the orange trees begin to show their full beauty, when the level rays of the sun make the fruit glow like luminous balls of radiance out of the green shadows; till each tree seems hung with crimson lanterns.

Pointer was blind to them, too, as he turned away, past Bosio's corner with the bust of Dr. Bennett, around to the bank.

CHAPTER 23: MRS. NORBURY IS MISSING

On the third day of the *Fetes du Citron*, the day on which Pointer had returned to Menton, Norbury drove off in a lorry to Sistrron. He needed to get a wheel of his new tractor straightened. He had hardly left, when a car drew up at the house and Mr. Squires, the manager of the English bank at Menton, got out. Rackstraw and Laroche met him on the step. They were just returning from a ramble. "Is anything wrong at the farm?" Squires asked, shaking hands.

"Not that I know of," said Rackstraw.

"What makes you ask?" came in unison from Laroche and from Pelham who had just appeared on the wide, much broken stone step.

"I passed Norbury's shepherd and offered him a lift. He refused it. And his manner was so grim. Yet, as a rule, these Provencals are a cheery, easy-going lot."

The bank manager and Pelham were introduced, and Pelham seemed curious about Du-Metri's manner. "He was driving the farm's show-cart, I thought," he said.

"He told me that his daughter had felt ill," explained Squires, "and that he left her and the cart down in Menton with some relatives. He seemed very—well—upset. Perhaps disappointment is the explanation of it . . . I saw him and a very pretty girl driving in the procession. These Provencals are like children—easily vexed. But this is not what I came to the farm about."

Mrs. Norbury came out then, and Squires explained that he had returned sooner than was expected from Turin, and had just heard of Inskipp's terrible end. What could have been the motive? Mr. Inskipp's solicitor, Mr. Parnall, he went on to say, had been inquiring at the bank about a transaction of Inskipp's which would, of course, in the normal way have been treated as confidential, but in view of what had happened to Inskipp—there followed a general talk as to what that could have been. Then the manager, prompted by Blythe, returned to the explanation of what had brought him to the farm, which was to hand over to Parnall a list of the numbers of some thousand-franc notes which had been taken away by Mr. Inskipp some time before his end. "Oh, dear me, yes, they were paid over to him in mid-November." Further than that Mr. Squires' revelations did not go.

He sat awhile with Mrs. Norbury in her sitting-room, and then, as her husband had not yet returned, the bank manager decided to take advantage of the chance offer of an empty taxi returning to Menton from the village, and left with his hostess an envelope containing a copy of the numbers of the notes in question to be handed to the supposed solicitor when he should return.

Mrs. Norbury stood at the gate and saw him off, then she turned to Pelham who seemed very much at a loose end, and who had sauntered after her and her guest.

"Mr. Squires said something to me just at the last moment about having been passed by my husband's shepherd on his way up here. That must mean Du-Metri. But Du-Metri and Sabe are in Menton! They won't get back till about nine to-night at the earliest." Mrs. Norbury went back to the house, and Pelham, after a moment, followed her. Was this of any importance, he was asking himself, and decided that it was not.

When Pointer stepped in at the English bank, he was shown into the room of the bank manager who had just returned.

"Mr. Parnall? I've but this moment got back from Norbury's farm, where I left with Mrs. Norbury for you the list of the numbers of the banknotes handed by us to Inskipp." The manager shook hands. He then went on to express his shock at learning of Inskipp's terrible and unaccountable end. He told of his own talk with the dead man about the reputation of Maitre Francois at Clermont-Ferrand. Apparently Inskipp had been given the famous lawyer's name, but was not quite sure of his standing. He, the manager, got the idea from the talk that Inskipp wanted to be sure that any money paid over to the avocat would be used scrupulously according to the instructions. He had also got the notion that there was some question of divorce on the carpet—which was, as he had told him, Maitre Francois' special, though by no means exclusive field.

"But now about his murder—have the police any clue?" he asked, lowering his voice as though the criminal might be one of his own clerks.

"I suppose they have," Pointer admitted "they're sure to have, I should think. Perhaps an arrest is quite close. Let's hope they get the murderer. Now about the numbers—can I have another copy? I suppose the one you left for me at the farm was securely sealed in an envelope?"

"Sealed? No." The manager looked uneasy. "No. Certainly not. The envelope flap was not stuck down. I had no idea the numbers were confidential. French notes! Surely there was no point even in giving you the list? After all these months." Mr. Squires was rattled by the suggestion that he had been at any fault in the matter. "I left the list with Mrs. Norbury, who promised to hand it to you herself. But—frankly—the three other men staying at the farm—Rackstraw is the only one I know—looked at the list, too. Just glanced at it, you know."

Pointer did not hope for much from the list, except as the starting point for laborious inquiries later on. He left the bank with yet another copy of the seventy-five numbers. He was able to dart across the road to the post office and try his luck at the telephone again. This time he was put through, and after a longish wait, he heard Pelham's voice.

"*'Ello! 'ello! Q'est que c'est?*"

"It's Parnall speaking," Pointer replied. "On my way back to the farm. How's everything?"

"Damned funny," was the reply. "Mrs. Norbury has disappeared. We're hunting for her. Norbury's beside himself. A postman was bashed over the head an hour ago on his way down to Menton not far from the farm— nothing whatever was taken, he swears. Apparently he was just slogged for the fun of the thing. And it was just about then that no one could find Mrs. Norbury. She's still missing. We've hunted high and low."

"What visitors have you had at the farm to-day?" Pointer asked at once.

"The bank manager from Menton. No one else. He left for you a list of the notes which he had once given Inskipp. Norbury is certain that the man who did for the postman must have laid his wife out somewhere. By the way, we're quite alone, there's no one in the house. So what are my orders?"

"Don't let Norbury out of your sight on any account whatever," said Pointer urgently. "He runs the greatest danger every moment that he's alone. Don't tell him so, but hurry off and find him at once—at once, Pelham! And stick to him like his shadow. I'm coming as soon as I can get there."

Pointer dashed the receiver on its hook and ran to a garage but a step away, where he was able to hire a first-class motor-bicycle. In a moment he was skimming out of the town. Once beyond its limits, he let her all out, and roared up and down the mule paths as though on a switchback. Could he get to the farm in time? Would Pelham obey orders absolutely, or forget and look for Mrs. Norbury—whom he probably would never find, since she had been missing for an hour. Mrs. Norbury would know every nook and corner of the farm and the country-side, and Pointer believed that she had put her knowledge to practical use.

About an hour after the bank manager had left, Mrs.

Norbury came to herself where she had been dropped on the floor of the barn. Her throat felt as though it had been circled with a ring of fire, as well it might, for the strangler's marks on it, plum- purple, explained why she had lost consciousness. What she did not understand was why she was alive—not killed outright. She knew that death had swept so close to her that she had heard the rustle of its wings. What had saved her? Not mercy or pity, that too, she knew. Then she heard Rackstraw's name being called just outside the barn on the floor of which she was lying. And she understood that a call had saved her—for the moment.

The door of the barn was shut, but she could crawl to it, and then—when the speakers had passed out of sight, she might be able to slip out. She found that she could not move an inch in its direction. As some people cannot jump from a sinking ship or a falling plane, her muscles refused to obey her will. Or was it that beneath the surface-will another will refused to give the command? Mrs. Norbury had looked murder full in its horrible face—the shock had been profound. Her mind refused to right itself. She heard Rackstraw's voice. She heard Blythe and then Laroche . . . she knew that now was the time to call for help and escape the doom so very close at hand. But she could not stir—she could not make her tortured throat let one sound pass. She cowered closer to the floor where she had been dropped, when a hand had all but touched the unlocked door of the barn where she was clutched in a silent death-struggle. She lay motionless while the voices receded. Then came a sound at the door and she sank still lower on the boards. But it was the noise of the door being locked, of the key being swiftly pulled out, and then there was again only the receding voices, talking about the fete down in Menton.

Now she was locked in—to be the more completely at the mercy of the murderer when he could slip back unnoticed. At that, the power of motion at last came back to her body. She staggered to her feet and unbolted the shutter of the unglazed window. Heavily, stiffly, she clambered through the opening, and swung the shutters shut as best she could with a couple of swift jerks. She might have only a few minutes' grace in which to hide. And all her dulled mind was concentrated on hiding till it should be dark, and she could really escape. She was not capable of any sweep of thought. She was still too stupefied with her danger. But inside a little circle her mind moved swiftly and surely. Where could she hide? Nowhere, was the answer. Nowhere. There was no hay kept at the farm, no fodder for cattle. That meant no hayricks, or barns, or lofts. The trees? Mrs. Norbury had never climbed a tree in her life, even supposing that there was one nearby that could have hidden her. The grain and corn in the fields were but a span high as yet. In the house, too, there was nothing that would detain a searcher. Yet she had but to raise her voice and she would have been safe. But she could not even get one sound out from those squeezed cords. Also, there are those—of which she was one—who in moments of extreme peril seem to revert to some distant age, before speech—before cries—were possible. To such, a shout—a word—is the last thing that the cornered mind suggests.

Flight, soundless—and noiseless. Concealment. Absolute silence—these alone occur to such brains. And Mrs. Norbury, standing trembling outside the barn, could think of no possible spot in which to hide. The scarecrow facing her swayed and seemed to bow grotesquely. He had been rifled of his straw for the cart, the "Mas Provencal." True, some one had stuffed rags in place of the straw, but they were already slipping out as he swung in the breeze.

A wild notion came to her. She ran to him where he stood, not in the field of maize which was a mass of trim little hillocks, Norbury had not allowed any careless foot to be put on those laborious ridges, but in a corner of the lemon orchard. In a second she had stripped off her dress, made, like all her dresses. in one. For a moment she stood in her shorts and trim underbodice, then she flung her rolled-up dress far into the nearest hedge. That done, she ran to the scarecrow and pulled on the trousers, old ones of Norbury's, spread the stiff, square, head cloth of the dummy over her own head, and tied it around her neck with the same piece of half-rotten rope, slipped into the overcoat, and put the battered hat rakishly on one side of her head. Her feet were far short of the openings to the trouser legs, her hands far above the edge of the sleeves, for she was a little woman. A broken rake was close by, probably it had been used to collect the straw. She drove it with one strong thrust deep into the earth at the foot of the scarecrow to about the right height to support her in a half-sitting position. Then, each hand holding a bundle of rags, she slipped her arms through the rope bracelets which had fastened the scarecrow's arms to the wooden cross-piece, and took up her position. The cloth had had two black buttons sewn on in place of eyes, she had torn them off, and in so doing tore the weather-beaten calico. That was all to the good. She could see out with ease. Half-seated on the teeth of the rake, half-standing on a big stone which had been placed at the foot of the scarecrow to brace it upright, she waited, her heart beating almost to suffocation. If she could pass muster— and she believed that she could—she might hope to escape when darkness fell.

It seemed a long time before she saw a man walking swiftly towards the locked door of the barn, saw him look about him, quickly take a key from his pocket, unlock the door, and, stepping inside, shut it behind him. But only for a moment. The next, he was out again and rushing round to the window through which she had climbed. Back again, he stood at the door, apparently trying to guess where she had gone, and Mrs. Norbury's heart began to flutter so wildly that she thrust her arms still farther into the bracelets—if she fainted again as she had when the fingers had closed so cruelly around her neck they might have to bear her full weight.

An hour later Norbury ran into Laroche just outside the gate of the farm. The Frenchman had just been told at the post office of an extraordinary and savage attack on the village postman, who was taking the post down to Menton as usual, when, hearing a sound behind him, he turned in the same instant that a blow stretched him senseless on the path. When he came to and looked over his box of letters, which he carried like a pedlar in front of him, swinging by a leather strap around his neck, he made certain that nothing had been taken, though everything had been searched and tossed about. There had only been an exact dozen of ordinary letters, besides five registered ones, and some packets. All were there. In fact, as he had reported at the post office, everything was exactly as it had been, bar the addition of a big lump on the top of his head.

Norbury seemed only amused at the recital, and suggested a falling branch off a tree as the criminal. But a little later he burst in on the four men sitting having cocktails, with a very worried face.

"Where's my wife? Has any one seen her? She's nowhere to be found."

The others said that since lunch they had not seen Mrs. Norbury. Norbury went over to his wife's desk in a corner of the room. Lying on it he noticed the envelope left by the bank manager. Sticking down the flap, he went himself to put it in Parnall's room. Then he went out calling his wife's name. The uneasiness in his voice communicated itself to the others. They jumped up—all except Blythe, who had just opened a couple of to-day's newspapers left by the Menton bank manager for the guests, and who was staring at the front page's headlines.

"Whin-Browning Poisoning Case Solved in Dramatic Fashion."

The other paper had the same sized lines but its heading ran:

"Mrs. Whin-Browning Innocent. Warrant Withdrawn. Is She Still Alive?"

He sat plunged in the reading of the columns below while Rackstraw, Laroche and Pelham hunted with Norbury for his wife. But they hunted to no purpose.

"She's gone down to Menton with the bank manager," expostulated Rackstraw.

"Without telling me? Leaving us to get supper for ourselves!" Norbury said sharply.

Pelham said that Mrs. Norbury had not gone with Mr. Squires.

"I'm wondering now if that postman met a madman," Norbury went on. "I don't like my wife's absence—after that tale of his! I want to know where she is."

"What about trying the dog?" suggested Laroche finally.

Norbury took the dog off the chain, but Hero was no bloodhound. He was a sheepdog as much as he was anything, and went by his eyes, not his smell. Nor did he understand in the least what was wanted of him. His freedom seemed to him a heaven-sent opportunity to pay off some old scores with the cat. That done—or rather, attempted—he went and lay down at the foot of the scarecrow.

Laroche laughed.

"Strikes are in the air—Hero has struck too."

But from the motionless scarecrow a low, hissing sound had reached Hero's ear.

"*Posso!*" It is the Provencal word to send a dog off, just as *Fut!* is used for a cat. Hero knew those two syllables well, which he alone could hear.

He rose and slunk back to the men who wanted him to do some incomprehensible thing—play with his mistress's gloves apparently. Once more he gave it up, and lay down, this time at Norbury's feet, who marched him off to his kennel and chain.

Suddenly a sound reached the others. It was a cry

from the room they had just left. Blythe reading the papers as though his life depended on it.

They stepped back hurriedly to see Miss Blythe snatch the papers from him and run with them up to her own room. She had just caught sight of the headings.

"Has she won a prize for a crossword puzzle?" asked Laroche. Edna was wont to pass long hours at that amusement.

"I don't know," replied Blythe in an oddly shaken voice. Then he, too, hurried after Edna.

"Look here, Norbury"—Rackstraw had had enough of hunting for the lady of the house—"you're working yourself up needlessly—and getting the wind up for nothing. Mrs. Norbury is safe and sound, probably in Menton. If not, then at the village shop in Castellar—"

"It's closed during the afternoons of the fete," said Norbury.

"Then she's having her hair waved. Anyway, she's safe somewhere."

But Norbury went on hunting, and so, therefore, did Pelham, for he had just answered the telephone a few minutes earlier. And so finally, as though to make up for his negligence of just now, did Blythe.

Rackstraw tailed behind looking very disgusted with things.

"Why don't you get Du-Metri to help? That bank manager fellow said he passed him on the way up here," he suggested.

Norbury did not trouble to stop, he only called out that Squires was talking through his hat, that he didn't know Du-Metri by sight.

This was the scene which Pointer found when he whizzed up on his machine.

CHAPTER 24: A SCARECROW IS THE MAIN INCIDENT IN THE ROUNDING-UP OF A MURDERER

"Mrs. Norbury?" Pointer asked, as Pelham went to meet him.

Pelham shook his head.

Norbury came up and told again of the strange incident of the postman and of the savage blow that had stunned him.

"It looks to me as though my wife might have seen the incident, recognised the man perhaps, and been laid out too," he finished.

"Or heard of it, and got frightened," Pointer suggested. "Suppose we all go round the farm calling out that everything's all right. That there's no danger in her coming out now? Has any one questioned Miss Blythe? From one of her windows she may have seen Mrs. Norbury."

"Miss Blythe!" called Norbury instantly.

Out over the balcony leant Miss Blythe in prompt response. The men stared at her in bewilderment. This was not Miss Blythe, surely! This was her younger and very pretty sister. As to whether she had seen Mrs. Norbury after lunch, Edna said that she had—quite latish. She had seen her going out of the gates dressed as though for a call—that way! She pointed.

"What did I tell you, Norbury?" said Rackstraw triumphantly. "I knew it!"

For answer there was a shout of: "That's the man! There he is! *Halte la!_*" Norbury fired as he shouted. He was a very good shot indeed, but he only hit the branch of an old olive tree, for Pointer had struck his arm up with his walking stick.

"Don't fire at that scarecrow, Norbury—your wife's inside!"

Pointer shot Pelham a meaning glance as he let go Norbury's arm which he had grasped.

There was a gasp from the men around, as Pointer strode to the scarecrow. They saw him cut the rope-bracelets and gather up the extraordinary figure in his arms.

"It's Mrs. Norbury, all right!" he added to the others, "she's fainted."

At that moment two cars swung in through the gates. His burden in his arms, Pointer wheeled to face them. Pelham tightened his grasp of Norbury, who asked him what the devil he meant by keeping him away from his wife.

But the commissaire getting out of the first car saved Pelham a reply. One swift glance expressed polite surprise at finding the chief inspector holding the farm scarecrow tenderly in his arms. But Pointer silently made for the dining-room, while the men from the second car grouped themselves around Norbury.

"In the Name of the Law," said the commissaire. "On sworn information I detain you, Frank Norbury, for the murder in England of John Inskipp on the fifteenth of January. You will be handed over to the representative of British justice in due course, and be taken to England to stand your trial. *Vive la Republique.*"

Like a wild animal's was Norbury's leap for the orchard.

Pelham had been utterly taken by surprise. He had held Norbury back to save him from danger, not because of any suspicion of him. Now he would have rushed forward but Pointer's calm voice through the dining-room windows checked him. "Better leave it to them, Pelham!" The chief inspector knew how susceptible the French can be, when it is a question of an arrest on French soil. It was a pity that the others were too far off to have a chance of stopping the running man, for the police had made the mistake of thinking of Norbury—in spite of the accusation against him—as the Norbury whom they had hitherto known. They had left a place open in their circle, and he had dashed through. Pointer felt sure that he was making for some definite objective known only to himself, prepared by himself within the last couple of hours for this emergency—improbable though it had seemed. A ladder against a wall somewhere, and a car on the other side he rightly guessed, and once in the car, there would be scant hope of capture, with Italy so close. Norbury would know the frontier twists and turns like any smuggler. He would be sure to have plenty of friends among those gentry, too, on both sides of the frontier. Once let him get clear of the farm, and he stood a very good chance of escape. He was running, too, like a trained athlete. Pointer bent over the scarecrow that he had laid on the sofa. So he did not see the tall figure that rose suddenly in front of Norbury and closed with him just before he reached the hedge. Du-Metri had muscles of iron. He needed them.

The gendarmes were at his side in a moment. It took the three of them to master Norbury, who fought first for freedom, and then for the possession of one of the policemen's revolvers. Once he broke away for an instant—once he all but got the revolver in his grasp. Round and round on the ground the tangled heap surged, all arms, and legs, and heads, and boots, but in the end the policemen rose, pulled a handcuffed, very battered Norbury to his feet, hauled him to the car, slung him in, tumbled in after him, and drove off. The scene had had a nightmare quality of lack of speech about it, which suggested something seen in a motion-picture show.

"I wish I'd had a cinema camera," said Rackstraw breathlessly. He had not offered to join in the struggle.

"I found a note to Sabe slipped in the basket of confetti," came, in heavy breathing, from Du-Metri.

"Asking her to meet him at the wine vats—to meet him—my daughter!" Du-Metri became too Mentonnais to be coherent. One of the gendarmes took him to the kitchen, while the guests at the farm followed the commissaire into the room where Pointer had laid what he claimed was Mrs. Norbury down on the farm's one sofa. He had already untied the rope around the neck which held the calico cover in place, and they all now saw the white little face inside it. They saw, too, the four purple bruises on the one side of her neck and the dark, single mark on the other where the strangler had got his grip on her.

"Brandy!" said Pointer. And held it to her lips—"if she can swallow"—but Mrs. Norbury could not.

He had to content himself with trickling a very little water between her parched lips.

"What happened here?" asked the commissaire, helping to fill the spoon. "I have your letter—but what is the reason of this?"

"The Menton bank manager left the numbers with Mrs. Norbury of the notes that he had handed Inskipp to the amount of a thousand pounds"—Pointer broke off to see if by altering the position of the unconscious woman they could get her to swallow.

"But Norbury knew we all knew the numbers," put in Pelham, "He didn't try to harm any of us!"

"Evidently, therefore, the notes didn't matter to any one but Mrs. Norbury," Pointer explained without looking round. "So she must have known some fact about them, and, I feel sure, taxed him with it. The two were in Marseilles together making purchases for the farm after the notes were paid to Inskipp by the bank. Finding that she had some dangerous knowledge—or proof—he evidently tried to strangle her, and only some lucky chance must have saved her life—for the moment—and given her time to slip into the scarecrow's clothes, and take its place in that orchard."

Edna hurried in the without asking any questions, relieved Pointer from his place at the head of the sofa. She, too, had been spellbound by the suddenness and the violence of the scene which she had watched.

"Money?" echoed Laroche, "ah, if Inskipp was killed

for money, it would be Norbury, undoubtedly! Some securities left here in his charge, I suppose, when Inskipp went to England, and which Norbury decided were too good to have to hand back? But where does the postman come in? Was that Norbury's doing too, hein?" He turned to Pointer, so did the commissaire, who had not yet heard the last piece of news.

"I think we shall find that Norbury had been told by his wife that she had posted some letter, possibly containing one of the notes in question, or some information, to the police, and wanted to secure it. I take it she said that, hoping to save herself when she saw how unwise she had been to tackle him alone in a room—or a barn—about the matter."

Mrs. Norbury gave a sort of gasping choke. Edna's massage had helped her to swallow a sip of brandy, and a few minutes later she was carried to her room where they left her with Edna and Sabe.

The commissaire and Pointer had a long talk in a room to themselves, guarded by a policeman with a bulging holster. Laroche shot Pointer a keen glance at the name and title by which the commissaire called him as he shook hands finally and hurried out to his car.

Pointer found that Edna, since the doctor was down in Menton, had, with the sublime confidence of ignorance, given Mrs. Norbury a strong sleeping draught such as she herself had so often had to take. It had calmed the woman almost instantly, and

she was now sleeping heavily.

"I hope I've done right," Edna said a trifle fearfully.

Like many other people, she asked herself that a trifle belatedly. But Mrs. Norbury appeared to be sleeping tranquilly. Pointer said as much. And then he asked her why she had said that she had seen Mrs. Norbury passing through the farm-gates dressed as for a call.

Edna flushed. "I did see her, but slipping round the corner of the barn," she confessed, "and her face—and her manner of doing it "she paused for a second. Then she looked full at the chief inspector. "*I* know what terror looks like—and feels like! Naturally one thought of Mr. Norbury—I never liked him. And I didn't think she did— much. So on the off-chance that it might be of use to her I said that I had seen her making for the opposite direction from the one she had really been taking."

She stopped to look down at the sleeping figure. By this time the arrest of Norbury for the murder had been discussed over and over again by the guests at the farm.

"I suppose there's no question of his being acquitted?" she asked now, in a low voice.

Pointer said that he did not see any possibility of such a miscarriage of justice.

"And she will be pilloried everywhere as a murderer's wife. A ghastly fate. I like Mrs. Norbury." She folded an outflung hand into a more comfortable position. "She's straight. And she's any amount of grit. She would make a splendid pioneer. I'm thinking of taking her with me on the world-tour which I'm planning after my affairs are cleared up. She will probably be free from giving evidence against her husband by then—and will be glad to come. We may find some spot on the other side of the world where we can start life afresh. My mother will come too."

They talked for a few minutes and then Pointer slipped out again. Laroche stopped him to ask after Mrs. Norbury. That done, the Frenchman hesitated a second.

"How in the world did you guess that she was hidden in the scarecrow?" he asked curiously.

Pointer did not explain. On the way to the farm, rushing up hill and down dale, he had decided that it alone would offer any chance of concealment to a desperate woman. And inspecting it with very carefully-veiled intentness, he had, just at the last, seen the eyes move. He was not certain, however, but that Mrs. Norbury was in hiding in order to learn some vital fact in the case. It was only when he saw that Norbury, too, had seen the eyes move, and saw him in the same instant draw his revolver, that he had to act.

"Do you know, I all but called attention to the fact that the dog had lain down at the foot of the scarecrow when we wanted him to hunt for his mistress," went on Laroche, as the other remained silent. "Norbury was turned away from him, scanning the hedges, and it was on the tip of my tongue to say that Hero seemed to mix up Mrs. Norbury and *l'dpouvantail*—but because it hardly sounded polite, I left it unsaid. My mother complains that I have no notion of manners. But I shall be able to tell her that it was precisely that that saved a life—for I think he might have caught on to the idea then at once—eh? And you would not have been there to save her!" Laroche looked really moved.

"Just as well you didn't make your little joke," Pointer agreed. Norbury is very quick, I fancy, in spite of always referring to himself as a slow-witted farmer."

Laroche nodded assent. "And he is absolutely ruthless—and heartless absolutely—and only cares for money. A true farmer in some ways," said Laroche. "As I said just now, if money was the motive for Inskipp's murder, Norbury could have been predicted to be the answer. And he deceived us by his earnest desire to find his wife. There is no deception like truth. I have been expounding the reasons to Pelham. By the way, since you are not a solicitor, nor called Parnall—what is he? And what is his real name?"

Pointer explained that Pelham had not needed an alias. He himself had.

" I have been hearing from Pelham the really formidable chain of deductions that led you here," Laroche continued, "Or would you call them guesses?"

"No, routine work," replied Pointer, passing on, while Laroche burst out laughing.

In the morning, they found that Mrs. Norbury had waked up quite her usual self; and to Pointer's relief he discovered that she had no reluctance whatever to giving away her husband. Chiefly from genuine horror of what he had done, but partly also from the growing dislike of

the man, that Edna Whin-Browning had divined. Mrs.
Norbury had wanted back the money that she had put
into the farm so as to be able to leave him. As Pointer had
thought, she had recognised one of the numbers of the
notes when, after the manager had left, she had read
through the list carefully. For when they had gone to the
Marseilles at the end of December, she had noticed that
Norbury was always slipping away from her. She
suspected some other woman, and had followed him—to
five banks. Watching, she saw him change a thousand-
franc note in each. He paid, too, for their purchases,
entirely in thousand- franc notes, and had dealt—though
she had not noticed the significance of this—entirely with
shops where he and she were not known. She bought back
one of the notes which he had just changed, found that it
was perfectly good, but kept it. It was the number of this
note which she had read on the list handed in by the
manager. And when Norbury refused to explain how he
came to have had it in his possession at Marseilles, it was
her false assertion that they would soon see about that,
as she had just explained, when and how it had come into
her possession, and posted the explanation to the Menton
police which had led him, when he found her gone from
the locked barn, to hurry after the postman in rubber
shoes, stun him, and search his postbag. What had saved
her life had been, as she thought, Laroche calling and
looking for Rackstraw who was late for a proposed jaunt
over the hills together. Norbury, who had snatched his
wife by the throat in a passion of murderous fury, knew
that in another minute the Frenchman would try the door
of the barn—and that it was unlocked. His wife hung
limp in his grip. He dropped what he thought was her
dead body on the floor, stepped out, walked on with
Laroche, slipped back to lock the door of the barn when
Rackstraw joined them, and then went on a little way
with Blythe and Pelham. It was the latter's chance
insistence on questioning Norbury about some of the
lemons in a farther orchard which had given the half-

dazed Mrs. Norbury time to hide in the scarecrow.

Had his shot killed Mrs. Norbury, her husband would afterwards have sworn that he saw a stranger slipping behind the hedge, and fired at him—if indeed any one had noticed that the scarecrow was sagging still more after the shot. Had they not done so, he would have claimed a miss and disposed of her body during the night, and what had really happened to his wife would have always remained a mystery. Just as it would have, had he really strangled her in the barn.

Pointer was called several times to the telephone that evening and once even at midnight. The name of Oreille seemed to occur a good deal, and after the last time that he was summoned the chief inspector looked as though a load were off his mind. Christopher only glanced at him now and then as he made an occasion to pass, but he had been promised that, on the return journey next morning, he would be told everything, and he was patient. Besides, he was much more interested, hearing the answers to questions, the first of which concerned himself, than with any queries about Oreille.

"Look here," said Christopher, as he and Pointer stood on the platform at Menton and watched the train swing out that was carrying Norbury back to England between two very burly fellow-passengers, who kept always one or other hand thrust through his arm, "Look here, I know the cat must only look at the king, far less question his Majesty, but why did you tell me over the telephone, when Mrs. Norbury was missing, to take such care of Norbury? Why stuff me about his being in danger?"

"I wanted to prevent his finding his wife at some moment when he was by himself, and immediately finishing her off," Pointer said gravely.

"—as he would have done!"

"Also, it's ghastly work pretending to be friends with a man whom you believe to be a murderer," Pointer's voice took on a deeper note, "let alone suspect of being on the verge of a second murder. You would have had to talk to him—sympathise with him—perhaps drink and eat with him—take his hand—I assure you, there's nothing harder to do! So I thought I would spare you that —if I could. Also," his eyes twinkled, "I don't know how good an actor you are. And it takes uncommonly good acting to deceive a man who's watching for the shadow of the rope. Norbury was not to be suspect that he was suspected. But there's our train just coming in."

The two were only going as far as Nice and the British Consulate-General for to-night. When they were seated in an empty compartment, Christopher leant forward.

"Thanks for sparing me. I certainly should have loathed the job and equally certainly should have bungled it," he said. "But when did you first suspect Norbury? I had no idea—somehow I never thought of him. He looked what he called himself—such a typical farmer."

"When did I first suspect him?" Pointer was in no doubt about that. "When 1 first got to the farm and learnt that the dog was let loose at night. His kennel was near the scarecrow from which the clothes were taken. That couldn't have been done noiselessly, and he would have barked at any one but his master. That seemed to show that Norbury was either an accomplice or the murderer. Probably the latter, since there seemed no need of help in this crime. But that was only my notion. The Whin-Browning complication had to be cleared up first."

"Did he rely on it to throw off suspicion, do you think?" Pelham asked, "since he knew about them."

"I think he counted most of all on the tramp-effect of the dead body passing muster for genuine," Pointer said, "as it would have done but for two women both having claimed the body."

"As it would have done but for you!" Christopher protested energetically, "My uncle told me how you saw through that disguise—and that the clothes had come off a scarecrow, and then found that the scarecrow had stood in a maize field near a lemon grove. Then, that in France, lemon orchards are to be found only at Menton—which led you to the Farm of the Golden Goat."

"A straight line, and purely routine work," said Pointer quickly. Since the arrest he had found copies of all the letters to Oreille and Oreille's actual replies, and copies of all the letters to and from Inskipp about Mireille first from Florence Rackstraw.

There was a short silence. Christopher, as well as the others at the farm, had been told about the money obtained by Norbury from Inskipp in the name of a fictitious Mireille. Rackstraw had given Pointer a very intent look, but he had made no observation when the chief inspector had said that Norbury had evidently taken the portraits of the so-called Mireille from his— Rackstraw's—photographs, and then invented a character to fit which would be sure to captivate the romantic, lonely Inskipp.

"Frankly," Christopher said now, "I can't imagine what set Norbury off on the idea of the lovely Mireille. A girl who was dead before he ever saw her portrait! It worked—up to a point. But how did he come to think of it? It seems so out of his line of country. Laroche can't sleep at night, he tells me, for puzzling over it."

Pointer explained the origin of the trick that had been played on Inskipp. Spite on the part of Florence Rackstraw—and a desire to humiliate Inskipp's very soul when she would have the joy of telling him of the deception, which had set a ball rolling that in the end had led to Inskipp's murder. "Mrs. Norbury suggests that it was when Norbury was hunting for the mother's address to let her know of the daughter's tragedy that he found those copies of the letters written by Florence to Inskipp that we have just discovered among his personal papers. Sabe's evidence, too, will be taken about the change in the postmarks just after the death of Miss Rackstraw."

"Sabe seems only excited about Norbury's arrest—not in the lest heart-broken," put in Christopher, who had a soft spot for the pretty Mentonnaise.

"That's all. Her father feels that he paid back

handsomely whatever score there was to settle, by collaring Norbury so usefully. Luckily for Sabe, Mrs. Norbury was on the qui vive about the girl, though she had not thought of connecting her flightiness with her own husband. She suspected Rackstraw or even Blythe, of being the trifler, she says."

Again there was a pause, as the train carried them along the wonderful coastline at which neither man so much as glanced.

"Norbury was starting to sell his farm—without Mrs. Norbury's knowledge. The place was bought in both his and his wife's names, but I think he would have managed to swindle her out of her share in the proceeds," Pointer said next.

"Trust him!" The fervour of Christopher's tone meant just the opposite.

"You think that Norbury would have sold—and vanished?"

"I do. He was getting things ready, and he was a good planner."

"Just what did the Whin-Browning story stand for in his plans, do you think?" asked Christopher after another pause.

Pointer's explanation started earlier in the tale.

"When Norbury knew that he would have to pay back that thousand pounds and risk being prosecuted and convicted, he foresaw that probably Inskipp would have to be killed." Pointer was lighting his pipe.

"And when did that dawn on him?"

"When he saw an envelope handed to Inskipp from Clermont-Ferrand in another writing than Oreille's, he must have suspected—wrongly, as it happens—that Oreille had fallen down on the task of completing the hoodwinking of the poor victim. When he watched Inskipp's appalled face, he guessed that the game was up. We know now that Norbury came down late for dinner and excused himself with a tale about wandering around corridors and not finding lift or stairs. I shouldn't be surprised if he had slipped into Inskipp's room and read that Clermont-Ferrand letter, left probably by Inskipp in his suitcase. Norbury's keys, we find, would have unlocked it. What he read would tell him that he would be wise to get Inskipp out of the way at once. He may have written the note as much to get a chance to read the letter from France, as with any idea of settling matters there and then, but once he read it, he would know that there was no time to lose. He went to the appointment carrying a small despatch case containing the clothes off the scarecrow, and the sock with the brass bed-knob in it. The sand he could get on the spot."

Christopher digested this swiftly. "And the Whin-Browning story?" he asked again. "I wonder why he didn't go all out on it."

"I take Norbury to be a man who dislikes to alter a plan," said Pointer. "The tramp scheme was simple and promised well. But should it go wrong there was the other to fall back on. Inskipp had supplied him with the name of the maid in Dover, thinking him a helper—or at least a sympathiser. Norbury talked to me, and he probably had to Inskipp, of his belief in Mrs. Whin-Browning's innocence—but he really was certain that she was guilty. That I'll swear. And because of that certainty, he imagined that she would be a perfect second-line of defence if by any chance things went wrong with his tramp plan. The success of that must, of necessity, largely depend on circumstances beyond absolute certainty."

"Inskipp might not have gone to the rendezvous," suggested Pelham.

"Exactly. Or there might have been other people in the shelter."

"Or a lamp might have lit up the interior too clearly?" Pelham again proffered. But Pointer shook his head.

"Norbury is a cautious villain. He had inspected that shelter before he chose it, we may be sure."

"And, of course, he wrote the letter to Rackstraw giving him every conceivable right in Inskipp's scenario—

" Christopher gave a reminiscent chuckle at the man's cunning.

"Of course. And so could point out afterwards how odd he thought it!" The detective officer, too, gave a grim smile, adding that there was nothing so easy to pass off successfully as a forgery when no suspicions were roused.

There followed a long silence.

"Mrs. Norbury's evidence about the thousand-franc note will stand any cross-questioning." Pointer's tone was one of deep satisfaction. "You can't bully Mrs. Norbury into changing black into white. And then, above all, the French police have got hold of Oreille."

Christopher was only mildly interested. "You seem very keen on Oreille, but I take it he stood for nothing in the actual crime, only in the deception?"

"His character meant the difference between life and death to Inskipp. Rather in Laroche's strain that, but I think it's true none the less," was the slow reply, spoken very gravely.

"You mean 'all the more,'" prompted Christopher, whose forehead was wrinkling as he thought over the other's last words. He did not follow the reasoning behind them, and said so after a short silence.

"As I see it, Inskipp's death, after his claim for the return of his thousand pounds, was necessary only because Oreille couldn't be trusted," said Pointer. "Otherwise, he would only have had to disappear, and Inskipp could never have cleared up the taking of the money, or the truth about Mireille, who would merely have 'disappeared' too."

Christopher frowned at his own dullness. "You run faster than I can," he said ruefully. "You're right, of course." There followed a short silence.

"Miss Blythe—that name is shorter—doesn't seem to dislike Blythe any more. He's showing up very well, I think."

"He finally realised that things couldn't have run on along his proposed lines much longer. And possibly—just possibly," Pointer's eyes twinkled, "he, too, may have found, during the months at the farm, that there are more agreeable companions than a captive."

"And thanks to you she's free—"Pelham gave a little crow of sheer enthusiasm.

This time Pointer gave him one of his swift, transforming smiles.

"That's a plum such as doesn't often come my way—though, mind you, every criminal caught means innocent people freed from the danger of suspicion, let alone of a false arrest—or a wrong verdict." And the chief inspector knocked out his pipe with a feeling that he could now enjoy a well-earned rest.

FINIS

Other Resurrected Press Books in *The Chief Inspector Pointer* <u>*Mystery*</u> Series

Murder at Bridge

When an afternoon bridge party attended by some of Hamilton's leading citizens ends with the hostess being murdered in her boudoir, Special Investigator Dundee of the District Attorney's office is called in. But one of the attendees is guilty? There are plenty of suspects: the victim's former lover, her current suitor, the retired judge who is being blackmailed, the victim's maid who had been horribly disfigured accidentally by the murdered woman, or any of the women who's husbands had flirted with the victim. Or was she murdered by an outsider whose motive had nothing to do with the town of Hamilton. Find the answer in . . . **Murder at Bridge**

One Drop of Blood

When Dr. Koenig, head of Mayfield Sanitarium is murdered, the District Attorney's Special Investigator, "Bonnie" Dundee must go undercover to find the killer. Were any of the inmates of the asylum insane enough to have committed the crime? Or, was it one of the staff, motivated by jealousy? And what was is the secret in the murdered man's past. Find the answer in . . . **One Drop of Blood**

AVAILABLE FROM RESURRECTED PRESS!

GEMS OF MYSTERY
LOST JEWELS FROM A MORE
ELEGANT AGE

Three wonderful tales of mystery from some of the best known writers of the period before the First World War -

A foggy London night, a Russian princess who steals jewels, a corpse; a mysterious murder, an opera singer, and stolen pearls; two young people who crash a masked ball only to find themselves caught up in a daring theft of jewels; these are the subjects of this collection of entertaining tales of love, jewels, and mystery. This collection includes:

- **In the Fog - by Richard Harding Davis's**

- **The Affair at the Hotel Semiramis - by A.E.W. Mason**

- **Hearts and Masks - Harold MacGrath**

AVAILABLE FROM RESURRECTED PRESS!

THE EDWARDIAN DETECTIVES
LITERARY SLEUTHS OF THE EDWARDIAN ERA

The exploits of the great Victorian Detectives, Poe's C. Auguste Dupin, Gaboriau's Lecoq, and most famously, Arthur Conan Doyle's Sherlock Holmes, are well known. But what of those fictional detectives that came after, those of the Edwardian Age? The period between the death of Queen Victoria and the First World War had been called the Golden Age of the detective short story, but how familiar is the modern reader with the sleuths of this era? And such an extraordinary group they were, including in their numbers an unassuming English priest, a blind man, a master of disguises, a lecturer in medical jurisprudence, a noble woman working for Scotland Yard, and a savant so brilliant he was known as "The Thinking Machine."

To introduce readers to these detectives, Resurrected Press has assembled a collection of stories featuring these and other remarkable sleuths in The Edwardian Detectives.

- The Case of Laker, Absconded by Arthur Morrison
- The Fenchurch Street Mystery by Baroness Orczy
- The Crime of the French Café by Nick Carter
- The Man with Nailed Shoes by R Austin Freeman
- The Blue Cross by G. K. Chesterton
- The Case of the Pocket Diary Found in the Snow by Augusta Groner
- The Ninescore Mystery by Baroness Orczy
- The Riddle of the Ninth Finger by Thomas W. Hanshew
- The Knight's Cross Signal Problem by Ernest Bramah

- The Problem of Cell 13 by Jacques Futrelle
- The Conundrum of the Golf Links by Percy James Brebner
- The Silkworms of Florence by Clifford Ashdown
- The Gateway of the Monster by William Hope Hodgson
- The Affair at the Semiramis Hotel by A. E. W. Mason
- The Affair of the Avalanche Bicycle & Tyre Co., LTD by Arthur Morrison

RESURRECTED PRESS CLASSIC MYSTERY CATALOGUE

Journeys into Mystery
Travel and Mystery in a More Elegant Time

The Edwardian Detectives
Literary Sleuths of the Edwardian Era

Gems of Mystery
Lost Jewels from a More Elegant Age

E. C. Bentley
Trent's Last Case: The Woman in Black

Ernest Bramah
Max Carrados Resurrected:
The Detective Stories of Max Carrados

Agatha Christie
The Secret Adversary
The Mysterious Affair at Styles

Octavus Roy Cohen
Midnight

Freeman Wills Croft
The Ponson Case
The Pit Prop Syndicate

J. S. Fletcher
The Herapath Property
The Rayner-Slade Amalgamation
The Chestermarke Instinct
The Paradise Mystery
Dead Men's Money

The Middle of Things
Ravensdene Court
Scarhaven Keep
The Orange-Yellow Diamond
The Middle Temple Murder
The Tallyrand Maxim
The Borough Treasurer
In the Mayor's Parlour
The Saftey Pin

R. Austin Freeman
The Mystery of 31 New Inn from the Dr. Thorndyke Series
John Thorndyke's Cases from the Dr. Thorndyke Series
The Red Thumb Mark from The Dr. Thorndyke Series
The Eye of Osiris from The Dr. Thorndyke Series
A Silent Witness from the Dr. John Thorndyke Series
The Cat's Eye from the Dr. John Thorndyke Series
Helen Vardon's Confession: A Dr. John Thorndyke Story
As a Thief in the Night: A Dr. John Thorndyke Story
Mr. Pottermack's Oversight: A Dr. John Thorndyke Story
Dr. Thorndyke Intervenes: A Dr. John Thorndyke Story
The Singing Bone: The Adventures of Dr. Thorndyke
The Stoneware Monkey: A Dr. John Thorndyke Story
The Great Portrait Mystery, and Other Stories: A Collection of Dr. John Thorndyke and Other Stories
The Penrose Mystery: A Dr. John Thorndyke Story
The Uttermost Farthing: A Savant's Vendetta

Arthur Griffiths
The Passenger From Calais
The Rome Express

Fergus Hume
The Mystery of a Hansom Cab
The Green Mummy
The Silent House
The Secret Passage

Edgar Jepson
The Loudwater Mystery

A. E. W. Mason
At the Villa Rose

A. A. Milne
The Red House Mystery
Baroness Emma Orczy
The Old Man in the Corner

Edgar Allan Poe
The Detective Stories of Edgar Allan Poe

Arthur J. Rees
The Hampstead Mystery
The Shrieking Pit
The Hand In The Dark
The Moon Rock
The Mystery of the Downs

Mary Roberts Rinehart
Sight Unseen and The Confession

Dorothy L. Sayers
Whose Body?

Sir William Magnay
The Hunt Ball Mystery

Mabel and Paul Thorne
The Sheridan Road Mystery

Raoul Whitfield
Death in a Bowl

And much more!
Visit ResurrectedPress.com
for our complete catalogue

About Resurrected Press

A division of Intrepid Ink, LLC, Resurrected Press is dedicated to bringing high quality, vintage books back into publication. See our entire catalogue and find out more at www.ResurrectedPress.com.

About Intrepid Ink, LLC

Intrepid Ink, LLC provides full publishing services to authors of fiction and non-fiction books, eBooks and websites. From editing to formatting, from publishing to marketing, Intrepid Ink gets your creative works into the hands of the people who want to read them. Find out more at www.IntrepidInk.com.

www.ingramcontent.com/pod-product-compliance
Lightning Source LLC
Chambersburg PA
CBHW070846250626
47159CB00003B/949

* 9 7 8 1 9 3 7 0 2 2 7 8 5 *